UNCERTAIN SOLDIER

UNCERTAIN SOLDIER

KAREN BASS

pajamapress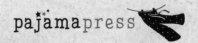

www.pajamapress.ca info@pajamapress.ca

 Canada Council Conseil des arts
for the Arts du Canada

 ONTARIO ARTS COUNCIL
CONSEIL DES ARTS DE L'ONTARIO
an Ontario government agency
un organisme du gouvernement de l'Ontario

 Canadä

The publisher gratefully acknowledges the support of the Canada Council for the Arts and the Ontario Arts Council for its publishing program. We acknowledge the financial support of the Government of Canada through the Canada Book Fund CBF) for our publishing activities.

Library and Archives Canada Cataloguing in Publication

Bass, Karen, 1962-, author   Uncertain soldier / Karen Bass.

ISBN 978-1-927485-72-9 (pbk.)

    I. Title.

PS8603.A795U63 2015   jC813'.6   C2014-906772-0

Publisher Cataloging-in-Publication Data (U.S.)

Bass, Karen, 1962-
    Uncertain soldier / Karen Bass.
[288] pages : cm.
Summary: It's World War II. Erich, a young German prisoner of war who dislikes Nazism, and Max, the twelve-year-old son of German immigrants, become friends when Erich is sent to work at a Canadian logging camp near Max's town. But with a saboteur haunting the logging camp and anti-German feeling running high in town, their friendship puts them both in danger.

ISBN-13: 978-1-92748-572-9
1. Friendship – Juvenile fiction. 2. Interpersonal relations – Juvenile fiction. 3. World War, 1939-1945 – Canada – Juvenile fiction. I. Title.

[Fic] dc23   PZ7.B388Un 2015

Cover design:Rebecca Buchanan
Cover images: background texture–Shutterstock/©isaravut; soldier walking–Shutterstock/©Chris Singshinsuk
Interior design and typesetting:Martin Gould

Printed in Canada by Webcom
http://www.webcomlink.com

Pajama Press Inc.
181 Carlaw Avenue, Suite 207, Toronto, Ontario Canada, M4M 2S1
www.pajamapress.ca

Distributed in Canada by UTP Distribution
5201 Dufferin Street, Toronto, Ontario Canada, M3H 5T8

Distributed in the U.S. by Orca Book Publishers
PO Box 468 Custer, WA, 98240-0468, USA

To Brenda,
You taught me that big sisters never stop nagging. So here, at last, is what you kept requesting: a story set in our part of the world.

To Hartmann,
You have shown me that having your heart broken in childhood does not stop you from being a good person unless you let it.
You didn't.

BEGINNINGS

The radio news sparked a storm in the kitchen, and soon the thunder of his father's voice rumbled through the house and rattled the window panes. Sheltered in his bedroom, Max hugged his pillow and pressed his forehead against the cool glass.

Outside, the barn cat—golden like the trees edging the garden—stalked between the potato plants, tail high like a flag. It lifted its head as if it sensed Max's gaze. The tail lowered and swept from side to side.

The voice grew louder. Angrier. At eight years old, Max didn't always understand grown-ups, but he understood that tone of voice. He wished he could be a turtle and hide safe inside his shell.

"They should have stayed out of it," his father boomed. "Bad enough the British foolishly declared war, but how could the Canadian government be so stupid?"

Soft tones, too quiet to blossom into words, filled the pause. Max held his breath. His mother could sometimes calm the anger.

"Idiots," his father bellowed. "The only good thing is that it will be short. Our armies will crush the British and Canadians if they decide to fight. But they won't: the Poles aren't worth it."

Max chewed his lip. Who are our armies? Shouldn't "our" army be the Canadians? Mother says I'm a Canadian because this is where I was born.

A door slammed. Max flinched. A minute later he watched his father march across the yard toward the barn, arms swinging. He always stomped like that when he was going for a drink. Mother didn't like the schnapps to be kept in the house. Max didn't like it anywhere. Its smell reminded him of paint.

His father disappeared into the barn as the sun began to set. Through his door Max heard muffled crying. He blinked rapidly, wishing he understood what was going on.

7 MAY 1943, NORTH ATLANTIC

Fear was in the air, thicker than the salt rising from the waves. Tension gripped every sailor Erich passed. The closeness of the night, the utter darkness, unnerved him. As he stepped onto the bridge, emergency lighting and the blackness pressing against the glass combined to shudder alarm through his frame. He snapped to attention and saluted, ignored the itching of his scalp.

His captain nodded curtly. "Seaman Hofmeyer. Good. Our primary radioman is in sick bay and Brust doesn't understand the English chatter we're picking up. See what you can do."

"Yes, sir."

The radio operator had his headset off and extended toward Erich when the Seetakt operator cried, "Captain, three ships on screen."

Erich felt the headset drape over his outstretched hand, but his focus was on the captain. Everyone's was. The man swore, marched to the radar screen and bent over the cringing operator. He straightened, clasped his hands behind his back and frowned into the black night beyond the glass. His voice was monotone. "There are no other German ships in the vicinity. British ships, then. Verdammt! They're executing a pincer movement."

Seconds stretched. The smell of sweat filled the room. The captain turned. His somber gaze fell on Erich. "Seaman Hofmeyer, I no longer require your knowledge of English. Get to your battle station." *He signaled his second-in-command.* "Sound the alarm."

The Seetakt operator reported, "All three ships are closing on our position."

Erich let the radio headset slide from his fingers. Sirens wailed as he flung himself out of the bridge and draped over the railing, fighting the convulsing fear trying to spew from his stomach. Three British ships. Closing. He didn't want to die in the Atlantic. Didn't want to die at all. Pull it together, Dummkopf.

Erich made his way midship. His antiaircraft gunnery sergeant slapped a life jacket against his chest. Erich's muttered thanks went unheard over the clanging alarm. He hunkered beside the stock of shells he would be expected to feed to the gunnery team. Sat on the jacket. Waited.

The ship hauled to port, the first of several course changes. The wailing stopped and now the only sounds were the frantic thudding of diesel engines and the slap of waves on the hull. Erich squinted into the darkness, straining to see the enemy. His eyes ached. Salt air stung his dry lips. Let this end. Please let it end.

It did. In a cacophony of wailing sirens and streaking flares, and a hissing that ended in a mighty whump. The ship jolted, almost throwing Erich to the rail, then trembled and groaned. Flames blossomed aft, illuminated the deck, the damaged bridge. Another explosion. Then, the order: abandon ship.

Men yelled, scrambled for lifeboats. Screams mixed with the sizzle of flames. Fear rooted Erich to his post. Oily smoke billowed, hiding the madness. He coughed. His gunnery sergeant shook him and yelled, "Get off! We're breaking apart. Sinking!" He pushed Erich toward the rail.

Below, the ocean yawned black and unfathomable. Then the blackness erupted in flames.

Broad hands pushed Erich and he fell toward the fiery sea.

1:

20 OCTOBER 1943,
CAMP 133, NEAR LETHBRIDGE, ALBERTA
(6°C/43°F)

Erich dipped his toast in the egg yolk and chewed slowly. The crisp and soft textures melted together in his mouth as smoothly as a waltzing couple. Beside his plate, a bowl of porridge steamed. He finished his egg, set the bowl on his plate, globbed jam on top of the cereal, and stirred it into swirls of red.

Nikel, his bunkmate, laughed. "You eat like you're seducing a beautiful woman."

Erich smirked. He scooped a spoonful of porridge and looked Nikel in the eye as he cleaned off the spoon. "Mmmmmm."

Nikel's coffee sprayed out of his mouth in a fine mist. He laughed so hard his wide face turned as red as the jam. Konrad, one of Nikel's shipmates, chuckled and gave Erich's shoulder a good-natured tap. Like Erich, Konrad was on the work detail that unloaded food supplies from trains for the prisoner-of-war camp.

Theirs was the last of three breakfast shifts so they lingered over coffee while the mess hall cleared, men scattering across the sprawling complex of Camp 133. Some would be on the football pitch or in one of two recreation halls, the sick would be lining up at the hospital, and the ones with toothaches at the dentist. A few would be tending animals they had captured and penned, others would be gardening, indulging hobbies, or reading to pass the time. Many prisoners would be pacing the perimeter fence like animals in a cage.

Erich had heard a guard comment that the camp was the same size as Lethbridge, the Canadian town beside it. Both had more than 12,000 residents, but they were tiny compared to his hometown, Cologne's, population of almost 700,000. The guards rarely entered the camp, leaving the running of it to the German prisoners. As a result, Camp 133 was like a piece of Germany. Erich tried not to cringe at the thought. He wished the Canadians ran things. They seemed decent.

"You got a letter yesterday," Nikel said to Erich.

"My grandmother."

"Anything to share?"

Erich scraped the last porridge from the bowl. How could he tell them his German grandmother lived in England? She had written in German, probably so other prisoners wouldn't get suspicious about his English connection. Accusations of spying were dangerous. "Other than family news, she related some newspaper reports." The censors probably liked German prisoners getting the English side of the story.

"And?"

Erich swished his coffee and watched the waves.

Nikel snorted. "So the news is bad."

Konrad nudged Erich. "What did she say?" When Erich still didn't respond, Konrad nudged him harder. "Come on, Hofmeyer. You're acting like a child losing on the football pitch." He dropped his voice. "You can't believe we're losing, can you?"

Erich glanced around. Men wiped tables on the far side of the hall, working their way to the end where the trio sat. Nikel leaned forward. His eagerness surprised Erich. Few people here cared what a seventeen-year-old thought.

He answered directly. "Your ship sank over a year ago, Nikel. April of '42, right? Maybe we were winning then. Who knew the war would last so long? In January, the Afrika Korps lost Africa and Stalingrad fell. When my ship sank in May, Cologne was being bombed into dust. And at the end of July, Hamburg was almost leveled in one night. When was the last time you heard news about winning a battle?"

Konrad spoke through clenched teeth. "Shut up."

"He's right." Nikel's whisper was urgent. "You can't say such things here. Remember Gersten."

Erich lowered his head and swirled his coffee. Gersten was famous in camp. Like Erich, he had arrived at the beginning of August. On his second day, he'd casually mentioned how Germany seemed to be losing. That night he'd been dragged to the showers by masked men and beaten so severely he'd almost died. Now the sight of him limping with a cane was a clear warning that only Nazi-approved statements were allowed here. Erich rotated his shoulder. The mention of his ship had made the burn scars on his thigh and shoulder blade tingle. He peered at Nikel. "No one can hear us."

"Always assume someone can hear you."

Erich brushed crumbs from his denim prison shirt. "I'm going to the library."

Konrad grabbed his wrist. "You should destroy that letter. You wouldn't want the wrong people reading it."

"I'm carrying it. No one will find it."

Erich spent most of the morning in the library near a discarded copy of the *Lethbridge Herald*. Everyone said the Canadian newspapers were planted propaganda. He ached to read them anyway, especially after his grandmother's letter, but picking one up would announce that he read English. Other than his barracks commander, Bechtel, no one in camp knew he spoke or read the language, and since Bechtel had ordered him to spy on the Canadian guards he couldn't reveal his secret. After abandoning some Friedrich Schiller essays that he might have been studying if he'd been allowed to attend university, he picked up a copy of Goethe's *Faust*, and recalled a passage he had memorized for school:

Woe! Woe!
Thou hast her destroyed
The beautiful world,
By a mighty fist.

His grandmother's descriptions of Hamburg's destruction formed pictures in his mind of charred corpses, mangled bodies, and streets turned to rubble. She'd said that English newspapers were reporting Germany's claim of 100,000 dead. Erich rubbed his eyes. Too many people were dying. Were his parents safe in Cologne? He hadn't heard from them since April, or from his brother in the Luftwaffe, though that would be a shocking first. He wanted it to end. He didn't care if it was because Germany lost. Quietly, Erich slid the book back into its spot. He paused, hand gripping the shelf, as he spotted Gersten hunched at the far table. The man must have felt his gaze, for he raised his head. His scarred cheek and crooked nose gave a desolate air to his blank expression. Stomach tight, Erich left the library, pausing outside the classroom where prisoners were learning English.

"I am hungry," intoned the teacher.

"I am hunga-ry," repeated the class.

"May I have some food."

"May I haf zum fooot."

Erich spotted Nikel in the second row. Sighing, he returned to the barracks where at least a dozen men were writing letters, carving wood, even knitting. Anything to pass the long days. At least knitting was useful, the items in high demand now that winter was drawing close. He stretched out on his upper bunk. Hash marks in the wall by his head counted the weeks since the long train ride that had delivered him to this camp in an ocean of prairie. Arm draped over his eyes, Erich thought of happier days. Imagining his grandparents' cottage, its half-wild garden hedged in by stone walls, made longing swell inside his chest. His breathing rasped.

It took him several minutes to realize that silence was radiating through the room. The feeling of people being around him retreated with muffled treads. He pressed his arm hard against his eyes. Only one man could clear a room like that.

A full minute passed before barracks commander Bechtel spoke. "Get up, Hofmeyer."

Erich could swear no one had eavesdropped in the mess hall. What he'd said could earn the label of defeatist. He swallowed, and dropped from his bunk. He kept his focus on Bechtel's wide features, pretending confidence. As commander of the barracks, Bechtel had interviewed him when he'd arrived, as he did with all new arrivals, to make sure he wasn't planted by the Canadians to spy, and to determine his loyalty. Bechtel was suspicious of anything less than fanatic. All the barracks commanders reported to a panel of the highest-ranking Nazis, the real power in the camp.

Two assistants flanked Bechtel. The one with a scarred forehead ground his fist against his open palm. The other, Erich thought of as "Burly." The pair had roughed him up after that first interview, and had beaten him when he offered no useful intelligence from listening to guards, even though they rarely came inside the wire. They'd beaten him four times now, each with increasing severity. Nikel had nursed his wounds when he'd refused to go to the hospital.

Bechtel motioned for Erich to advance. "So, Hofmeyer, you're now on the detail that unloads trains. What have the guards been saying?"

Erich released a slow breath. Not about this morning then. "They mostly give directions. Sometimes one will ask the other about a family matter."

"Three days ago someone else reported that one guard told another they would be sweeping the fifth row for contraband this morning. Yet you told me...what?"

Erich's scalp started to itch as inner sirens blared, *Danger!* He fought to keep his voice calm. "I told you nothing. The guard spoke too loudly, was too close to prisoners when he said it. He was fishing for spies."

"You're an expert, are you? So, expert, what happened this morning?"

Erich combed fingers through his hair and thought about books he'd read, then guessed. "Maybe guards were watching to see if we took the bait. If men set out sentries or cleaned up evidence of illegal activities, the guards took note. Now our work detail will probably be banned from working outside the fence."

Bechtel inclined his head. "It sounds as if the guards told you what would happen. The detail's leader, who the guards know speaks English and who relays orders, was taken for interrogation when the raid didn't happen."

A hardness in Bechtel's face made Erich want to run. Instead he ran his hand over his hair again. "But if I'm right..."

"Why am I here?" finished Bechtel. "It wasn't your decision, Hofmeyer. You should have reported everything, suspicions included. This is more proof you are untrustworthy."

"More? But I've never done anything to put my loyalty into question." Fear quavered through the words. Erich's limbs turned to lead.

"Is that right? Step forward."

Step? He wanted to run and never stop. Away from these fanatics, from this camp, from the whole war. Erich had to mentally order his feet to move. They dragged across the floor.

"Arms out." Bechtel nodded to Burly. "Search him."

"Scar" blocked the aisle. Burly patted Erich's arms and torso, rolled loose cloth and released it. He found the letter where Erich had tucked it under his waistband against his spine. Horror threatened to turn his midsection in on itself. He closed his eyes but Gersten's face haunted him. As Bechtel read the letter, threads of understanding wove together. The other spy on the work detail was Konrad. Had Bechtel ordered him to watch Erich? Vomit edged up his throat. He swallowed.

Bechtel waved the letter. "You believe this propaganda?"

Erich swallowed again. "My grandmother wouldn't lie. What good is propaganda here? We're already prisoners."

"So you're as defeatist as her? I'll get word to the Fatherland to have her arrested as a traitor. How pathetic, Hofmeyer. You've sent your grandmother to her death. Are you pleased?"

That made no sense. *Word to the Fatherland....* How could that affect her? Of course! Like all correspondence coming into the camp, the return address on his grandmother's letter was blacked out; Bechtel didn't know it had come from Stratford-upon-Avon in England. Erich fought to suppress a smile.

"You think I'm joking?"

"I doubt you ever joke." Tension corkscrewed as fresh fear jolted through Erich. He could see Bechtel was done talking. For once, he wanted to strike first, but could barely clench his fists. He slid his foot backward but Burly grabbed him from behind.

Scar advanced. Burly released one arm and plowed a fist into Erich's kidney. And again. A shockwave of pain rippled out from the hit. Erich's vision doubled. In desperation, he swung at the wrong Scar. The real Scar nailed him in the jaw. Pummeled his stomach.

He didn't remember falling. Hardly felt the kicks. Until a rib cracked. He bellowed.

"Enough!" Bechtel barked. Over the ringing in his ears, Erich heard, "...permission from council...then finish..."

I'm dead.

The next thing Erich knew, agony jarred him awake. Orderlies rolled him onto a stretcher. Nikel, blurry at the edges, appeared alongside. He leaned over and whispered, "What will you tell the doctors, Hofmeyer?"

Through swollen lips, Erich replied, "I tripped."

A smile crinkled out from Nikel's eyes but quickly retreated. Erich inhaled sharply as he glimpsed a guard behind the orderly. If Nikel had asked for their help, he would be in danger too. The stretcher bumped something, and pain jarred him into oblivion.

Erich woke in the hospital. Nikel and a doctor stood nearby, and Nikel was trying to speak English. "Mussen...Muss. Avay. Jetzt. Now. Ja?" He switched to German. "How do I say he's in danger?"

"I'm sorry," the Canadian doctor said. "I don't understand. An orderly can translate."

"No," whispered Erich in English. "He's trying to...tell you"—he spoke slowly, forcing the words past the pain—"that I'm...in danger."

Both men stared, surprise stamped on their faces. Nikel whispered in German, "You speak English?"

Erich replied in English, "Yes, I speak English. Fluently."

"That isn't in your records," the doctor said.

"They were trying to get me...to spy on...guards."

"Trying?"

Erich nodded. The doctor raised his voice. "I must consult my colleague." He disappeared beyond the oval fence of white curtains.

"*Scheisse*," Nikel clamped a hand on his high forehead.

A single laugh escaped Erich's lips. His ribs contracted painfully and he gasped. In German he whispered, "You're in danger now too, Nikel. I'm sorry."

They silently awaited the doctor's return. "My colleague agrees you must be transferred to the military hospital in Lethbridge for treatment." His voice dropped. "When you have recovered enough, you'll be questioned to decide your future."

"Nikel goes too." English. It felt strange to be speaking it again.

"Your friend? I can't authorize that."

Erich spoke urgently. "Please. He stood by me, called for guards, came here. They will beat him, or worse." He took a breath that quivered along his ribs, squinted against the pain. "We both stay or both go."

"I'll see what I can do."

"*Vielen Dank.*" The doctor looked puzzled. Erich realized he had spoken in German. He translated, "Thank you."

The doctor inclined his head and left. Nikel squatted so close Erich could feel warm breath on his ear. Could smell coffee and egg. "Tell me what you said."

"I may have gotten us released from this prison." Another painful breath. "But wherever we go, we'll still be behind barbed wire."

2:

16 NOVEMBER 1943,
LETHBRIDGE (19°C/66°F)

"Do you understand why we are questioning you, Seaman Hof-meyer?" The Canadian intelligence officer removed his wire-rimmed glasses and rubbed the bridge of his nose. "We need to understand the situation and your role in it to determine how to proceed."

Erich shifted on the wooden chair and rested a palm against his ribs when they twinged. They were much better. He had recuper-ated quickly in the military hospital.

"The doctor reported that you said you speak English fluently, even if you haven't done so since coming here. Odd that your records from England didn't mention it. The burns you sustained might have kept you incoherent, I suppose." The officer studied the file. "You were in an English prison hospital for two months?"

Erich nodded.

"Third-degree burns to isolated parts of your body, received, I suppose, when the ship you were on sank?"

Another nod. Erich had been lucky compared to some. The ward had been full of burn victims, a room filled with unbearable stench, harrowing moans, sometimes screams. The worst ones had lived in agony for days or weeks before sinking into death. Not a restful place. Erich tried to block the memories.

The officer sighed. "At least tell me why this reluctance to talk."

Erich's fingers slid halfway over his freshly shorn scalp before he realized it and dropped his hand. He hadn't known he was so nervous. He was glad for the haircut, though. His dark hair and blue eyes often invited comparisons to Hitler's. And he had to smile at the comments as if pleased, when he wanted to shout that his straight nose and high cheekbones were nothing like Hitler's doughy features. "If I talk, I might as well commit suicide."

The man's eyebrows arched. "Fluent, indeed. We're aware there are fanatic Nazi elements in the camp, some now targeting you. We need to know more to keep you safe."

Nazi elements. Erich almost laughed. The Nazis outright controlled the camp, and would so long as prisoners were left to run things. Fear kept everyone in line. Negative comments were seen as undermining morale and weren't tolerated. As Erich had learned. Now this officer wanted names? Was he insane? "I won't be a traitor to my country."

A sigh. "If I return you into Colonel Taylor's keeping at Camp 133, will your *countrymen* welcome you?"

Erich shook his head.

"Will they beat you again, possibly kill you?"

Erich shrugged, as if he didn't know the answer. He knew.

The officer rubbed his nose again. "What do you want, Seaman Hofmeyer?"

"I want to be left alone."

"From what your friend has told us of the beatings you've received, I doubt your fellow prisoners will allow that."

Nikel had spoken to them? Was he safe? Something in his expression must have betrayed Erich's thoughts because the officer said, "Your friend is on the premises. He's fine." He twiddled with a pen. "Why do you think your barracks leader targeted you? Is it because you speak English with no trace of German accent?"

Erich stared at his left hand gripping his thigh. No, it was because he hadn't responded with enough fervor when asked about the Führer. He had given quiet agreement when Bechtel wanted loud declarations of loyalty unto death. The commander would have sliced Erich open if he'd dared to voice some of the things about the Führer his grandparents had told him, like rumors that say he froths with rage when opposed and how he puts revenge ahead of common sense. Erich couldn't think the man a god like so many people his age. This intelligence officer would like that, but Erich said nothing.

The officer continued his questioning. "Is it because you have family in England, so he suspects your loyalty is divided?" Erich jerked his head up. The officer nodded. "You know all correspondence is read by censors. We know you received a letter from England."

Erich stood, winced at his ribs' protest, then eased over to the window. In the reflection he saw the guard leave his post and advance. A curt order from the officer returned him to blocking the door. Erich shifted his gaze from the reflection to beyond the window. No fence topped by coiled barbed wire marred the view. The late November wind tugged the last leaves from a tree, tossed and twirled them before carrying them away.

He had to get away from the camp. It was out there, a shadow on the edge of the town. The shadow of the valley of death.

"There might be a solution to your dilemma." Once again, the officer seemed to be reading Erich's mind. When he stayed facing the window, the officer continued. "Given that prisoners seem to manage communications between prison camps, there is only one camp that houses anti-Nazi POWs, where you might be safe. But it takes time to determine if you qualify. It's easier to rate you as low risk, which allows you to volunteer for a work camp."

Erich considered that. "But the sugar beet harvest is done."

"This is a different work project, just starting. The work camps involved are all a good distance from Camp 133."

"Would Nikel go too?"

In the glass, the officer's reflection turned. Erich felt his gaze. "So you're interested? Given that he's a cheerful worker here at the hospital, I'm certain I could get Petty Officer Nikel onto the same work detail. What is your relationship?"

Erich knew that to win this chance at survival he had to talk. "We're friends." *The older brother I wish I'd had.* Outside, a woman walked away from the building. A coat hid her form, but not her shapely legs. A wind gust sent her hat tumbling down the sidewalk and she chased it, showing more leg.

"Were you a member of the Nazi youth organization? What is it called?"

"Hitlerjugend." Erich blinked. "Hitler Youth. I joined in 1939 when it became the law."

"Not before?"

"I wasn't interested in group activities, except some football. I mean, soccer." He rested his palm on the cool glass, remembered the thick wavy panes in his bedroom window that had distorted the view. His room had been the only safe haven in their house, the one place his brother had been forbidden entry.

"What were you interested in?"

"I studied, read a lot, played piano." This was already tiresome.

"And your parents? What do they do?"

"My father is an industrialist with two factories near Cologne. My mother volunteers for charities."

"Is your father a member of the Nazi party?"

"He has to be to get government contracts. I don't know if he *wants* to be." Erich returned to his chair. Spine stiff, he stared over the officer's head.

"Do you have a good relationship with your father?"

"He has an older son for that." Seventeen years hadn't been long enough to figure out why Gerhard despised him. His best guess was that his brother, even at three years old, had hated that someone—even a sibling—might take any of his parents' attention.

He had channeled that hate into endless cruelties that had grown as they got older. At twelve, Gerhard had pushed nine-year-old Erich down the stairs and he'd broken his arm. When his parents had asked, Erich had said he'd tripped. After that, caution and avoidance became a way of life. Mostly. Once in a while he'd felt compelled to poke the bear.

The intelligence officer jotted notes. The questioning followed the same lines for awhile. The talk came, as Erich had known it would, to his grandparents and why they lived in England. "They supported the Weimar Republic and didn't like the change of government."

"Did they ever talk to you about such things?"

"Yes. I spent summers there, before the war started." Erich remembered the summer of 1939. He had been thirteen and had arrived home in Cologne three days before Germany invaded Poland. If he had stayed in England one more weekend, he might have been trapped in Stratford-upon-Avon for the duration of the war. Except the trap was in Germany, where Father refused to let him attend university, saying he was too young, but insisted he do his mandatory military service. He had wanted Erich to join the air force, as Gerhard and many young nobles had. Erich had joined the navy instead. His one act of defiance.

And this was where it had landed him. A prairie flatter than a becalmed sea. He missed rolling hills, forests, rivers guarded by medieval towers, sidewalk cafes in Cologne and the soaring buttresses of the cathedral. Visiting his grandparents in England. Seeing plays. Stopping on a stone bridge spanning the Avon to watch scullers whisk under the arches. Riding the old chain ferry. Lunching in a pub in a half-timbered house. His grandmother teaching him to waltz when he wanted to learn swing dance.

Freedom.

"Seaman Hofmeyer? You look pale." The intelligence officer stood. "I have obviously questioned you too long. You must be tired."

Erich didn't trust his voice, so nodded.

The officer motioned the guard forward, then held up his hand. The guard stopped behind Erich. The officer said, "We need to have another conversation or two about your background and such, but I'm certain I can get you assigned elsewhere. One thing. Technically, prisoners must volunteer before joining a work detail. Are you volunteering, Erich Hofmeyer?"

Returning to Camp 133 would mean more beatings, maybe disfigurement like Gersten's, maybe death. Erich swallowed. "Yes. Whatever it is. Yes."

3:

11 DECEMBER 1943,
HORLEY (3°C/37°F)

Max crouched behind a spruce tree and planned his approach into town. Of all the days Mother could send him to the general store, she had to pick Saturday. Busy, bustling Saturday. And it would just get busier as the day went on. By evening the place would look like a rotting log with the bark pulled off: bugs scurrying everywhere. *Stomp them. Stomp them all.*

Horley only had three streets. Where did all the people come from? Every person from every farm for ten miles must flock into town on Saturdays. Normally Max's family went earlier in the day.

The sun crept toward the horizon. The longer he waited, the farther he'd be walking in the dark. Night came early in December. He considered whether it would be better to make the whole trip under cover of darkness. The farm was only a mile away. But Mother was sick and she'd worry as it got later.

Max lurched to his feet, afraid he'd never move if he didn't start. He made sure the coast was clear, then strolled onto the road as if he hadn't been hiding for half an hour. His pant legs were wet below his knees.

At the first street he swung right, past one clapboard house, then cut through Mrs. Johnson's yard. He emerged on the next street beside the alley that ran behind Main Street's businesses. Mr. Miller's truck was parked by the loading dock of his general store, Miller's Mercantile. Because he had to go to Woking to get freight from the train, it was the only vehicle in the area driven regularly. Since the war had started, adults complained about gas rations.

Max eased through the employees' door beside the waist-high loading platform. The storeroom was lit by one lantern hanging from a ceiling hook. A trio of unlit lanterns stood on a shelf by the inside door. Shadows wobbled in the corners.

He pressed his ear against the inside door and strained to listen. A low hum vibrated through the wood, but no kid noises. He cracked the door open an eyeball's width. Mrs. Johnson and Mrs. Wilks talked in the canned goods aisle. Mr. Miller's grown daughter, Frances, arranged an Ivory Soap display. Wrapped bars were scattered around her feet, as if someone had knocked them over. Maybe that's why no kids were in the store.

Silently, Max slid sideways out of the storeroom and leaned against the door to close it. So far, so good. The smell of woodsmoke filled his nostrils. Maybe it was the other scents in the store, but the smoke here always smelled tangier than at home. He scanned the store again; still no students. *They've all disappeared, zapped by alien ray guns, but none of the adults have realized it yet.*

Max slinked along the back shelves then sidled up to the counter, hoping Mrs. Miller would serve him without noticing he hadn't stood in line. He stopped by the candy jars with their tempting rainbow sweetness and tried to catch her eye.

Someone nabbed his collar and dragged him backward. "Rude child, sneaking to the front of the line. You're big enough to know better," Mrs. Williams said.

"Well, what do you expect?" the woman behind her added. Her voice dropped, but not low enough to avoid Max's notice. "Germans are so rude. Have you heard that awful language?" She sniffed and peered down her pointed nose.

Max lowered his head and shuffled toward the back of the line of women. Exactly what he hadn't wanted. It would take too long. Halfway down the line, a hand on his shoulder stopped him. Mrs.

Lane's face was softened by kindness. She was sort of their neighbor. Her husband owned a logging camp two miles past their house, in the hills. And her son was a prisoner of war in Germany, which was probably why she always looked a little sad, even when she smiled.

"How many things do you need to get, Max?" she asked quietly.

"Only three."

She pulled him into line in front of her, keeping her hand on his shoulder. "That will only take a minute. You and I can get our things together." He nodded his thanks.

Behind them, two disgruntled snorts sounded. Max glanced back but his gaze landed on the potbellied stove and the men surrounding it, sharing a hot drink and a visit. One said something and all the others laughed.

Under the laughter came a whisper. "It's hardly surprising *she* would defend the boy. Did you hear what they're doing at the camp?"

Mrs. Lane's hand tightened on his shoulder; she had heard too. He wished he could ask her what that meant. She gave him a slight smile. "Your mother doesn't often send you on errands, Max. Is everything okay?"

He half turned, to face her better, and froze at the sight of a head pressed against the big window to their left. He bit the inside of his lip as Richard Anderson's face twisted into an ugly mask.

"Max?" Mrs. Lane pulled his attention away from the boy.

"She's sick," he replied, and turned forward, gaze on the navy coat in front of him.

"Nothing serious, I hope." Mrs. Lane seemed determined to keep talking.

Max shook his head, shoved his hands in his plaid coat's big pockets and hunched his shoulders. How could he turn invisible if she kept talking to him? The line inched forward.

The other women forgot about him and resumed chatting. Mrs. Lane finally turned to talk to Mrs. Johnson, who had left her conversation by the canned beans.

All of the women wore wool winter coats, unbuttoned in the warmth radiating off the stove. The men gathered around it had shed theirs. But Max kept his coat buttoned for a fast getaway. He was only one person away from the counter now.

The woman in front of him stepped ahead. Frances joined her mother serving customers and motioned to him. Max lunged at the counter. He handed over the list and family ration card. In less than two minutes, Max had a small paper sack with his mother's purchases, a sarsaparilla-flavored candy stick, and some change, which he squirreled away in his trousers' pocket.

He thanked Frances and glanced outside. Richard was still there, watching him like a brown-haired owl tracking a mouse. If Max snuck out the back now, Richard could race into the alley and catch him there. With no witnesses.

At least on Main Street the presence of adults might save him from a beating. Richard was almost two years older, half a head taller, and spent all his spare time thinking of new ways to torture Max. *Zap him now, you stupid aliens. Before I get outside.*

Dragging each step to prolong reaching the door, Max kept his attention on his stick of hard candy. He wove his fingers around it, index and ring fingers on the top and the other two fingers on the bottom, like it was a post and his fingers were the split rails of a fence.

Someone swung open the door. "Don't block the way, boy. Get out if you're going out."

Without looking up, Max stepped outside. The wooden slats of the veranda were swept clean under the store's overhang. Richard had been to the right the last time Max had looked, so he swung left.

Ahead, a cluster of men talked on the sidewalk, two feet beyond the store's porch.

Max sped up. Footsteps followed. A hand clutched his neck. Richard's harsh whisper brushed his ear. "Hitler doesn't deserve candy."

Richard snatched the sarsaparilla stick and shoved Max hard. He'd been inches away from the two steps leading down to where the men talked. He took flight. Smashed into a broad back and fell onto the pile of packed snow beside the wooden sidewalk.

The man he'd hit spun and hauled him up. Max's eyes widened at the sight of Constable Mason, the RCMP officer from Spirit River.

The policeman kept ahold of his collar and lifted Max so only his toes touched the ground. "What are you doing, boy?"

"N-nothing. I was pushed."

Mason looked and only saw Richard, ten feet away, focused on the sarsaparilla candy he was sucking. The policeman leaned close. "Don't lie to me." He straightened and studied Max's face. "I know you. Your dad is Helmut Schmidt. I was just at his farm making sure he's behaving himself." He gave Max a little shake. "Maybe I'll have to keep an eye on two Germans in this town instead of one."

"No, sir. It was an accident. Honestly." Max quietly added, "I was born in Canada. I'm not German."

A sneer curled the policeman's lip. "The apple doesn't fall far from the tree. I'll be watching you. Cause trouble and I'll arrest your father and you both."

He scooped up the bag, shoved it against Max's chest, and pushed him away. Max leaped over the ridge of snow and bolted down the snow-packed road, toward the edge of town. His heart thudded so loudly in his ears, he couldn't tell if anyone was following.

Someone in that circle of men would tell Father. Then he'd be in trouble at home.

Superman rockets out of the sky and carries Corporal Mason by the scruff of his neck to his own jail, then flies away. I want to fly away. Somewhere where there's no war, where no one cares where Father was born.

A single raven swooped over his head and soared across the field, as if taunting him.

4:

13 DECEMBER 1943,
LOGGING CAMP (5°C/41°F)

"Have you ever imagined such a dismal hinterland, Erich?" Nikel rubbed his upper arms.

Erich studied the two men cutting down a tree with a crosscut saw. The smooth rhythm, back and forth, give and take. Like a dance. He blinked when Nikel said, "Erich? Are you listening?"

Nikel used to call him Hofmeyer; he wasn't sure he'd ever remember to say Johann. Out here, the military stiffness from prison camp drifted away, like smoke from a chimney. That, he liked. "I heard. I disagree with dismal. We're a world away from anything, but it's beautiful. Snow in Cologne turns instantly gray. This whiteness almost hurts the eyes."

They had come to the logging camp at night; even their march from one train to another in the small city of Edmonton had been in darkness. Though with no blackout—strange after years of war—they had been able to gape at the streets, homes, and stores decorated for Christmas. The military truck leading their odd parade had carried a dozen guards armed with flashlights. A police car had trailed them, headlights illuminating the big red circles sewn onto their new winter jackets. At least the night trek had meant few civilians could gawk at the enemies marching through their midst.

Prisoners had debarked at various stops during the train ride, fifty here, twenty there, eighty here, all going to different work camps. This camp was a small operation and had only ten Germans. Greber, Conkle, Weber, and Koch were working in the sawmill. Erich, Nikel, Rudolf, Schlenter, Lerhmann, and Hubart were assigned to cut trees.

They were lumberjacks. Amusing, considering many Germans thought Canada was a nation of lumberjacks. Now trees here would feel the bite of German axes because the Canadian lumberjacks were all in Europe, cutting down German soldiers. Not so amusing.

Erich peered past the two Canadians to where he'd seen movement in the trees. A shadow, fifty meters away. Just over fifty yards—life would be easier here if he used the Imperial measurements he'd learned in England. He sidestepped for a better look. Saw it again. He waded through knee-deep snow to get closer. The unidentified animal blended with the evergreens, its dark form vaguely horse-like. Were there wild horses here?

"Timber!" one of the lumberjacks shouted.

Timber meant—

Loud creaking spun Erich around. A tree leaned toward him. More creaking. *Pop, pop, pop.* Small branches broke off in collisions with other branches. The tree listed more. Erich took three steps and dove. The tree crashed down beside him. A jagged branch sliced along his jaw as he rolled away. On his back, he stared at the spider web of branches outlined by blue sky. Mushrooming snow blocked the sight, settled on and around him as he heaved air.

Erich brushed off the dusting of snow. A lumberjack loomed over him, his face the shade of his red plaid jacket. "What the hell kind of stupid move was that? You never walk round a tree being felled. Dammit, you stupid Jerry, don't you know anything about felling trees?"

Erich's heartbeat rattled. He touched his glove to his throbbing jaw. It came away red. "I was raised in a city larger than most in this country. Where would I learn to chop trees?"

The blond man, in his early twenties, spat a gob that landed near Erich's head. "Jeez-uz. The Jerry speaks like a bloody Englishman and is just as clueless. What's Henry expect us to do with that? Even Christmas would be better than these two. At least he's a good worker."

A person named Christmas? Erich rolled onto his hands and knees. Blood dripped off his chin onto the snow. He wanted to crawl away and mope, but he needed to appear strong. He pushed up, steadied himself on a slender white trunk, met the man's dark gaze. "So teach us." Why wasn't this hate-filled man a soldier?

The man spat again, hitting Erich's boot. "Teach you, huh? Okay, Jerry, grab an ax. The tree needs delimbing. Let's see if you can do that without losing a foot."

"Frank," the older, bearded lumberjack said, "shouldn't he get that cut looked at?"

"What do I care if he bleeds to death? One less Jerry is no skin off my nose."

In German, Nikel asked Erich if he was okay. Frank spun and pointed a finger at him. "No damned Jerry-talk out here. Speak English or shut your trap." He raised his voice, as if Nikel were deaf. "Understand? Speak English!"

Nikel nodded warily. Erich mouthed that he was fine. It stung like a dozen wasp bites, but the bleeding was slowing. Dampness cooled on his throat—it probably looked like a knife-wielding madman had attacked him. He ignored it and faced Frank. "Johann didn't mean anything. He only started learning English in the prison camp."

"Better teach him more fast, Jerry."

"My name is Erich Hofmeyer."

Frank whipped out a grimy handkerchief and blew his nose. "Grab the ax, Jerry."

He ached to hit this man, but getting into trouble was a one-way ticket back to prison camp, where Bechtel and his goons waited to finish him off. Beside Nikel, the other lumberjack held two axes.

He handed one to Erich with a forced smile. "Name's Chuck. Work hard, don't give Frank any lip, and he might ease off."

Doubtful. Erich took an ax. He had chopped firewood during Hitler Youth camping trips so his feet weren't in danger. He followed Chuck's instructions on how to delimb the tree. Nikel watched closely. The crack of ax blades against wood echoed sharply.

Dripping sweat, Erich struggled past tree limbs already cut to get at the ones under the trunk. Even wearing gloves, he felt blisters forming. Done, he rested while the lumberjacks measured the naked trunk with a long stick, cut it in two, then hooked giant tongs to the log and chained it to a patient horse.

"I'll skid it out." Frank took the horse's reins. "I need some fresh air. Stinks like sauerkraut here." He clicked his tongue and started down the path. The horse nickered and followed.

Chuck pointed. "Grab that metal half moon for measuring diameters. I'll teach you how to pick a tree. Normally you cut down five or six trees, then each limb half of them. Henry wants you working by yourselves real soon, so pay attention. Learning how to bring a tree down safely is the trickiest part." He eyed Nikel skeptically. "Translate if you have to, quietly. The landing ain't far. Frank won't be long."

The day dragged on in a blur of sore muscles and aching hands. The only good thing was that darkness came early in this northern wilderness.

My new life. It would be hard, but if he stayed out of the way of falling trees, it wouldn't kill him.

5:

13 DECEMBER 1943, LOGGING CAMP (5°C/41°F)

In the log cookhouse at dinner, men sat at two long tables flanked by benches. The one near the side door had been claimed by nine boisterous Canadians who made room for the two Veterans Guards. They had accompanied the prisoners from Lethbridge to prevent escapes but had counted heads only a few times. At the other table ten German prisoners ate their stew and bread. The loudest thing on that side of the room was the hiss of two coal oil lanterns. Erich's exhaustion went so deep that his bones ached more than his muscles. He longed to sleep.

Irritated mutterings from the next table drew Erich's attention. Something about leftover stew and no pie again. Someone mentioned a kitchen helper having quit.

The side door banged. The Canadians fell silent and gave their attention to the man standing near their table. Henry Lane, owner of the operation, wore a casual authority as he surveyed the room, nodded to men, then scanned the prisoners. His gaze stopped on Erich. He crooked a finger. "Come on, son. My wife wants to clean that cut."

Erich touched his jaw. He'd washed his hands but had forgotten his neck was caked with dried blood. He got his coat off a peg by the back door and skirted around the Canadians.

Frank said, "Need me to come, Henry? Or a guard? So Jerry minds his manners?"

"He'll be fine, Frank." Henry left without looking back.

The frosted night was ghostly; a half-shrouded moon gave the yard a gray cast. Erich had expected it to be colder. Henry was halfway across the yard and moving fast. Erich quick marched, or as close as his weary legs could manage. The Lanes' house had a room built on to the east side with its own entrance. The boss's office, someone had called it.

From the office steps, Erich surveyed the small camp. The mill operation was to the left behind a screen of trees. A barn, storage, and hay sheds were tucked near more trees behind the house. The cookhouse, windows glowing with soft light, stood with an icehouse between two dark bunkhouses. The one closer to the barn housed the Canadians. The other one was surrounded by a corral of high fence that went up to one side of the cookhouse, giving the prisoners access to it through double doors. A locked gate beside the cookhouse would be opened in the morning when the prisoners went to work.

The door behind Erich creaked. "Stop gawking and come in. Leave your boots on."

Erich hung his coat on the peg by the door. He touched the bloodstained collar. Every injury he got seemed to be on the left side. Could a body be half cursed?

"Sit down." Henry indicated a stiff-backed wooden chair beside the desk. In the thirty hours since arriving at camp, Erich hadn't seen Henry without his plaid hat, even indoors, and hadn't realized he was bald as a shorn monk. Hatless, he appeared about the same age as Erich's father. Henry perched on the corner of the wooden desk. "Chuck told me what happened. Could've been a darn sight worse."

"Yes, sir. I was careless. It won't happen again."

Henry chuckled. "I've heard that plenty." Louder, he said, "Mildred, is the water hot? We're ready."

A woman used her ample hip to nudge open the door between the office and kitchen, then backed in carrying a large basin. "Get off my work space, Henry." He retreated to his chair. Mildred kept her gray gaze on her handiwork as she washed Erich's jaw and neck, ignoring his protests that he could do it himself.

Henry set a bottle of whiskey on the desk blotter. "Her rooting around has it bleeding a bit again."

"I don't need a drink."

Henry snorted. "Not wasting this on your belly, son." He handed the bottle to his wife.

She tilted Erich's head to the side and dribbled whiskey along the cut. He hissed. "Hush, now," she said. "We can't let it get infected."

When she was done, Henry thanked her and asked her to leave them.

"How old are you?"

Was he too young to be a lumberjack? Erich was tempted to lie, but it didn't seem wise. "Seventeen. I'll be eighteen in February."

"So you were sixteen when you enlisted? They're letting boys do that in Germany?"

"Sometimes. I'd finished my secondary education, so my father gave permission." Erich's lips compressed, recalling his father's refusal to let him attend university.

"You graduated from high school at sixteen? That's early, isn't it?"

"Yes, sir." Erich shrugged. "Mother always said I was her thinker."

Henry studied him for a minute, opened his desk drawer, removed a sheet of paper, and laid it in the middle of the blotter. Then he leaned back and folded his hands across his middle. It was an alphabetical list of the prisoners, their names and ranks. Hofmeyer was in the middle. Erich asked, "Why is my name underlined?"

"You're the thinker. You tell me."

"I had some trouble with a man back in prison camp, but otherwise..."

Henry snorted again. "The answer's in your voice, son." Puzzled, Erich brushed at his short-cropped hair, only starting to grow out from his hospital stay. Henry poured himself a finger of whiskey and downed it.

Erich gave up and requested an explanation. Henry rested both hands on the paper. "I deal straight with my men and don't figure I should treat you differently. Fact is, you could disappear, get different clothes, blend in. You sound more English than German. Understand?"

Erich nodded. It *would* be easy to give his words a nasal sound to imitate Henry. He could say he was going to Edmonton to sign up for the army. That might get him a ride. People might shake his hand instead of spitting on his boot.

Henry broke into his thoughts. "What are you going to do, son? Can I trust you enough to send you out that gate every morning?"

"If I tried to run away—"

"I'd have a search party on your trail so fast you'd be running scared. Darn scared. We hunt to put meat in our icehouses. All the men and boys, and half the women around here, are good shots with a rifle."

"And if I survived being recaptured, you'd ship me back to camp." Henry Lane's amber eyes reflected the lamp light. Erich said, "Honestly, sir, I'll do anything to not be sent back. I *can't* go back." A half laugh escaped. "I don't even know where I am. I know I'm young, and I grew up in a city, so you might regret keeping me on, but I want to try."

Clattering came from the kitchen. It became percussion accompaniment to quiet singing. A hymn, Erich thought, though it wasn't familiar.

Henry tilted his head and listened for a moment. "What city?"

"Köln. Uh, Cologne."

"That place has a fancy cathedral, doesn't it?"

Erich nodded.

"Still standing?"

"The last I heard."

"The missus always said if we ever travel, she'd like to see it. That and the big one in Paris. Me, I'd rather see a castle."

Erich imagined the cathedral, with pillars soaring above the nave and choir. The organ music could swell to fill the interior and infuse him with awe. With Cologne being so badly bombed, Erich doubted he'd ever re-experience that.

Henry broke into his thoughts. "We're in northwest Alberta, an area called the Peace Country, named after the Peace River twenty or so miles north. And it dumps into the Arctic Ocean about a thousand miles north. Want to see an atlas?"

Erich's muscles tensed. Was this a trap? At Camp 133, prisoners weren't allowed to see maps. He shook his head. "I don't need to. We probably traveled more than the length of Germany to get here from Lethbridge. And it took five days to get there from the east coast of Canada. I'm on the other side of the world from my home. What else do I need to know? Except for falling trees, I'm probably safer here than anywhere." Erich lowered his head as thoughts of home washed over him. Even with his father's criticism and his mother's blindness to it, he wanted to be there so badly it felt like a rat gnawing his intestines. He wanted to nestle into the wing-backed chair in his room with a book and block out the world.

Henry stood. Erich followed. The man extended his hand. Relief clogged Erich's throat as he shook it. The man was shorter than Erich by half a head, but his grip was iron. "Around here, son, a man's handshake is as binding as any contract drawn up by a fancy lawyer in a big city. Don't let me regret this."

"I won't. And thank you."

"For what?"

"For not calling me Jerry."

6:
15 DECEMBER 1943,
SCHMIDT FARM (3°C/37°F)

Father slapped his hand on the table. The milk in Max's oatmeal rippled and washed up on the shores of mushy islands. He kept his head down and stirred his breakfast into a pool of quicksand. *The man sinks to his waist, calling for help. Struggling makes him sink faster. Superman rockets down, saving him just as he goes under.*

Max shoveled a glob of oatmeal into his mouth. Father demanded he look up. He gobbled another spoonful, then obeyed. When had Father's hair started crawling off his head? His forehead shone white above the line where his hat usually sat. His thick eyebrows folded toward each other. He pointed his spoon at Max and a clump of oatmeal dropped onto the oilcloth tabletop. "I told you not to get in trouble, especially not with the police."

"I didn't—"

"Don't lie to me!" His roar made Max wince. "Miller was drooling, he was so eager to tell me what three men had told him, how you'd attacked a policeman."

Max bit the inside of his cheek. Anything he said would be talking back, even if it was to explain what really happened.

"Now they'll watch you, looking for an excuse to return. That snooping pig, Mason, searched the barn and house on Saturday after Sven told him I'd asked to borrow his rifle. You can't trust anyone. The Swedes are supposed to be neutral."

Max returned to his oatmeal as Father began his familiar rant about having his rifles taken away when the war started and having to report to the police station in Spirit River every two months. All because he was a German immigrant. Worse, most of his friends and neighbors avoided him now, even though they knew he'd emigrated from Germany in 1929, four years before Hitler came to power. Even though they knew he'd come to Canada because of Germany's failing economy, because he'd wanted to farm his own land. Just like them.

He smacked his coffee cup down and the spilled liquid oozed toward the edge of the table. "They expect us to be ashamed of being German. Don't you *ever* be ashamed, Max."

Max's head popped up as if yanked by a puppet string. "But at school—"

"No buts! You are German. Hold your head up and be proud."

Max bit the inside of his cheek again, so hard he tasted blood. *The bomber dips low over the school, drops its payload, and banks away. Red and orange blossom in the icy blue sky.*

"Thanks to that *verdammten* Sven, I wasn't able to butcher the hog. Mason didn't care, and he wouldn't help." Father's tone was thickly laced with something other than anger. Max was used to anger. This was...frustration maybe. Or worry.

Max sat back, extended his arm and ran the spoon around the rim of the empty bowl. Last year they'd had to butcher the pig by sinking an ax into its brain. Father had hated that so much he'd sworn to get his hands on a rifle this year. Max often wished he hadn't stayed in the barn to watch. "Maybe Mr. Lane from the logging camp could help. Or Alf."

By the sink, Mother kneaded bread. "Alf is also Mr. Lane to you, Max. Be respectful."

"Yes, Mother. They pass by on the way to town. I bet they'd stop."

Father's eyebrows finally met. "I don't have time to traipse two miles into the hills to have another neighbor refuse to help."

"I could go." Max's breath cut off. He hadn't meant to offer, but he liked Mr. and Mrs. Lane. And she always had dessert around because of cooking for the lumberjacks. Max licked his lips.

"Maybe." Father's voice was gruff. "But not until Sunday. I need you after school to help work on the interior of the new pig barn."

Max released a disappointed sigh at having to wait. "Yes, sir."

"Get to school." Father turned on the radio and opened the newspaper. As he did every morning in the winter, he read local news while waiting for the radio's national news, which included what was happening in the war.

"Brush your teeth first, Max," Mother said.

Max carried his dishes to the sink and got his toothbrush out of the cupboard beside it. Mother always left a glass of water on the counter for him. He dipped the toothbrush into it, added paste, and stood beside the red hand pump while he scrubbed his teeth. He swished the toothbrush in the water to clean it, and left the glass beside his breakfast dishes.

Mother tapped her cheek. He pecked it. Voice low, she said, "Thank you for offering to talk to the Lanes. It's hard for your father to ask for help."

Max nodded. Reluctant agreement was almost the same as approval from Father, who usually only growled or barked. He was surprised he'd been given permission to try. Maybe Father was more worried than he'd let on about having to butcher the pig with the ax again.

That was a new thought: his father worried. He always seemed so sure of himself, like everything he said was an absolute fact. No questions allowed. Ever. Obedience was the key to keeping Father's anger away, most of the time.

Max hurried out the door. Some students got to ride horses to school, or even horse-drawn sleighs, but Father thought a mile and a half was too close to let Max take the horse for the whole day. Maybe Father knew he'd be tempted to ride right past the school.

To the east, the sky was gray but the sun hadn't risen. The night's chill clung to the morning, making snow crackle underfoot. When the cold air seeped through his pants and long johns, Max sped up, swinging the lard pail containing his lunch and marching like a soldier. Soon only his cheeks were cold.

"It's a long way to Tipperary, it's a long way to go. It's a long way to Tipperary, to the sweetest girl I know." Max sang under his breath, a song from the Great War that soldiers were singing again. *I'm marching off to fight*—What if the war was still going when he was old enough to join the army? No matter what the other students called him, he was a Canadian. So he'd enlist and fight the Germans. But Father had two sisters back in Germany. He could kill a cousin and never know it.

His arms swung lower and lower until they hung by his sides. His pail bumped his thigh with each step. He shoved his free hand into his coat pocket as he considered fighting for Canada. Father wouldn't like it. And what if he had to fight beside Richard Anderson?

By the time Max got to town he had decided he'd take a train as far as he could and then sign up, so he wouldn't be in the same battalion as anyone from Horley. No one in Vancouver or Toronto would care where his father was born. Would they?

The sun poked over the horizon. Mr. Miller was sweeping off the general store's sidewalk as Max passed, so he greeted the man. His broom-like moustache twitched as if he were pursing his lips. Three blocks later Max was through the town, and his least favorite place in the world came into view. The white clapboard building with evenly spaced windows along its side looked innocent enough, but it was infested with bugs. Isn't that what you'd call people who liked to bug you?

Miss Williams emerged from the double doors and stood on the wide top step. She lifted the wooden-handled bell and clanged it.

Ding, ding. The low morning sun glinted off the brass. *Ding, ding.* Children raced from every corner of the grounds to get in line. Max lengthened his stride but didn't run as he turned into the yard. Miss Williams chided him for being last. Everyone stared. Max lowered his head.

The school was also the community hall and a church on Sundays, so the students sat at tables instead of desks. The youngest students sat closest to the teacher's desk. Being in grade seven, Max was in the second-last row. Only the grade-eight students, including Richard, sat behind him. No one ever sat beside him.

A spitball hit the back of his head, then another. *At least I have a window seat.* After they had sung "O Canada" and recited the Lord's Prayer, the teacher told them to get out their mathematics. She was more of a supervisor. Their real teacher had enlisted and gone to fight. Miss Williams helped the younger students with their correspondence lessons and left the older ones to work alone. But she was strict about everyone being quiet.

Max finished his lesson before math time ended, so he asked to use the outhouse. Miss Williams consented. He got his boots and coat on and escaped outside. He slipped into the the slant-roofed shed beside the outhouse and patted a few horses, pausing to stroke one coarse black mane. The animals' body heat and the sweet manure smell made the small stable feel airless. Max scurried to the outhouse. Whichever parent was supposed to supply toilet paper for the week had forgotten, so he dipped into his emergency supply in his inside jacket pocket.

The smell wasn't too bad when it was cold, so he lingered as long as he dared. It wasn't long enough. When he stepped outside a hand grabbed his collar and propeled him toward the snowbank. Richard plopped onto his back and rubbed his face against the hard-packed snow. Ice scraped his cheeks like kittens scratching.

Max struggled and thrashed, hardly able to get a breath. His cry for help stuck in his throat. His lungs shrank into stony lumps.

After several agonizing minutes, Richard pulled him to his feet and shoved him toward the schoolhouse so he tumbled over the piled snow along the path and broke through the ice crust to soft powder below. He rolled onto all fours and gulped in air. When he pushed to his feet, his hands were red and stinging.

Richard threw a snowball and hit his shoulder. "Doesn't matter where you hide, Hitler. I'll always find you."

7:

16 DECEMBER 1943,
LOGGING CAMP (6°C/43°F)

The clanging of an old saw blade signaled the end of the work day. The blade hung from a tree at the landing where skidded logs were collected. *Whang-ang-ang-ang.* The gonging shimmied through the air. Erich stopped delimbing and lurched toward the skid path. He flopped into the nearest snowbank. Nikel said in careful English, "You good, Erich?"

"Chain me up and skid me out of here, Johann. I'm too tired to walk."

Frank joined Nikel. He rubbed his dark blond stubble, then hit the sole of Erich's boot with the flat face of his ax. "I'll gladly string you up, Jerry."

The words drove Erich to his feet. At least he only had to walk to the landing. From there, one man rode a skid horse and led the others while everyone else perched atop logs on the sloop. Uncomfortable, but better than walking. The sloop was a sturdy wooden frame with wooden cross pieces as the base. The fronts of the side beams were carved like sleigh runners. Four vertical posts on each side edge held logs in place. *A raft on runners.* Most men sat near a post for something to hang onto.

The men piled on, the Canadians at the front by the driver, German prisoners at the back. The driver, Alf, was Henry Lane's brother. He had the same small stature but had a darker complexion with a friar's ring of black hair and bushy black eyebrows. He told everyone to hang on and flicked the reins, setting the two horses into motion.

A faint chugging became audible—the steam engine that powered the saws in the mill. Ten minutes later the road curved and the horses strained at their harnesses with ears pricked forward. Lehrmann muttered, "I hate this part." The horses started trotting. The snow road dipped into a valley and the horses picked up speed down the hill. The rig swayed. By the time they hit the bottom of the draw, men were swearing in both languages. Erich clung to the logs.

The horses loved that downhill run. Their momentum carried the rig halfway up the incline before they had to lean into their harnesses. When they topped the rise, the camp spread out before them. The horses swung left, past the fence of trees, pulled the sloop to the sawmill's loading dock, and stopped. Clouds of steam puffed out of their nostrils.

Alf ordered everyone off the sloop and waved at the sawmill crew. The sawmill's steam engine fell silent and lumberjacks lined up at vises to sharpen their axes for tomorrow. A young redhead named Jimmy arrived with the four skidding horses and rode toward the barn. The rhythm of the day's end, a country dance in four parts.

The thought of more stew slowed Erich's steps. He missed the food at Camp 133. The cooks there made meals that tasted fresh from a German grandmother's kitchen. When he got close, a cheerful din escaped the cookhouse. He leaned against the log building, enjoying a moment alone. Nikel appeared from behind the log bunkhouse, returning from the outhouse. Erich met him by the door.

They stepped inside and were engulfed by a smell that was definitely not leftover stew. Some kind of roast. Fresh buns. They shared a grin, hung up their coats and waited for a turn at the wash basin. Erich unwrapped the bandage strips securing his blisters. Though red and raw, they didn't look any worse than this morning. The harsh soap made them sting.

Behind him, Chuck said, "You'd better not be bleeding into the water like yesterday."

Erich flexed his hands. "That's what comes of having a heart-less teacher."

Chuck's expression tightened, then relaxed. "I'll show you heart-less. Tomorrow you and John will fell your first tree. The crosscut will give you blisters in different places." He sneered when Erich threw the towel at him.

Nikel whispered in German, "Why do they call me John?"

"That's English for Johann."

Nikel slid onto the bench, leaving the end spot nearest the kitchen for Erich. The tin plates were on the table instead of piled at the serving window that opened to the workspace. Mrs. Lane pushed through the door of the kitchen carrying a meat platter. "Don't get used to being served. This is a treat for tonight. Tomor-row you can line up as usual." Everyone was quiet as she served the Canadians.

A girl appeared with a second platter. Her shoulder-length tawny hair shone a half dozen shades in the lantern light. She looked up from the meat, revealing eyes of amber and emerald. Her cheeks tinted rose, maybe from exertion or maybe from knowing all eyes watched her.

She set down the meat at the table of silent Germans and retreated, returning with a pitcher of gravy, then a big bowl of green beans with a plate of buns balanced on top. With each trip Erich noticed more details. She looked close to his age. An apron hid her curves but he glimpsed them when she turned. Even in clunky shoes, her legs were shapely.

Finally she brought a heaping bowl of mashed potatoes. Erich drank in her features. Fine eyebrows, slightly upturned nose, lips that would be curved if they weren't pursed in concentration. Nikel spoke in German, "She's a girl, Hofmeyer. Remember those?"

A few of the prisoners laughed and added to the ribbing.

"It's been too long. He doesn't remember. He needs a kiss to jolt his memory."

At the sound of German, color drained from the girl's face. She froze half a step from the table. Her hands began to shake.

Still speaking German, Rudolf said, "Introduce yourself, Hofmeyer."

The girl's eyes widened. The metal bowl slipped from her grip and bounced off the edge of the table. Potato splattered across the table and floor, but only caught one heel of the fleeing girl. Alarmed, Erich jumped up to help her. But before he'd taken two steps, a body slammed into him. Air whooshed out when he hit the floor. He fought to inhale. A hand held his head down, his cheek and nose pressed into a glob of potato. Something sharp poked his side.

"Move an inch, Jerry," Frank said, "and this knife will separate your ribs."

Men shouted at Frank. Some yelled for him to stop, but someone said, "Finish it." Erich couldn't move. A knee pinned his shoulders. The hand trapping his face against the floor pressed harder, and the other still held a knife to his ribs. He saw German feet and legs. His fellow prisoners gathered by the head of the table, silent witnesses to his humiliation. From the corner of his eye he saw some clenched fists. Was his impulse to help the girl actually going to start a fight?

A door slammed. The prisoners' boots retreated a step, as if a warning shot had been fired. "Frank Janowski, put that knife down!" Henry Lane bellowed. The knife clattered onto the floor. "Get off that boy," Henry added, "or so help me I'll fire you on the spot."

The knee lifted from Erich's shoulder blades. Frank pushed up from the hand pressing on Erich's head. He squinted his eyes against the pressure. Hands grabbed and lifted him up. He found himself surrounded by his fellow prisoners. Behind the Canadians, the gray-haired Veterans Guardsmen observed, apparently curious to see if Henry Lane could control things.

"You okay, son?" Henry asked. Erich nodded and Henry turned to his brother, Alf, who usually ate with the men. "What happened?"

"Not much. Like all of us, the boy was watching your new kitchen help. When she was setting potatoes on the table, someone said something in German that upset her. Don't know what. She bolted. The boy started after her and in a flash Frank had him on the floor."

Henry marched to the huddle of prisoners. He eyed Erich. "What'd they say?"

Erich rubbed his cheek to get some feeling back, and to hide his chagrin. "They were teasing me about not remembering what a girl looks like."

"Why'd you chase her?"

Erich stared at Henry's boots. "I wanted to find out what was wrong. That's all."

"You gonna believe that piece of Nazi shit over me?" Frank demanded.

Henry was in his face in a heartbeat. "I didn't ask for your two cents, Janowski. Everyone knows you carry enough grudges to fill a boxcar. If you can't see yourself clear to work with these men," he said, indicating the prisoners, "then you can leave with a week's pay. But I'm shorthanded and need every worker. Let me know what it's to be."

Frank made to spit but swallowed when Henry crossed his arms. Gazing at the floor, Frank nudged some potatoes with his boot. "If I wasn't flat-footed, you know I'd be killing Nazis. There ain't much I can do besides fell trees. I'll stay."

"Good. And there'd better not be any accidents out there."

Frank sneered at Erich. "I won't cause any, but it ain't my fault some of them are dumber than sacks of hammers."

"Don't mistake inexperience and stupidity. You're only stupid if you make the same mistake twice." Henry stared at Frank until the younger man looked away. Then he scanned the Canadians. "Listen up. Their fighting days are done. You want to fight, go enlist. We can work together if we try. Some of these German boys come from cities and that means we have to show them the ropes, but that's how it goes. Danged if I'll make this speech again. Any of you can't hack the new arrangements, talk to me tomorrow and I'll give you the same deal I offered Frank."

He strode into the kitchen, came out with a stock pot and set it on the prisoners' table. "That's all the potatoes left. Eat before it's ice cold. There's saskatoon pie waiting."

The redheaded Canadian, Jimmy, whooped. "Saskatoons are my favorite."

Laughter shattered the tension and everyone took their seats. Schlenter leaned across the table in front of Nikel and whispered to Erich, "What is saskatoon pie?"

"I don't know. I just hope it tastes better than leftover stew."

19 DECEMBER 1943, LOGGING CAMP (-3°C/27°F)

Fire licked at him. With frantic kicks he dived, left the screams and flames behind. Pulled through the water, past the oil slick, past thrashing men. His lungs wrenched, needing air.

Erich woke up gasping. Cringed at the crackle of fire, until he realized it was the barrel-shaped stove being stoked. He was in a log bunkhouse in western Canada, not in the Atlantic. The cold air at this end of the room prickled over his arms and his scars tingled. He rubbed the puckered skin on his shoulder. Heard screams echo in his mind. Shivered, but not from the cold.

He had learned quickly that this bed by the door, forced on him by the other prisoners, was preferable to the ones by the stove. The men in those beds cooked from heat, threw off their blankets then froze. He could burrow under his covers to create a warm cocoon.

The door flung open and thunked against coats hung on pegs as three men entered. A blast of cold air rolled inside. Erich swore and pulled his blankets up. Nikel, one of the three, laughed and slapped Erich on the hip. "You missed breakfast. I brought you toast and jam."

Erich groaned at the prospect of a long day on an empty stomach, then remembered it was Sunday. That's why Nikel hadn't woken him.

The need to use the outhouse drove Erich up. A chest separated each bed from the next. He lifted the lid of his crate, yanked out clothes, and quickly dressed to brave the cold. When he returned he announced that what he missed most were flush toilets and hot showers. Several men threw things at him and suggested he return to Camp 133, since the prison camp had both. He shook his head and reheated his toast on the flat surface of the stove.

The morning ticked by. Men chatted about home. Not the war or how they'd come to be prisoners—too many raw memories of dead comrades and bloody battles. Better to focus on the good, like who was waiting for them and what they'd do when they returned. Some dozed. Erich wrote to his grandparents, a letter he'd never mail, a record of his time here. He wrote in English to keep his thoughts private from his roommates.

At noon, Alf called them for lunch. As they filed into the cookhouse they waved at the guard sitting outside their gate. Inside, fixings were laid out to make sandwiches. They were enjoying coffee and a dessert called rhubarb crisp when the Canadians entered. The two groups ignored each other. Erich ate a second dessert. He'd had rhubarb in Germany, mostly in tarts, and was surprised to see it here. It was warm and sharp, sweetened by whipped cream lobbed on top. His grandparents would puzzle over this airy topping, so unlike the clotted cream they used. He preferred the whipped cream.

It had warmed considerably outside and the Germans lingered in their enclosure. No watchtowers, just a lone guard who barely looked at them and the knowledge that stupid actions led back to Lethbridge. Rudolf took his knitted cap—called a toque by the Canadians—filled it with snow and closed it up with an extra shoelace. It made a misshapen football that hardly rolled, but Erich joined the game.

Ten minutes later, Alf yelled to get their attention. The men stood in a wary cluster as he opened the gate, then invited them to play outside the fence. The guard was gone. When no one moved, he said, "No one'll shoot you, for Pete's sake. Come out and play where there's room to run, like normal folks."

When the men turned to Erich with questioning looks, he translated, then asked the older man, "We're prisoners. Why would you do this?"

"You're men. You shouldn't be cooped up like chickens. We put up the wire because some folks wanted it, but you've all worked in the bush or the mill and come back each night. You've proved you're dependable. Keep it up and we'll get along."

Again Erich translated. When the looks of distrust eased on the German faces, Erich knew Alf had won their gratitude. He thanked Alf. The others ran past him, found chopped wood to mark goals and tramped the borders of their makeshift pitch.

In the blacksmith shop beside a lean-to shed, one Canadian clanged away, pounding metal. Some Canadians sat on the steps of their bunkhouse and some on the cookhouse stoop. Neither guard was in sight, though shadows moved behind a cookhouse window.

Erich stood in the middle of the yard and inhaled the tart spruce scent of the nearby sawmill. This moment, with no guards and no fences, tasted like freedom. More filling than toast by far.

At the house, the only clapboard building in a collection of log structures, the serving girl sat on the step and talked with Jimmy. The youngest local, it was no surprise he'd be talking to her, though she'd never spoken to any of the men in the cookhouse. Jimmy smiled and laughed a lot as they talked. He seemed to know her.

A clump of snow caught Erich on the shoulder. Nikel said, "Stop staring or she'll think you mean her harm." Erich scowled at his friend, who laughed. The game began in earnest.

9:

19 DECEMBER 1943, LOGGING CAMP (-3°C/27°F)

Every day that week Richard and his friends had caught Max, at recess or after school. They surrounded him, called him Hitler as they shoved and sometimes hit him. No one ever interfered, certainly not Miss Williams, who preferred the warmth inside the schoolroom to supervising recess.

Max was relieved to have a long list of chores on Saturday. When Mother offered to let him take a break to go buy a piece of hard candy, he declined. Why buy candy that would wind up in Richard's pocket? Instead he retreated into a comic-book world.

The church service on Sunday was Anglican, so his parents, Lutheran like all good Germans (Father said), stayed home and listened to *Back to the Bible Hour* at eight o'clock in the morning. Mr. Manning, the preacher, wasn't Lutheran, but Max figured his father didn't care so long as he wasn't Anglican.

After an early lunch of rye bread and bear stew—the meat came from Mrs. Johnson, who couldn't abide bear in her raspberry patch or in her pot—Father gave Max permission to walk to the logging camp. Mother made him promise to be back before dark.

Horley perched on the north fringes of the Saddle Hills, and the hike south to the camp took Max higher into a forest of poplar and spruce trees, with some birch. The trees seemed to have stepped back to form the road and stood shoulder to shoulder, watching Max pass. Birds chirped to the front and behind but never near him, like the girls and younger students at school. The older boys were more like hungry ravens pecking and tearing into him.

He sighed, wishing for the thousandth time that his father had bought a farm to the southeast, in the Westmark community where other German families had settled. Then maybe he'd have a friend.

Two years ago his sister, Bertha, had moved to Grande Prairie to work and finish high school so she could become a nurse. She wrote every week, but without her around Max spent a lot of time in his bedroom with his comic books. *Superman* and *Johnny Canuck* were his favorites, though he couldn't buy *Superman* anymore since the government had banned non-essential imports from the United States—but Superman was very essential. He always won against evil. *Jeepers, who wouldn't want the strongest guy ever to save them? I sure do.*

The road entered the big yard between a massive barn and pen on the right and the Lanes' home on the left. Some horses stretched their necks over the fence, hopeful Max had a treat. He didn't, but he stopped to pat a reddish bay with a white blaze. It pressed its face against Max's jacket and snorted.

The stutter of indistinct voices rose from the far side of the house. Then laughter. Max headed toward the noise. Beyond the barn, clusters of lumberjacks smoked on the steps of the first bunk-house and cookhouse. Their attention was on the yard and no one noticed Max. A dozen more steps revealed another group of men.

Max halted. These men were in matching sweaters and blue jeans with red stripes running down the outside seams. They were trying to play soccer with something lumpy and black. No one in Horley played soccer. They played baseball in the summer and hockey in the winter. Max's grandmother had mailed him a soccer ball the Christmas before the war started, but no one had wanted to play so he had only ever kicked it around with Bertha.

The men reshaped their so-called ball by stuffing more snow into what looked like a black toque. They tied it closed with something. Max almost laughed. No wonder it was lumpy and wouldn't roll.

When the men resumed playing, their voices rose and Max's jaw slackened. They were speaking German. And no one was getting mad at them.

A hand clamped onto his shoulder. He jumped. Alf Lane's friendly face peered at him and he relaxed. "I swear you've grown a foot since summertime, Max. It must be that blood sausage of your mother's."

A smile tugging at his mouth, Max gave a one-shouldered shrug.

Alf leaned close. "How'd your face get scratched? You get fresh with a girl?"

Heat crept across Max's cheeks. "I...slipped on some ice."

Alf pushed his lined hat back on his head. "Slipped, eh? Not with help, I hope."

Before Max could respond, some of the men playing soccer shouted and pumped their fists in the air. The lumpy hat they'd been kicking sat on a line scraped into the snow between two pieces of wood. The other men started arguing with them. Max pointed. "Who are they?"

"Prisoners of war."

POWs? Max searched Alf's face for a hint of teasing. There was none. "G-German prisoners?" Alf nodded and Max added, "Where did they come from?"

"Germany, I expect." Alf winked. "They're from the big prisoner-of-war camp down by Lethbridge."

"What are they doing *here*?"

"With the war dragging on, we're mighty shorthanded, so we joined a program to use prisoners."

"They're slaves?"

"No. They get paid credit for each day worked, plus room and board. We treat them fair." Alf squeezed Max's shoulder. "Henry wouldn't have it any other way. You know that."

Max nodded. He'd never heard anyone say anything bad about Henry Lane. Or Mrs. Lane, before that whisper in the store: *"It's hardly surprising she would defend the boy. Did you hear what they're doing out at the camp?"* That must've been about the Lanes using German prisoners. Max wanted to ask if people were angry at them. The words jammed in his throat.

"Did you hike up here for a visit, Max? Maybe you smelled Mildred's pies?"

Max smiled hopefully. Alf laughed. He steered Max toward the house. "She likes baking in her own kitchen. Let's see if we can beg a piece of warm rhubarb pie."

At the corner of the house a squishy thud behind Max made him turn. The toque turned soccer ball was a flattened lump near his foot. He picked it up.

A prisoner with short dark hair ran up to him. A grin narrowed eyes as blue as a lake in sunshine. "Thank you. Not that it could roll away." He took the snowy toque from Max's unresisting grip. He spun and called out in German, "Time out to refill the ball."

Max stuffed his hands into his pockets and watched the prisoner untie the toque's lace. He had spoken like Mrs. Williams, who came from England, not like his father with his thickly accented English. Alf nudged him into motion. "You speak German, don't you, Max?"

"At home." He glanced back. "That prisoner speaks English really good."

"Yes he does. He must've had a good teacher."

Max nodded to Jimmy, who was sitting on the steps with a girl he'd seen at some community suppers and dances his parents forced him to attend. Jimmy nodded back, his constant smile plastered in place like it had been painted there. The two wriggled to the side to let Max and Alf pass.

The second Alf opened the door, heat washed over them and tangy rhubarb filled Max's senses. He closed his eyes and inhaled loudly. Alf laughed. "Mildred, I sure hope you have a piece of pie you can spare for this boy so he doesn't suck all the air out the room smelling it."

Mrs. Lane paused from rolling out pastry dough on waxed paper at the far end of a large wooden table. "Of course, I do, Alf. It's your piece though."

The older man pretended alarm and winked at Max. "We'll see about that."

At Mrs. Lane's prompting, Max hung his coat on a hook by the door and took off his boots. Rag rugs were scattered around the living room and kitchen, all one big room. The hulking black woodstove acted as a partition, its pipe feeding into a brick column in the middle of the room. Almost like walls were going to be built out from the bricks, but it had never happened. Max liked it, open and comfortable. Alf indicated he should sit at the table.

As he moved around the kitchen, getting plates and cutlery, Alf asked, "Where's my brother? I think Master Schmidt has business to discuss."

"I'm right here, Alf." Henry Lane emerged from a side door.

"Working on a Sunday, Henry? Your mother taught you better than that."

"And she tried to teach you to respect your older brother, but it never took."

Max lowered his head so they wouldn't see him smile. Alf snorted and set the plate beside Max. The fork on it clinked. A wedge of rhubarb pie took up most of the plate. "Gee, thanks." Max licked his lips and cut the tip of pie with his fork. As he was chewing, the tart and sweet flavors bursting in his mouth, Henry claimed Alf's pie and thanked his brother.

"So, Max, what brings you up the hill?" Henry took a big bite of pie.

Max swallowed, set down his fork, and rubbed his palms on his thighs. "He, that is, Father." He bit the inside of his cheek. Both men leaned toward him, elbows on the table, with matching looks of curiosity. Max swallowed again. "We'd like help killing our hog." He exhaled, relieved to have spat it out.

"Your father can't do that himself?" Henry skimmed a hand over his bald head. He looked a lot like Alf, except he was fair and Alf was dark-haired with an outdoorsy redness. "He did last year," Max said, "but he had to use an ax. And—"

"Messy?" Henry suggested.

"Some. Father really likes his pigs." Max sighed. "It's a hard way to kill something."

Both men nodded. Mrs. Lane said, "Can't he shoot the pig?"

Henry replied, "The government took away all the German immigrants' guns."

"Oh dear. I'd forgotten. You could take your rifle and shoot the pig for him, couldn't you, Henry?" She wiped her nose with the back of her hand and left a smudge of flour.

"I believe that's what Max is hoping."

Max nodded and stuffed more warm pie into his mouth.

Alf said, "Sven Ahlberg told me Helmut asked to borrow his rifle. Sven was nervous as a hen with a coyote sniffing around."

Max jabbed at his pie. "Sven told Corporal Mason and he searched the farm, looking for weapons. Father only wanted to borrow it for a day. He knew Sven was busy with clearing roads for the district."

Henry shook his head. The pie in Max's stomach curdled. His head drooped.

"Son?" Henry's quiet voice urged Max to look up. He speared a piece of pie. "I was shaking my head over Sven. I wasn't refusing you. I go into town every Wednesday. If it suits your father, I'll stop by with my rifle this week."

A slight smile lifted the corners of Max's mouth. "Yes, sir. I'll tell him. Thank you."

"No need to thank me. It's what neighbors do."

Not all neighbors. Through the discussion, Alf had polished off his pie. Now he pushed his plate away. "If business is done, I've got something you can help me with, Max."

Max chewed and swallowed quickly. "Yes, sir. I don't have to be home until dark."

"That's good. Because I've been sanding and waxing the runners on Joey's sled, and I need someone to try it out."

Joey was Joseph, Henry's son who'd been captured by the Germans. Henry huffed. "What in the Sam Hill are you doing that for? Waste of time."

"It was hanging in the barn. That's my territory. Looking after what's in the barn isn't a waste of time." Alf jigged his eyebrows. "Besides, you never know when someone might happen along who enjoys a bit of fun. Remember fun, Henry? Ring any bells?"

Henry stood. "I have work to do. Go sledding for all I care. Just don't break that thick head." He nodded to Max and marched toward the side door.

Alf winked again. "It won't be me on that sled. You'll be careful, won't you, Max?"

His head bobbed. There were no good spots for sledding on his farm. It was on the side of the hill, but the slope was too gentle. The Lanes, though, had a deep valley on the east side of their yard. Max wolfed down the last two bites of pie, eager to go sledding. When he dropped his fork, he glanced at Mrs. Lane, only now realizing she might be upset at the mention of her son. She gave him one of her sad smiles. "Go on, Max. I hope you have gloves."

"Yes, ma'am." Max took his plate to the sink, thanked her, and scurried to the door.

He trotted after Alf to the barn to get the wooden sled, with its metal-trimmed front crosspiece curved like the wings of an airplane. He slid his arm between the flat deck and the runners. Alf swatted the back of his head. "Don't hit any trees."

Max jogged across the yard, past the stalled soccer game, past Jimmy and the girl, past the wide expanse on the left that was Mrs. Lane's vegetable garden in the summer. He stopped at the top of the hill and studied the terrain. December's unusual warmth had settled the snow, which was great for speed now that it had dipped below freezing. The spot that was packed down the most was the logging trail used by the horses and sloop. That looked too rough.

With his route planned, he backed up half a dozen steps, gripped the sled in both of his hands, and sprinted forward. One step from the slope he launched himself, flopping onto the sled and shooting down the hill.

His gleeful shout echoed across the valley.

10:

19 DECEMBER 1943, LOGGING CAMP (-3°C/27°F)

Erich retreated from the argument over whether the other team had scored. The men huddled around the pathetic knitted cap, more squished egg than ball. The boy who'd arrived half an hour ago trotted across the yard carrying some style of snow sled.

The redheaded lumberjack and the girl strolled after the boy, who launched himself over the rim of the hill. Curious, Erich followed. Conversation sifted across the snow.

"James Fraser," the girl said, "I'm no child that you can taunt in such an immature way."

"Everyone calls me Jimmy, but I like that. Will you call me James all the time?" Jimmy was red-cheeked and grinning.

The exchange seemed to give the girl pause. "If you wish."

"I do wish." He grabbed her hand. "Let's see if Max will let us give the sled a try."

"Unhand me, you oaf."

Jimmy released her. His grin widened. "The twisty way you say things is nice."

"Do stop being so horrible."

"Is horrible your favorite word?"

"Is nice yours?" They faced the valley.

Erich wondered about her accent. It had a hint of British, but nothing like his grandfather. Had she lived in England? Now he was more curious. He stayed a dozen steps behind them, unsure how his presence would be taken. Behind him, the sad attempt at a soccer game restarted. The toque lasted maybe six kicks before it was useless again.

Max—twelve or thirteen, Erich guessed—reappeared pulling the sled. He was coated in snow and grinning. His smile disappeared when he spotted Erich. The others turned.

After an awkward pause, Jimmy said, "Hello there. Want to join us?"

The girl recoiled slightly. Jimmy didn't seem to notice. The boy, Max, watched him, waiting for an answer, it seemed. Erich slid his hands into his pockets. "I'd like to watch."

The girl scowled. Jimmy turned back to the boy. "Can I give it a try, Max? You only got three-quarters of the way down. I can beat that if I stay on the trail."

Max held out the tow cord that looped from one side to the other of the front crosspiece. "You'll crash. Too many pockmarks from the horses."

"Ha. Just watch."

Erich sidled closer to the slope to see the whole valley. He kept Max between him and the girl, squirming inside to recall her reaction to the Germans that first night and the resulting chaos. She'd served the men from the kitchen since then, through the large window, and never looked at the German prisoners.

With a shout, Jimmy copied Max's technique, flopping onto the sled as he sailed down the hill. The sled bucked, hit a hole and rocketed off the path. Jimmy held tight, even when he rolled. He landed with the sled on top of him.

"He isn't moving," the girl said.

"I told him to stay off the horse trail," Max commented.

Erich pushed his fingers through his half-inch long hair. "Should we perhaps see if he's alive?" Shock seemed to ripple across the girl's features. Erich lowered his voice. "Is something wrong?" Down the hill, Jimmy struggled to his feet and began to brush himself off. Erich tried again. "What did I say to earn that look?"

"Y-your accent..." She blinked. "Are you...mocking me?"

Erich had worked hard to learn to speak like his English grandfather. Did she expect him to have a heavy accent like the other prisoners? "I don't understand. This is how I speak English."

"Like someone from England?" Her voice thrummed with tension.

"I suppose. Are you from England?"

She made a sound of disgust. "Of course I am. Everyone says my accent is quite distinct."

"It sounds a little faded." A frown settled on her brow. Erich backpedalled. "I mean, you must have lived in Canada for some time." The frown grew deeper.

"As it happens," she snipped each word, "I have lived in Canada since I was eight. Nine years."

The boy's gaze darted back and forth. The tension was so thick even he noticed. The boy turned toward her. "I'm Max. When did you start helping Mrs. Lane?"

The girl glared at Erich for three more seconds, then smiled at Max. "Nice to meet you, Max. At least someone here is polite enough to introduce himself. I'm Cora Edwards. I heard about the job from my cousin and only started a few days ago."

"You'll like it. The Lanes are the nicest people I know."

"They are kind." She smiled, and it seemed to light up her whole face.

What would a man give, Erich wondered, *to have her look at him like that?*

Jimmy reached the top of the hill. "Gosh, that hurt. Who's stupid idea was that anyway?"

Max and Cora laughed. Jimmy offered the rope to Erich. "Sure you don't want to try?"

"After your spectacular tumble? No, thank you. I'll learn Max's technique first."

Jimmy laughed. "I need to see if coffee's on in the cookhouse. Warm me up. Want to join me, Cora?"

"I'll watch Max ride, thank you. Then I have some letters to write."

Jimmy shrugged and handed the sled to Max. "You were right about those hoof marks. They were real bear traps." He gave Max a playful tap on his shoulder. "Say hi to your sister. She'll remember me from school. Is she still around?"

"She's working in Grande Prairie, saving to go to nursing school."

"Good for her." With a wave he limped away.

For a moment the three were statues. Then Max shook himself. He extended his hand. "I'm Max."

"Erich Hofmeyer." He shook Max's hand. "Nice to meet you." Max's eyebrows rose, which puzzled Erich. "Was that the wrong thing to say?"

"No. I've never had anyone say it is all." Max spun and charged the hill. He took the path he'd ridden before, turned the sled at the last moment and extended his path.

No one ever said it was nice to meet him? Erich pondered that.

"I do wish you'd stop speaking like an Englishman," Cora said.

He raised his eyebrows. "Would you rather I spoke German?"

She flushed. "I would rather you didn't speak at all." She spun and stalked to the house. She disappeared inside at the same moment Max trudged to Erich's side.

"Did you say something to make her mad?"

Erich sat on the ground and rested his forearms on upraised knees. "Apparently it was how I said it, not what I said."

"Girls are strange." Max sat on the sled beside Erich.

"They are, strange yet so appealing."

Max whipped off his toque and rubbed it over a blond crewcut, mopping up sweat as he gave a doubtful look that rounded his green eyes.

Erich chuckled. Max looked embarrassed so he changed the subject. "Why don't people think it's nice to meet you?"

Max shrugged and bit his lip. Erich waited until Max said, "My last name is Schmidt."

"You're German?"

"No. I was born in Canada."

"With a German name."

Max sighed. "And a very German father."

"I have one of those too."

"Well of course you do. You're from Germany."

"True. But not all fathers insist their sons enlist at sixteen."

"You're sixteen?" Max's voice rose, cracked. This time his embarrassment spread, a red stain on his neck and ears.

"Seventeen, but I was sixteen when Father signed my enrollment papers. I had wanted to go to university. I'll be eighteen in February. How old are you?"

"Twelve. I'll be thirteen in March." He propped his chin on his cupped hands. "The only twelve-year-old in the world with no friends."

"There aren't any other students nearby with German parents?"

"Not in this district."

Erich squinted at him. How would he have felt to be twelve and friendless? He hadn't been like his older brother, collecting friends the way some people collect stamps, but he'd had a few boys to chum with. He studied the valley and recalled the loneliness that had consumed him when he'd first joined the navy and everyone had shunned him because he was so young. Some of them had harassed him because of his English skills, which had gotten him assigned to be a backup radio operator. That loneliness had felt as vast as the

North Atlantic. It hadn't been until he'd met Nikel in Camp 133 that it had shrunk a bit. But being nine years older, Nikel often felt more like a kind older cousin than a friend.

A movement across the vally caught his eye. Max saw it too and pointed. "Coyote."

"It looks like a wolf." Erich shifted as the cold wormed through his blue jeans.

"Smaller. I usually see them alone or in pairs. Maybe I'm a coyote. And the boys at school are wolves who always gang up on the loner."

"I've run into wolf packs."

Max gave him a startled look. Erich shrugged. "Two-legged wolves, I mean. Back at the prisoner-of-war camp."

"Is that why you're here?"

"Mostly."

The coyote, gray and white with a hint of brown, stared at them for a long moment. Then it disappeared into the shadows of the forest.

"It seems we're both like that coyote." Erich rose into a crouch to get off the wet ground.

"Loners?" Max suggested.

Erich nodded. "But we could try banding together, if you want."

The wide smile told Erich he'd said the right thing. He only hoped it didn't make things worse for Max.

11:

24 DECEMBER 1943,
LOGGING CAMP (-1°C/30°F)

The week proved grim. The closer Christmas came, the quieter the men became, each lost in memories. When home was half a world away, the thought of Christmas wasn't cheerful.

Christmas Eve. Erich felt at a loss. Even thinking of a jewel-eyed serving girl couldn't keep his mind off home. And that was more like torture, given how Cora had snubbed him the two times he'd spoken to her this week.

Someone kicked the door. Erich, being closest, opened it. Henry stood on the threshold, hidden behind a large wooden box. Erich helped set the box on his bed.

"Evening, boys. Merry Christmas."

The men stayed on their beds. A few replied with a half-hearted, "*Frohe Weihnachten.*"

"Christmas can't be happy when you're so far from home." Henry frowned into the box, as if he knew that feeling. "We have to make the best of it. I always give my workers something small on Christmas but was told you give gifts on Christmas Eve." He cleared his throat. "Got something in here for each of you and two of Mrs. Lane's Christmas cakes to share. So, have at it."

"Will we work tomorrow?" Erich asked.

"On Christmas? Of course not. Monday's soon enough to get back at it."

A few of the men didn't follow Henry's quick reply. Erich's translation brought smiles and nods.

"One more thing," Henry said. "I called the warden at your camp in Lethbridge. I convinced him we're too danged far from anywhere to worry about any of you escaping. You'd freeze to death if you tried." He waited while Erich translated for those who didn't understand. "He admitted he could use his guards at the big camp rather than here doing nothing. They're leaving on Monday." He paused again for Erich, then waited until the surprised whispers died. "Alf and I are sort of unofficial Veterans Guards now. We'll act like that if we have to, but we'd rather just be your bosses. It's up to you."

When Henry left the bunkhouse, everyone expressed their pleasure at the turn of events. Their attention turned to the box. Nikel suggested they gather round the stove for their gift opening. Two fruitcakes wrapped in waxed paper sat on ten small packets in brown butcher's paper. At the bottom were ten bottles of beer and an opener. The men brightened. They laughed as they unwrapped their gifts of identical work gloves.

They opened the beer, cut into the cake and shared Christmas stories.

Schlenter told how excited his children were to light the four candles on the Advent wreath.

"My family strolls the Christmas market every Saturday it's open. I miss cider and gingerbread," Nikel said.

"The mulled wine is better," Conkle insisted.

"I always liked St. Nicholas's visit on the sixth. A shoe full of sweets," Rudolf said, his round face beaming.

"I only got a switch in my shoe growing up," Hubart replied.

Everyone laughed. Anyone with pictures of children, wives, or sweethearts showed them off.

Erich told about the Christmas his grandparents had given bicycles to both brothers. Gerhard had crashed his on ice the day after Christmas and had taken Erich's, leaving him the one with a bent fender and crooked tire. His grandfather had helped him fix it, leaving him with the better, though dented, bicycle. Laughter flickered with warmth.

Erich wolfed down cake full of nuts and dried fruits he hadn't seen in ages. His parents would be celebrating with Gerhard, if he had leave. Having the eldest son to fawn over, they wouldn't miss him, but his grandparents might. Not half as much as he missed them.

Another knock at the door and Alf walked in. He wished every-one a Merry Christmas. The response was louder this time around. He handed a medium-sized box to Erich. "A present from a friend."

"Oh! *Ein Fräulein.*" Nikel brushed at his brown hair like a girl, making the men laugh.

"No girl is sending me anything," Erich replied as the heat crept over his cheeks.

"Not a girl. But the giver said you might want to share this."

Nikel cleared his throat, motioned for Erich to open it.

"*Ja, ja.*" Lehrmann took a swig of beer and spoke in German, "Show us the gift before we run out of cheer."

Alf said, "What are you waiting for? Open it."

Erich smiled as he untied the string. It was an Ivory Soap box. Either someone was sending him a message about hygiene, or they'd had no other box. He lifted the flaps. Stared with mouth open. He looked up at Alf. "Who would do this?"

"Max. He said it was his, but it's hardly been used. He didn't think you'd mind. So what is it?" Alf crossed his arms.

Erich lifted a brown leather soccer ball out of the box. The silence was profound. A real ball. Well stitched. The stamp said it was German-made. Erich handed it to Nikel, who gave it an approv-ing squeeze. It made its way around the circle, each man patting or squeezing it.

When it returned to Erich, Alf said, "Does it pass inspection?"

"It's beautiful," Erich replied. "*Wunderschön.*"

Everyone laughed, and nodded. Erich raised his bottle. "To Max."

"*Prosit!*" the men all responded.

12:

24 DECEMBER 1943, LOGGING CAMP (-2°C/28°F)

Max curled up on the couch in the Lanes' cozy home, adjusting to the strangeness of being in someone else's house on Christmas Eve. They'd always celebrated at home. But Bertha had stayed in Grande Prairie because of a bad cold, so being home would be strange too. When Henry Lane had stopped to help Father kill the pig, they'd decided to put it off until the following week. He'd invited the family to share Christmas Eve. And here they were. Had Father felt obligated to accept because Henry was going to kill their pig? Max had been so surprised when his mother had told him, he'd almost dropped his cup of hot Ovaltine.

Now he could hardly move, he'd eaten so much. Mother had brought her special occasion favorite: venison rouladen, thin rolled steak stuffed with bacon, onions, pickles, and mustard. Plus roast potatoes and red cabbage. Mrs. Lane had served fresh buns, green beans, and two kinds of pie, rhubarb and saskatoon. Max couldn't decide so he'd had one of each. He'd passed on the Christmas cake. He burped up the taste of saskatoons but didn't mind. The fat purplish berries were a favorite.

Henry's atlas was open beside him. Normally he liked maps, but now he rested his hand on his stomach bulge as Father visited with Henry at the table and Mother helped Mrs. Lane decorate the tree beside the brick chimney. Thankfully, Cora was visiting relatives, otherwise the adults would probably force her to play a game with him. The only thing worse than not having a friend was someone playing with you because they had to.

Mrs. Lane hung each handmade ornament Mother handed her.

"I would love to put candles on the tree," she said, "but Henry thinks it's dangerous, too many paper decorations. Back in Saskatchewan, we had glass ornaments, but we didn't think they'd survive the trip. I still miss them. I might ask my sister to pack them and send them anyway."

"But you have tinsel. Very lovely," Mother said. "You could burn candles near the tree and they would reflect off the tinsel."

"That's a wonderful idea." They worked silently until Mrs. Lane said, "I suppose lamplight would work. Maybe I'll use some extra coal oil lamps. Did you have electricity back in Germany? I miss being able to turn a switch and instantly have light good enough to read by."

Mother blinked. "You had electricity in Saskatchewan?"

"Oh yes. We lived in the capital, Regina, before we traipsed into the bush. This lumber company is Henry's dream. He grew up in a logging camp in Ontario. There weren't many trees in Regina so here we are."

"Yes, we had electricity in our hometown. But it was impossible to stay. No jobs, and Helmut dreamed too. He wanted to farm his own land. So here *we* are." She stared at the ornament in her hand.

Max could almost see the thoughts on her face. This time of year she missed her family. Her mother was still alive. And Mother had a brother and a handful of cousins she tried to keep in touch with. That was extra hard now.

Stomping outside announced Alf's return. Max popped to his feet and was halfway to the door when Alf closed it. Max searched his face. "Did they like it?"

"Like it?" Alf laughed. "Max, I've never seen a room of grown men so close to tears. They passed it around like it was a holy treasure. A few looked like they wanted to kiss it."

Max grinned. His father asked, "Are you now going to tell us what you gave that fellow?"

He bit the inside of his lip. Mother might not like that he'd given away something her mother had given him. "I saw the prisoners last Sunday, trying to play soccer with a toque they'd stuffed with snow. So I gave them my soccer ball."

"Oh, Max." He cringed at the sad note in Mother's voice.

He gave her a pleading look. "I don't have anyone to play with anyway. At least someone can enjoy it. Maybe I can come here on Sundays and play with them."

The disappointed frown lifted. "You're very generous."

"Yes, he is," Mrs. Lane agreed.

"Let's have a beer," Alf said. "We can toast Max like those boys in the bunkhouse did."

Max's ears heated at the thought of someone toasting him. Alf poured full glasses for the men, half for the women, and a quarter for Max. Father looked ready to deny Max, but Henry gave him a tiny nod and he nodded back. They all raised their glasses.

"Merry Christmas, everyone," Henry said.

"Merry Christmas!" they echoed.

Max was sipping his beer, trying to get used to the sour taste, when the singing began. At the table, the men exchanged glances. Mrs. Lane slipped her arm around Mother's waist. "I didn't think enough men were left in camp to form a choir. Those with family or friends nearby left at noon."

Max tilted his head. "That isn't English."

The sound swelled, the tune recognizable as "Silent Night." Henry opened the nearest window an inch. The hymn wafted through the crack and filled the room.

Mrs. Lane said, "I don't understand the words, but that makes it seem like we're being serenaded by a musical instrument. It's lovely."

The sound rose and fell, brushing over Max like a breeze, raising goosebumps. He rubbed his arms. Mother smiled, with tears glistening.

Silence. Max held his breath, wondering if they would continue. Alf joined Henry at the window as another song started. "O Christmas Tree," again in German. No one moved as the singing swirled through the room with the fragrance of spruce tree, Christmas cake, and pie.

That song ended. Across the yard, someone yelled, "Don't you Jerries know any English songs?"

This silence was longer, then one voice unraveled in the night. Max knew it was Erich. The words were too clear to be anyone else. "Good King Wenceslas looked out, on the feast of Stephen," he sang. "When the snow lay round about, deep and crisp and even."

"Don't know that one," Henry commented.

"I think it's an English carol. Didn't Mary Williams sing it once at a community Christmas concert?" Mrs. Lane replied.

"Brightly shone the moon that night, though the frost was cruel, When a poor man came in sight, gath'ring winter fuel."

Max puzzled over how Erich could know an English song. He listened to the words, the song of a king being kind to a poor man. It ended with, "Ye who now will bless the poor, shall yourselves find blessing." It felt like Erich had chosen the song as a thank you. Max flung open the door, saw the men clustered in the middle of the yard, then raised his hand in greeting. Most of the Germans had turned back to their bunkhouse, but Erich spotted him and returned the salute.

13:

29 DECEMBER 1943, SCHMIDT FARM (-3°C/27°F)

The glow of Christmas drowned in blisters and blood.

As Father butchered the pig, Max stirred the pail of blood carefully captured off the drainage board. The door of the slaughter shed was open but the thick metallic smell still made him gag. He tried to breathe through his mouth, but then he could almost taste it. He wasn't sure which was worse.

A day and a half of swinging a hammer, building stalls in the new barn, had given his hands juicy blisters that had popped and bled and stung with every swing. Now they throbbed with each turn of the stirring stick, though bandages helped some.

All of this would be worth it when Mother served the first blood sausage and cooked the first pork roast. She made the best gravy. Max loved to pour so much over his potatoes that they looked like islands in a brown sea. The stench of blood faded as he imagined it.

He wished someone else could stir the blood. "Is Christmas going to come work for you this year?"

Father grunted. "I never know with him. If he shows up, he shows up. But we don't have money this year to hire anyone."

Max sighed and went back to imaging a pork roast feast. They'd heard that in Germany food was strictly rationed. Max couldn't imagine that. Sure, some things were rationed, like sugar and coffee and eggs, but most things were plentiful. And on the farm, a big garden, laying hens, wild game, and the butchered pig meant there was plenty of food.

"Okay, Max," Father said. "Get the pail into the icehouse so it cools off as quickly as possible."

"Yes, sir." The blood needed to sit for a day or two, and they couldn't leave it where it might attract animals. The cold-storage shed was always barred.

Max hoisted the metal pail. He'd heard the expression "blood is thicker than water"; Max decided it was heavier too. The pail pulled his shoulder down as he made his way out of the butcher shed and angled toward the icehouse across the yard.

"*Meow, meow, meow.*" The orange barn cat trotted beside him, head and tail high.

"Go away, Humpty." He called the cat Humpty-Dumpty because it had fallen out of the hayloft when it was small and had broken its front leg in a crooked landing. Very uncatlike.

It continued to mew loudly, as if it were starving. Max kicked in its direction and almost slipped. He changed hands and slowed down as he neared the house. Mother, working at the sink, waved behind the window.

The shoveled path from the door to the icehouse was uneven. Today was barely above freezing and the warm weather all month had softened the trail, so much that half the time Max's boots made craters.

He picked his way down the path. Above him, a raven croaked. Its shadow sailed across the snow, a bomb plunging down. "*Crawk!*" Max flinched, twisting away from the shadow and the diving bird.

His foot caught in a hole. He pitched forward.

The pail bumped the snowbank. Splashed over the snow. Over Max.

He sprawled on the path, too stunned to move. A streak of orange landed near his face. The cat's rough tongue licked blood from his cheeks.

"Max? Max, are you okay?" Mother called from the window.

How could he say yes? He was lying in the snow, covered in blood. This was a new and hideous meaning of *bloodbath.* Superman would have flown the blood to the icehouse without spilling a drop.

A bellow spiked fear through Max's chest. His heart thudded frantically as he rolled over. Father charged toward him. Max scuttled backward, leaving a red smear down the path.

"What have you done?" Father's face darkened to a purplish color.

"I didn't mean—"

"But you did!"

"A, a raven—"

"*Mein Gott!* You would blame a bird for this mess? You clumsy *Dummkopf.*" He kicked at clean snow beside the blood. "You come home from school every day saying the same thing. 'I fell. I tripped. I slipped on ice.' I should have known better than to trust you with the blood."

"I'm sorry!" Max sat up. He wiped at his knees, spread the sticky mess. The smell made him want to gag. He swallowed hard.

"Sorry will not get us blood sausage!" Father's neck bulged with cords of muscle. The bulges pulsed. "Sorry will not squeeze more blood from that butchered hog!" Blood sausage was Father's favorite treat, more than anything sweet. Max clutched his knees so his hands wouldn't shake.

Father took a step forward, splatting into the gelling blood. Beside his foot, the cat licked the snow rapidly, glancing up every few seconds. Father made a low noise, almost a growl. His hands squeezed into fists. "Get over here." Each word was said slowly, with no space for dispute.

Max wanted to refuse. He'd never seen Father so angry. Instead, he scrambled up and eased his foot forward, then his other. Finally, he stood within Father's reach, on top of the scene of his crime. The pail sat in the snow, its mouth facing Max in an empty scream. Behind Father, Mother came out of the house in shoes. She held her brown coat closed under her chin.

Father's fists loosened, tightened, again and again. Max squeezed his eyes shut, waiting for the blow. Father had never hit him, though the threat had often simmered below his words. His tone alone never allowed for disobedience.

This hit would make anything Richard could dish out seem like a tap. Max tried to keep his breathing even. *I am Superman. I am strong as steel. Nothing can hurt me.* A sound of disgust made Max open his eyes. Father raised his open hand. Grabbed his cap and slapped it against his thigh. He spun and marched away, past Mother who sagged with relief.

Max dropped to his limp noodle knees. The cat startled, then resumed licking up globules of blood. On the roof's peak, a raven tilted its head and stared at Max as if he were a slaughtered carcass.

14:

31 DECEMBER 1943,
LOGGING CAMP (-8°C/18°F)

From the edge of the dark yard, Erich scanned shadows and inhaled woodsmoke scent. The light spilled from cookhouse windows and the prisoners' bunkhouse. The Canadian bunkhouse was dark; all the men gone to a community dance. It was so quiet, so different from the city bustle he'd known his whole life.

He had taken the sled from where Max had propped it against the house, and now he sat on it to keep dry. He pivoted so his back was to the yard as he fought his blue mood. Tonight was the last night of the worst year of his life. He had fallen from a sinking ship into a burning sea and had been pulled out by men he was supposed to consider enemies. He had suffered through burn treatments and had been shipped halfway around the world to a prison camp where men wanted to kill him for not being a fanatic. (Sometimes he wondered if his brother had sent word to torment him.) To escape he'd fled here, to this camp with conditions so primitive they made him groan with frustration, though he kept a cheerful front. Or tried to.

Though the war seemed a distant nightmare, on the far side of the world people were fighting. Dying. Was his brother alive? Had his home been bombed? His parents still hadn't written. Would they rather he had died a hero? Were they ashamed of his capture? He was relieved to be out of the fighting, a sentiment at least his grandparents shared.

The moonlight escaped its cloudy prison, cast silver light across the valley. *Good King Wenceslas looked out...* Christmas seemed ages ago. A day of soccer games and laughter, thanks to Max. But all week, exhaustion had oozed from his pores and he'd barely been able to lift his feet by day's end.

To his right, footsteps crunched along the sloop's path. Cora— who obviously hadn't noticed him. He cleared his throat. "Good evening."

Cora gasped and clapped her hand over her mouth. After a few seconds, she spoke with a quiver. "You shouldn't scare people like that."

"Sorry." Erich drew his bare hands out of his pockets and gripped his knees. They were pale against his denim trousers. "I assumed you were away dancing like all the lumberjacks."

"I wouldn't be good company tonight."

"Holidays are full of ghosts."

Cora inhaled shakily. "Meaning?"

"Just that it's hard not to think of home and other holidays."

"So you came outside to escape the ghosts of New Years' past?"

"No. I had a choice of staying with a sick man in the bunkhouse or joining a card game in the cookhouse. I have no face for poker. And it's nice out here." When she said nothing, Erich asked, "How do you usually celebrate New Year's Eve?" More silence. He peered at the moon. At least she hadn't stomped off. "My parents would be hosting a large *Silvester* party, with champagne, hors d'oeuvres, a live band, men in uniforms or tuxedos, women in gowns. Everything sparkling. I hate those kinds of parties." But what kind of parties did he like? Not many.

Erich cleared his throat and filled the increasingly awkward silence with the first thought that surfaced. "At parties I was my parents' trained monkey. They made me perform piano pieces, Beethoven or Mozart. But when I was fifteen I played Smetana." He chuckled.

Finally, a grudging question. "What is Smetana?"

"A composer. Inferior Czech music, according to my parents and their friends. Music one never played in the Reich. They grounded me for a month." He laughed. "It was worth it."

"The Reich." She spat the words. "I hate how smugly you say that. As if it doesn't matter."

"I don't understand. I was only..." Why would she react like that? Then it hit him. The war. He spoke quietly. "Did you lose someone in the war?"

Rage-filled words erupted. "Lose someone! That makes it sound like I could find them. It was one of your bombs. It didn't *lose* anyone. It tore my aunt and uncle into pieces, then burned what was left of them. And here you are, safe and happy, as if their lives didn't matter." She gulped in air noisily.

Erich rose and stepped toward her.

"Don't touch me!" She started to walk backward. "And stop trying to be nice. You're not nice. You're German. I can't bear to look at you. I wouldn't be here if Mum didn't need—" She fled toward the house.

Erich sighed and stuffed his hands in his pockets, muttering under his breath. "Should I apologize for everything? For dropping bombs, sinking ships, shooting soldiers, blowing up tanks, killing civilians, arresting people. For starting the war to begin with."

The house door slammed. Erich winced. *I'm so useless around girls.* Though that wasn't the problem here. Would she like him if he told her about his grandparents in England? In the prisoner-of-war camp Bechtel had hated him because of that connection, so maybe it would count. Unlikely. He'd heard the rawness in her voice.

He kicked at the sled until its bow-shaped front faced down the hill, then he sat. He'd orginally come out for a midnight ride, with no one to see him take a tumble. Now that Cora had left, being alone felt wide and empty. *Stop feeling sorry for yourself.* He wedged his heels against the front piece and held the cord like horse reins. He rocked forward, kept rocking until he felt the sled inch forward. He pushed with one fist.

The sled took off. He glided down, night wind biting his cheeks, racing into semi-darkness as the snowdrifts flashed by. A grin split his face. And then he was airborne.

Erich flung himself to the side, twisted and hit the ground with a grunt. He lay for a moment in a crusty drift. At least he was uninjured. That might have gotten him sent back to Camp 133. He shuddered. Opened his eyes. White curtains of light rippled above the trees. Waves in a cosmic breeze. His breath sucked in.

"Aurora borealis," he whispered. Though he'd never seen them, he had read stories set in Scandinavia that had described them.

Part of the curtain turned pale green. The color danced and shimmered along the ribbon of white, arched high above the valley.

Erich exhaled awe. *It's gossamer. A veil between this world and the next.*

He stood and craned his neck to watch the magical lights. It was spectacular. He glanced toward the top of the valley, wishing he could share it with someone. But he didn't want to leave in case it disappeared.

The shimmering light show grew, filled the sky, and loomed over him until he felt himself shrinking. A speck. A fleck of nothing.

Alone under translucent curtains he could never touch. In a frozen world where he would never belong.

15:

1 JANUARY 1944,
LOGGING CAMP (-7°C/19°F)

Erich moved through the day mechanically. His body did what it was supposed to—sawed down six trees with Nikel, delimbed them, left them to be skidded to the landing on Monday.

The images of the night sky's stunning beauty played in his mind and the feeling of insignificance returned. A punch on his shoulder startled him. He frowned at Nikel. "What?"

"You've been standing with that ax sunk into the base of that limb for five minutes. Should I leave you here to dream or are you quitting for the day with the rest of us?"

Erich hadn't heard the gong of the saw blade. He yanked the ax free. "Isn't this early to be quitting?" He didn't mind. It had gotten colder overnight and was snowing lightly.

"So we only worked half a day. Henry didn't want us to work at all." Nikel headed to the skidding path. Erich followed, ax in one hand and crosscut saw in the other.

"Are you liking not working with Frank?" Nikel asked.

Erich grimaced at the feel of blisters inside his gloves. On Monday Frank had said they were ready to work alone, which had turned the week into a slog of aching muscles and new blisters. Quiet lunchtimes, sitting back-to-back with Nikel on a felled tree, made it bearable.

Two days ago, while munching a ham sandwich, Nikel had said, "The navy is the only place where the war is still fought with honor."

"What do you mean?" Erich had asked.

"War is cleaner on the ocean. The things you hear that our soldiers do to civilians or that the Soviets do to us—I don't even want to believe them. Except, with men like Bechtel in the war, I fear even worse is happening. And bombs rain down to destroy whole towns. Where is the honor in that? On the ocean, it's a game of chess. You position your ships, make your moves, and only your opponents are destroyed. Not civilians. Not towns. And when we capture the enemy, we treat him with respect."

Before Erich could argue there was nothing clean about the oil and flame that had killed so many of his shipmates, Nikel added, "Friend or foe, you treat people with respect, Erich. You are a true *Kriegsmarine*, even if you are so young."

They had shared a smile, and Erich had shared his cake, which delighted Nikel. The declaration had carried Erich through the afternoon.

"You prefer working with that young hothead?" Nikel's voice tugged Erich from his thoughts.

"No, I like that Frank is gone. Though working on New Year's Day is insane." The sawmill crew wasn't working, but they generally kept apart from the others. Erich couldn't recall why the lumberjack prisoners had decided the day would go faster if they worked. Henry had scoffed but said if Alf was willing to take them into the bush, they could work. Alf had agreed. Did he also have ghosts to avoid on holidays?

Erich's steps slowed. Were ghosts created in wartime more haunting? Like Cora's relatives? Did they produce sharper sorrow? Erich realized he had stopped. He exhaled, spoke to the still forest. "Pull yourself together, Hofmeyer. You survived the Atlantic, you can survive a cold shoulder."

He was the last prisoner to reach the landing. Alf harumphed. "Thought we were going to have to send out a search party."

"Then you'd have six lost Germans instead of one."

"That wouldn't be a problem, smart ass, not with Christmas coming."

Nikel scratched his head. "Christmas is a week past."

"Would it be a second celebration, a second Christmas, if we were lost?" Rudolf asked.

Alf rolled his eyes. "This Christmas is a person. One who works harder than any of you."

Erich vaguely remembered Frank mentioning someone by that name. It was an odd name for a person. The prisoners exchanged puzzled looks and shrugs.

Alf motioned everyone on board. The sloop had one layer of logs on the frame, making a floor. As the men jumped on, Schlenter said, "I hear Canada winter *sehr kalt*. This not *kalt*."

"Cold," Erich corrected. The man shrugged.

"Cold?" Alf balanced on two logs, reins in hand. "This ain't cold. Enjoy it, boys. Next week is a full moon. Then it'll get cold enough to freeze the brass balls off a monkey."

Erich laughed as he straddled a log to let his feet dangle over the end. Nothing could be colder than his first voyage on the Atlantic last February.

Alf's chucking noise urged the horses forward. Behind them, the tree trunks stood straight as the columns in Cologne Cathedral. The men talked in low voices, adding a harmonic hum to the runners' hiss. *Hymn in a northern forest.*

Movement flickered beyond the landing, like that black shadow Erich had seen the first day. What was it? He almost jumped off the sloop to investigate. As they approached the valley beside the camp they picked up speed. He didn't think they needed much speed to make it up the hill with such a light load, but Alf liked the run. With saw and ax wedged between logs behind him, Erich curled his fingers over the edges of the logs. The other men held onto vertical posts.

The horses began their downhill gallop, their hooves drumming a muffled tattoo against the snow-packed trail. In seconds they reached the bottom. They thundered across the narrow valley, past where he had landed in a snowbank the night before.

A clank. Alf shouted. The rear of the rig slewed left. Hit soft snow. Bucked Erich off. He tumbled. Men jumped, fell. The sloop swung back. Thunked to a standstill.

Erich scrambled up. Heard swearing. Alf worked to calm the spooked horses. Erich ran toward the sloop, saw Nikel on all fours by the trail, shaking his dark head as if to clear it.

Movement flashed on the hill. Max pelted down the slope and skidded to a stop. "Are you all right, Erich?"

"What are you doing here?"

"I came to see if you were playing soccer. I'd hoped..."

Someone started yelling in German, calling for medical help. Erich spun Max around. "Find Henry. Tell him someone is hurt."

With a nod, Max scrambled past the horses and up the hill like a hare. Erich and Nikel joined the men huddled around Schlenter's partner, Rudolf. The second-youngest German, older than Erich by two years, Rudolf groaned and clutched his thigh. His round face shone with sweat. The snow under his calf was red, seeping pink at the edges of a growing pool of blood.

Schlenter tried to tear away the trouser leg, but Rudolf cried out. Alf elbowed his way past the kneeling man, pocket knife in hand. "John," he barked, "keep my horses calm. Erich, tell this boy to hold still. Can't do anything if he's thrashing."

Erich knelt and cupped his hand on Rudolf's wide forehead, whispered in German, told him to not move, then explained each thing Alf did. How he cut the trouser leg off, exposing a jagged gash half hidden by a smear of blood. Erich didn't describe the cut. Alf sliced the trouser leg into strips, tied a tourniquet above the injury. Used another piece to roughly bandage it.

A bow saw looped around Rudolf's other leg. He must have been standing with his foot inside the D of the handle without realizing it.

When he was thrown off the sloop, the saw tagged along. Rudolf had probably landed on it. Alf sat back on his heels. "Anyone else hurt?"

A few complained about hard landings, an aching shoulder. "We're only banged up," Erich told Alf. "What happened?"

"Chain snapped near the right runner. Damned if I didn't check it this morning. I always check the chains and harnesses." His complexion was darker than usual. *Angry*, Erich thought.

Henry shouted from halfway down the hill, causing the horses to shy. Nikel calmed them, then waved to Alf, who was on his feet and limping toward his animals. He stopped and returned the acknowledgment. Stared at his raised hand. Rudolf's blood had stained it a red that matched his red-checked jacket. He washed his hands in snow.

Henry stormed past Alf, a blanket over his shoulder. He threw it at Erich. "Use this as a stretcher, one man on each corner. Get him to my house. Mildred's waiting."

He backtracked to the sloop, bent over the broken chain. Erich and three others spread the blanket beside Rudolf. Taking hold of his three uninjured limbs, they lifted him onto the blanket, arranged his cut leg snug against the other. They each twisted a corner of the blanket and wrapped it around a fist. Lifted. Rudolf groaned and rolled his head. Already the makeshift denim bandage was darkening, urging them to hurry.

Max jittered at the top of the hill. Henry had obviously told him to stay there. He walked beside Erich when they reached the tableland of the camp. His navy toque fell off, revealing his sandy crewcut. He scooped up the toque and jogged to catch up.

Erich said, "Open the door, Max."

The boy darted forward. His expression was solemn as the men maneuvered through the doorway, drawing groans from their patient, but he didn't looked shocked. Maybe injuries were common in this hinterland. Mrs. Lane directed them to the cleared off table. "One of you will have to help."

"Erich speak *gut Englisch*," Schlenter said. The other two agreed and headed to the door.

As usual, the men left the youngest to do the dirty work. Erich kept silent. He didn't think complaining would spark a beating, but he wasn't sure, and he'd had enough of those in Camp 133. He hung his coat on a peg. Max stepped in. Erich stopped him. "Stay outside."

"But I've seen blood. Lots of it."

Erich shook his head and closed the door on a disappointed face. He followed Mrs. Lane's instructions, removed the bandage, bathed the wound, fetched Henry's whiskey from his desk.

Mrs. Lane dribbled whiskey along the gash. Rudolf screamed, arched his back. Erich snatched a wooden spoon from the counter and told Rudolf to bite it. The screams became groans.

"What did this?" Mrs. Lane asked as she examined the cut.

"Bow saw. We had an accident with the sloop. Men were thrown off."

"We'll sew it up as best we can and give him a tetanus shot. A good thing Lethbridge sent medical supplies. The nearest hospital is in Spirit River. It's too far to go with an open wound. How are your sewing skills?"

"Terrible."

She glanced up. "Use this syringe to keep dribbling water over the wound while I sew. Otherwise the blood won't let me see what I'm doing. Then we'll bandage it."

Silence descended again. Rudolf cringed each time the needle pierced his skin. He was leaving teeth marks on the spoon. They were almost done when Henry came in. He was usually so calm that his glowering expression unnerved Erich. He paused, wondering if the anger would lash out, like it always had with Gerhard.

Henry's words were terse, bitten off. "Boy'll need a doctor. Alf's hitching the sleigh. Damned gas rationing."

He paced back and forth, his boots loud on the floorboards. Mrs. Lane hissed, drawing Erich's attention. He resumed rinsing the wound.

"Alf checked those chains this morning," Henry blurted.

Mrs. Lane's needle only paused for a second. "A chain broke?"

Henry halted, hands on hips. "Yes. But from the looks of it, I think bolt cutters were used to cut a link most of the way through."

The accident wasn't an accident? Erich's glanced at his jacket on the peg by the door, at the large red circle sewn into its back—the circle all the men joked looked like a bullseye.

There was no question who the targets of this attack had been.

The bunkhouse air thickened with the smell of wood and sweat. Heat rolled off the potbellied stove, and on its flat top, water steaming in a pot released white wisps. Erich watched the twisting vapor fingers dissipate and listened to the other prisoners.

The idea had simmered all day, during a lunch they'd made themselves, through a soccer game played half-heartedly. They talked, listened, wondered. Erich mostly kept to himself and worried. The realization had hit him as the sleigh carrying Rudolf had driven away: even so far from the war, there was no escaping it. The safety he'd felt during his first few weeks here was no more solid than the steam above the stove. Now they drew burlap curtains, shutting out the late afternoon shadows and prying eyes, and bared their suspicions with unconcealed fury. Erich shuddered at the strength of it and fought to conceal the growing lump of fear that threatened to choke him.

"One of the Canadians did it," Hubart said. "This is a message."

"For us?" Schlenter combed his auburn hair, his knuckles white and voice tense. "Or the Lanes? Alf was also injured. His knee was almost as big as our football."

"They don't want to hurt their bosses." Nikel rubbed his dark stubble. "They respect them."

"Right," Hubart responded. "They want *us* hurt. That only harms the Lanes by slowing down production, but it tells them using prisoners of war was a bad idea."

"Maybe it was someone from the community. They don't know us. It's easy to hate people you don't know." Lehrmann, ash blond head bent, whittled his nearly finished whistle. Several men nodded.

The shavings fell to the floor, looking like remnants of a haircut. Would Henry report the incident to the camp warden? Would they all be shipped back to the Camp 133? If so, Erich was a wood shaving in a pile, about to be cast into the fire. He swallowed hard and gripped his thighs to stop the quiver in his fingers.

"We need someone to befriend the Lanes, find out what's happening," Hubart said.

Silence. Erich's throat closed. He lifted his attention from the wood curls to find everyone looking at him. He shook his head. "I'm no spy."

Hubart pinned him with a pale blue gaze. "You speak the best English."

"You helped Frau Lane yesterday," Schlenter said.

"And the girl watches you. I think she likes you." Nikel added.

Erich's fingers dug into his thighs. Nikel had never sided against him before, and it cut surprisingly deep, like betrayal. "No. She cannot get past my being German."

"Charm her past it, Hofmeyer." Hubart smiled, but only half his mouth responded, the other corner being permanently turned down by a scar that cut across his cheek and chin.

"Won't happen. Her relatives were killed by a German bomb."

"You're mistaking us here, Hofmeyer." Lehrmann moved to Nikel's cot and tapped the back of Erich's hand with his knife. His lean face reminded Erich of the coyote he'd seen that day with Max. Erich pulled back from a savage grimace. Lehrmann pointed his knife at Erich's face, his voice a low growl. "You are our only option, so you have no option."

Just like in Camp 133 when he'd been forced to spy on the guards. Around the circle, heads nodded. Lantern light glinted off the knife's edge. Erich's stomach tightened.

A knock on the door muzzled the men. Lehrmann pocketed his knife and nodded at Erich to answer the knock. Max stood with a wrapped package offered in stiff arms. "Mother sent this for you, all of you. It's red cabbage and pork chops."

The thought of food turned Erich's stomach again. He handed the large package to Nikel. "You've bragged about being able to cook." The others chuckled, several told Max to thank his mother. Max gave Erich a smile and left.

"There's the way to find things out," Hubart said. "Even if the serving girl doesn't like you, that boy does. Use him."

Every face filled with anticipation. They expected him to use a twelve-year-old who only wanted a friend. Dread mixed with disgust. Erich grabbed his coat and escaped outside.

16:

1 JANUARY 1944,
LOGGING CAMP (-12°C/10°F)

Max kicked at the rug beside the Lane's door and waited for Cora to say he could stay. "My father will be mad if you send me home. He thinks, with the Lanes gone to Spirit River, that you should have someone with you."

"Because of those Germans." She set the parcel Max had offered her on the table.

Apparently she didn't know his father was a German immigrant. "No, he said you shouldn't be alone with a camp full of men." His neck heated. He stopped kicking and stared at his boots, waiting for a verdict. He added, "Henry stopped and asked us to check on you. Father agreed."

"But he didn't say babysit. As if you could. You're the baby here."

"I'm twelve." Max forced himself to look up. His parents complained about him not looking people in the eye. "And I'm as tall as you."

"So you could protect me if the big bad wolf huffed and puffed the door down?"

The heat spread from his neck to ears. "No, but... You could throw me in the way and use the distraction to get away."

A smile tugged at her mouth. "Oh, take your coat off. You can help me cook whatever this is."

"It's pork chops and red cabbage. I delivered some to each bunkhouse too."

"That's a lot of meat."

"Father just butchered a pig. I think he made a deal with Henry, um, Mr. Lane, to share some wild meat if Father does the butchering.

He's good at it." And he'd get more blood for sausages, which would be a relief.

"Well, I appreciate it. Pork chops are a nice change. Thank him for me."

Max hung up his coat. "It might have been blood sausage if I hadn't spilled the blood."

"Oh, that sounds gruesome." Cora took the package to the counter and unwrapped it.

"It was. I looked like I'd taken a bath in the stuff. It's really sticky."

"It spilled on you?"

Max joined her. "Mother made me help wash my clothes. It took three tubs of water to get them clean."

"I've never been terribly fond of blood sausage. A neighbor of Mum's gives us some every year. I can never get past its ingredients." She grimaced.

"It's Father's favorite. He was raging mad. He said I won't be allowed any, even if we do get more blood." Max bit the inside of his cheek. He was babbling because he was nervous. Father wouldn't want him telling Cora anything.

She gave him a curious look but didn't ask anything. She trimmed fat off the pork chops while Max peeled a few potatoes. Heat rolled off the stove, stroked their backs, and wrapped around them as they worked. Max half filled a pot with water from the hand pump and set it on the stove to boil.

"It's even quieter here than at our farm." He peered out the window at the glow coming from the cookhouse. Were the Canadians and Germans cooking together? Somehow, he doubted it. Whatever they'd been talking about in the bunkhouses, both groups had seemed strung as tight as new barbed wire fences.

Maybe the cookhouse was neutral territory. Or a battleground. He wished he could see inside, like Superman with his X-ray vision.

Cora stared outside too. "The war always seemed so far away until I came to work here."

Not to me, Max thought. He didn't say it aloud, didn't want to explain what school was like in case Cora decided to treat him the same way the students did. Most adults were better, but not all of them. Instead, he said, "Henry's son is a POW in Germany."

"Yes, Mrs. Lane told me. And she said Frank Janowski's family in Poland was caught in the fighting. And apparently, the gruff fellow, Chuck, has two nephews in the army and one is missing in action. And Jimmy told me his two older brothers signed up. He listed off some other men in the community too. It's such a small community, isn't it?"

Max nodded.

"My cousin, Elizabeth—I supposed she would be Miss Williams to you."

Max took an involuntary step back. "Your cousin is the school teacher?"

She rolled her eyes. "You say that like it makes her an enemy. School isn't that bad."

When Max didn't answer she continued. "Anyway, Elizabeth said there aren't enough men to go around at a dance. Isn't that silly? Men are off fighting in a war, and she's worried about dancing." She peered out the window again, not that she could see anything in the darkness except lamp-lit windows.

Their talk shrank to directions and questions about cooking, something that was fairly new to Cora. She had helped with cleanup at home, not cooking. That had been her older sister's job, she explained.

Silence shrouded the meal. After cleaning up, Max settled on the couch with the atlas, but his mind was on the sloop accident. "You weren't here when it happened, were you? I didn't see you."

"It? Oh, you mean the horrid accident. Alf had let me borrow that impossibly slow horse, Sugar, to ride into Horley and visit Elizabeth and her family. Jimmy went with me. Goodness, he talks non-stop."

Max nodded. Jimmy had a mouth like a steam engine running at full power. Hardly anything could stop it or slow it down.

"Tell me about the accident," she urged.

So Max explained everything he'd seen.

When he was done, Cora said, "On the ride back, I was frightened half to death when a Native man stepped out of the forest dragging a, oh, what do you call those sleds made out of crossed sticks?"

"Travois?"

"Yes. He was a bit ragged. Plaid jacket worn to a frazzle and patched trousers. He had a large knife strapped to his waist and a rifle over his shoulder. And the travois held a dead deer. I didn't know what to think."

"Sounds like Christmas. He comes to the farm sometimes, looking for work. He's a few years older than me. Sixteen, maybe."

"Why would you call him Christmas?"

Max shrugged. "That's what everyone calls him. Mother said it's because he usually shows up near Christmas and finds work through the coldest months, then leaves again."

"He was headed to the camp for that very purpose, so he walked with us. When I asked where he learned English, he said he'd spent a few years at the *white man's school* before running away to live with his aunt in the bush. Jimmy said Christmas's one uncle is white but doesn't like coming into town because there are too many people. Can you imagine someone thinking Horley has too many people?"

Max smoothed the open page of the atlas. Cora talked almost as much as Jimmy, in spurts. Maybe she was nervous too. It was hard work talking to someone you didn't really know. "You're from Grande Prairie, aren't you?" He touched its dot on the map.

"Yes."

"Do you miss it?"

"I miss my family, my friends, and electricity."

Max didn't know what to say to that. He had no friends and had never lived where there was electricity. He chewed the inside of his lip as pictures of the accident jumped into his mind again. The swerving sloop, the clanking, the neighing and rearing of the horses, the shouts. The blood. "When did you get back to camp?"

"That certainly is on your mind. I returned not long after it happened, I suppose. I can't recall. Chuck came out of the barn and offered to stable the horse. Maybe he saw it too. He appeared quite frazzled, even his beard was mussed."

Mention of the barn jumped Max's thoughts. "Why did Alf go to Spirit River too?"

"Henry insisted because Alf's knee was terribly swollen. He was very grumpy at being forced to see the doctor."

Max didn't comment. Or add what he knew, especially since he'd learned it by eavesdropping. When Henry had gone into the house, he'd listened at the door; Henry thought someone had caused the accident by cutting a chain.

"Enough talk about dreary things." Cora turned on the radio and picked up a book. Max listened to the last half of the hockey game on the big radio. After the news at nine o'clock, a music show came on: *The Red River Barn Dance*. Cora offered to show Max how to polka. He shook his head frantically and held up the atlas like a shield.

Cora made a circuit around the room, dancing with an invisible partner. She stopped and held out her hands to Max. "It's fun." He shook his head so hard his neck ached.

A noise came from outside. Cora held her finger to her lips. *I am Superman. Nothing can hurt me.* Max jumped to his feet. "I'll protect you." Before she could stop him, he rushed over and flung open the door. "Oh. Hi, Erich."

Cora peered down at Erich sitting on the top step. "Skulking?"

"Listening to the music. At least, I think that's what it is."

Her eyebrows arched high. "Well of course it was music."

The way Erich's shoulders drooped made him look sad. Before Max could ask why, Erich gave Cora a weak smile. "Yes. It just isn't what I'm used to. I didn't mean to insult you."

Cora looked down her nose like he was a weasel in the chicken coop. Maybe she saw the same sadness. Her hard look melted a bit and she pulled her sweater close. "What kind of music do you listen to?"

Max had heard the phrase "his face lit up," but he'd never seen it before. Erich straightened and gave a wide smile. "I like classical. That's what I play, but I love swing music. Benny Goodman and Jimmy Dorsey. Nat King Cole. There are even German bands. Once, when Father had business in Hamburg, I went with him and snuck out of the hotel to go to Café Heinze—" He cut off and gave a shrug.

When Erich stopped rattling, Cora said, "You like to dance."

Another shrug, but Max could tell it was a "yes." He almost groaned.

Before either of them had a chance to say another word, Frank stormed out of the darkness. "Get away from her, you filthy cabbagehead. Henry leaves and you sniff around like some dog—"

Erich sprang up. He stood in the light of the doorway working his jaw. Frank said, "Come on, you stinking Heinie. Take a swing. I know you want to."

"You aren't worth the price I'd pay." Erich nodded to Cora and walked away, hands in his pockets.

Chuck, previously hidden by the darkness, intercepted Frank when he moved to follow. They exchanged quiet words. Frank hung back while Chuck asked, "Did he hurt you?"

Max replied. "He was sitting outside, listening to the radio." Cora nodded agreement.

Chuck looked angry as he rested one foot on the first step and leaned forward. He acted like Max hadn't spoken. "Don't worry about Frank, Miss Cora. He's hotheaded but means well. One thing he's right about: Don't trust that German. Don't trust any of them."

As the two men walked away, Max spoke quietly. "Father says I should be proud to be German, but how can I be? No one likes us."

Cora's gaze rounded. And Max remembered she hadn't known that his father was German. Now she would hate him too.

17:

9 JANUARY 1944,
LOGGING CAMP (-9°C/16°F)

The week following the accident was crammed with enough tension to launch a torpedo. Every meal was an ordeal of strained silence.

Erich felt like he was strung up between the two groups. The Germans eyed him impatiently, wanting him to infiltrate the Canadian ranks; the Canadians shot daggers from their eyes if he tried to talk to them.

He joined in the Sunday soccer game, but his mind wasn't on it. When he missed yet another pass, Lehrmann yelled at him to pay attention or leave. He left, wandered along the trees hedging the sawmill, and studied a truck on blocks in the shed beside the blacksmith shop. His hand cupped the radiator cap. It looked like some of the delivery trucks in Germany, with high fenders and running boards. No tires. Gas in short supply. Like back home. Henry might not use the truck until this war ended and rationing stopped.

Not that these Canadians knew what rationing was. Their restrictions were so minor that it felt like feasting to Erich. Anything he asked for Alf seemed to find in his locked closet in the cookhouse.

Erich's grip on the radiator cap tightened. His pulse tripped. Would it look like he was considering stealing the truck? He glanced around expecting...what? Someone coming at him with a knife? Lehrmann was still playing soccer, and no one seemed to be looking his way except for the Native fellow. Christmas, as he was called, leaned against the west side of the house, arms crossed. Watching, always watching. Was he spying on Erich for the Canadians? His steady gaze across the yard was unnerving.

He was from a different world, unlike Erich in every way except one: both groups were suspicious of him. He helped in the sawmill and in the barn, and lived apart from the others in the hayloft. He even ate at a small table in the kitchen, as if he were a leper. As if being Native was a disease. Erich scowled at the young man's ragged clothes and recalled overhearing that Christmas liked living in the bush. Why would anyone choose to live rough when civilization beckoned? And why would he spy for men who disliked him?

He turned away and studied the blacksmith shop. Since none of the Canadians were around, maybe he could peek inside. Maybe he could discover something without having to betray Alf or Henry, who had been fair to all of them. And he'd shaken hands with Henry. Spying on him felt wrong, dishonorable, something no *Kriegsmarine* would do.

Trying to look casual, Erich strolled to the open door, squinted into the semi-dark log building. The two windows were grimy. Embers glowed in the fire pit below the smokestack with its upside-down funnel opening. This morning, the clang of the blacksmith's hammer had woken Erich. That man didn't care it was Sunday.

Tools were neatly arranged on a wooden counter along the far wall or hanging above it. Erich edged forward half a step as his eyes adjusted. Five wire and bolt cutters, hung by size from nails. No doubt a blacksmith used bolt cutters for all sorts of things. Like chains. His breath stalled as he noticed a gap between the largest pair of cutters and the next smaller.

From the shadows to the side, a huge hand swept Erich against the door frame. The grizzled blacksmith, Sam, barely taller than Erich, easily had twice the muscles. He grabbed Erich's collar and squinted down his wide nose. "What you doing in my shop, Jerry?"

"I was only curious. I've never seen a blacksmith's shop." The man squeezed, pushed his hand up, and Erich's heels rose off the ground. His voice shrank to a hoarse whisper. "You keep your tools like my grandfather does, not a hammer out of place."

"Can't be looking for a hammer in the middle of a job. If metal cools before you're done you've got a weak meld." Sam held Erich in place for long seconds, then lowered him and spat a wad of tobacco juice near his feet. Sooty fingers curled around the doorjamb, nails rimmed black. His bulk blocked the view inside.

Erich's legs quivered. He wanted to leave but knew he might not get another chance. "You're missing a pair of bolt cutters."

"Yup. I ordered a replacement but it's slow coming."

"Did they go missing on New Year's?" Erich's mouth dried out as Sam's ruddy complexion darkened more.

Fear clawed up Erich's throat as the big man crowded him back against the door frame. "If one of you Jerries took 'em, I'll use 'em to beat you senseless. Tell your buddies that."

"None of us took them. Why, when our gate is always open? But maybe if you find them, you'll find whoever cut the sloop's chain." Amazed he'd got the thought out, Erich tried not to flinch. The seams of Sam's coat looked ready to burst. Someone that muscled could cut through chain with the right tool, and making that tool look stolen would divert suspicion.

"What's going through that cabbage brain?" Sam poked Erich's chest with a thick finger.

Erich rubbed his chest. "N-nothing. I want to find out what happened so no one else gets hurt."

"That so? Then maybe you should talk to that pecker Hitler, tell him to stop the killing."

"I meant here. I...I've never even met the Fü—Hitler. He wouldn't listen to someone my age even if I could talk to him."

"Yeah. You're just a piece of kindling for him to toss on this bonfire he started."

The man's anger scraped over Erich and he swallowed hard.

"What's wrong, Jerry? You like the idea of fighting and dying for your precious leader? You one of those bootlicking Hitler Youth turds?"

"No." Erich worked to smooth his ragged breathing, to hold the man's gaze. Look a man in the eyes if you want him to believe you, his father always said.

The blacksmith spat another stream of brown juice into the snow. He eased back half a step. "If I was younger I'd be in Europe killing pricks like you. I was too young last war, but my cousin died stopping the Huns. That's when we should've ended things. Should've killed all the Jerries then. Would've got that damned leader of yours, wouldn't we? Wasn't he in the Great War?" Erich nodded. Sam said, "Yup. A few firing squads last war would've fixed it. Wouldn't've had no brown-shirted pipsqueaks stirring up trouble. Hell, you and lots of other goose-stepping cabbageheads probably wouldn't've been born, would you?"

"Probably not." Erich stuffed his hands in his pockets as his breathing slowed. The man's venom contrasted with something Erich's grandfather had said on that last weekend in Stratford: more mercy by the Great War's victors might have prevented the fight that loomed that summer. It hadn't meant anything to Erich at the time.

The blacksmith growled for him to scram, so Erich walked to the ravine. Halfway down the hill, he waded through snow to a tree leaning in the arms of its neighbor. He brushed snow and frost away and reclined on the trunk to study branches and sky. Back home it was cloud, rain, wet snow, cold winds. Here, the crisp air and the vast expanse of blue sky amazed and relaxed him. The trees, covered in crystalline coats of something Alf called hoarfrost, looked as if they had donned their ballroom best. Touching the frost made crystals tinkle to the ground, leaving the branches with peach-fuzz coating. The unexpected beauty of this place stirred Erich with the desire to play music again, something he hadn't done since enlisting. Sam's words returned. *I'd be in Europe killing pricks like you.* Being surrounded by enemies was lonesome. Exhausting. Even nature's splendor couldn't change that.

He heard the footsteps long before they reached him. Erich abandoned sky-gazing and sat up, curious why Lehrmann had sought him out. He shivered.

"It's nice here. Quiet." Lehrmann broke off a branch and examined it, as if deciding if it was good for carving. "I saw you talking to the blacksmith."

"So?" Erich strove for a casualness he didn't feel.

"Did you discover anything useful?"

"Just that he thinks all our soldiers from the last war should've been shot, including the Führer. He thinks it would have stopped this war."

Lehrmann's straight nose and thin lips gave him a regal aspect. He snapped the branch. "Our Führer is invincible. Nothing could destroy him."

"As you say." The same response he'd always given in Camp 133 when loyalty to the Führer was expected. Erich could never express his real feelings. Every German soldier had sworn an oath of loyalty to Hitler and apparently Lehrmann took his oath seriously.

Lehrmann took out his pocket knife—the one Alf had given him for carving a week after they'd arrived—and sharpened the end of the stick. When the point was done, he twirled it between two fingers. "Is the blacksmith the saboteur?"

"He's strong enough, but the shop isn't locked. Anyone could've taken the cutters."

"Keep asking questions. None of them care who did it. Not even Henry Lane."

Erich's stomach hardened into a ball of dread. "And if we find out?"

"Then we'll decide as a group what to do." Lehrmann stabbed the pointed stick into a crack in the bark. The crunch of the man's retreating steps sent a shiver down Erich's neck.

The stick quivered to stillness.

Erich's knees were folded almost to his chest. The small metal bathtub made him feel like a child in a sink. He had dunked his head in the water to shampoo his hair before he had stripped down and crawled into the tub. Soaking off a week of sweat took awhile.

Heat from the cookhouse stove kept the chill at bay. It was colder again today. Tomorrow's full moon would tell if Alf's prediction of a cold snap was true. Erich thought of the Eastern Front, of frostbite so bad men's feet had to be amputated. Surely it wouldn't get that cold here in Canada. Alf was exaggerating to tease the gullible Germans.

Voices rose and fell from the dining hall, but he was alone in the kitchen, window and door to the other room closed for privacy and to keep in the heat. Erich stood, toweled his upper body, stepped onto a rug of woven rags, dried off, wrapped the towel around his waist and tucked it snug. The stove's heat bathed his chest and legs. His hair almost touched his collar now. He flicked it and rubbed the sparse stubble along his jaw. He only needed to shave once a week, so he combined the task with his bath. Each Sunday evening he was clean from toe nail to hair tip, jaw included. It lasted less than twenty-four hours. His nightly rinse from the waist up in the bunkhouse barely dinted the built-up sweat. Funny what became a luxury. At home he would never have gone so long without a shower.

Erich opened the shaving pouch containing his safety razor, brush, and soap cake. A worn-out mirror was propped on the top shelf of the stove. In it, everything was shades of gray. He dipped the round brush in the water, twirled it on the soap to build up lather. The brush was almost to his chin when the door opened.

A silhouette in the murky reflection moved closer. Stopped. Sucked in air. The prisoners didn't care about anyone's state of undress. Erich's skin tingled. Before he glanced over his shoulder, he knew it was Cora. The stove's fire crackled.

"G-Goodness. I had no idea..." She trailed off.

Why didn't she leave? He wasn't sure what to do. He kept his back to her as his body reacted to the nearness of a girl. *Think of something else, Hofmeyer.*

From across the room she choked out, "What—" Paused and tried again. "How did you get those scars on your shoulder? They must be terribly painful."

"Not any more." *Think of the ship sinking, not of her feminine softness. Think of the men howling, burning, splashing through flames that ate them alive.* His breath puffed out. "The ship I served on... There was burning oil when it sank." He didn't explain further.

The heat from the stove was unbearable. He retreated a step, clamped his right hand onto his left shoulder. The center of the burns still hadn't recovered feeling. The scars were always starker after a bath—the doctors had said they'd be sensitive to heat and cold for a long time.

"It must've been horrible." Her voice held a world of sorrow. This was rare—her speaking to him without anger. Erich didn't dare move.

Cora veered to the sideboard and curtained cupboards containing baking supplies. Erich snatched his shirt and slipped it on. As he buttoned, she said, "I didn't mean to interrupt. Mrs. Lane's stomach is upset. It sometimes happens with a weather change. She gets such a bad migraine it churns her stomach." Erich marveled at how she was babbling. "Baking soda and water often settles her stomach and we used the last of it at the house to make raisin scones this afternoon. She was feeling fine then—" She filled a small bowl with baking soda from a tin and turned, looking relieved at the sight of his shirt.

"Raisin scones sound delicious."

"Henry and Alf ate them when Frances didn't show."

Understanding dawned. "We scared your visitor away. The prisoners, I mean."

"Undoubtedly." The critical tone returned like a slap. She picked up the bowl of baking soda and started for the door. She paused beside it. "You...are strangely troublesome."

Erich had to bite back a smile. Did she know she was quoting Shakespeare? "Of all the insults you could hurl at me, strangely troublesome is mild. I thought you'd call me a vile worm or a scurvy fellow."

She looked puzzled.

"Shakespearean insults. My grandfather used to teach them to me."

"What a strange grandfather. I thought your government only liked German things, which Shakespeare certainly isn't."

The smile disappeared. "My grandfather has no connection to the German government."

"Did he teach you speak English?" Erich nodded, so she asked, "Where did he learn the language so well?"

Uncertainty made Erich hesitate. Would she believe him if he told her the truth? "Mrs. Lane needs her baking soda."

Irritation flashed across her face and she pushed out of the kitchen. Too late, Erich realized his mistake. She had been talking to him like a person instead of an enemy.

18:

12 JANUARY 1944, LOGGING CAMP (-3°C/27°F)

Hubart snatched the letter from Erich. His pencil broke and smeared across the bottom of the page. Erich had been reclining, knees raised, against the cool log wall that was his headboard. He had been so intent on describing Alf's belief about the weather changing with the full moon that he hadn't noticed the other man approach.

He bolted upright and reached for the paper. Hubart stepped back, his frown a deep trench. The scar tugging at the side of his tightly closed mouth was white.

"Give it back," Erich demanded. For a second he saw Gerhard's face. His brother always found a way to haunt him.

Hubart crumpled the page and threw it at Erich. "You're writing in English. Why?"

"So swine like you can't read my thoughts." He smoothed the paper against his thigh.

The sneer touched only the left side of Hubart's mouth. "What are you hiding? Are you writing reports to your English masters in Camp 133?"

Erich stopped smoothing the paper's wrinkles. Everyone in the bunkhouse watched. Though it was cool in this end of the room, beads of sweat formed along his hairline. He forced himself to hold Hubart's hooded gaze. "That's ridiculous." The nine men kept silent. Erich rose and retrieved the handful of papers from under his mattress. He tossed them on the bed. "Read them."

"You know I can't," Hubart growled. "None of us can."

"Get someone to read them to you. Jimmy maybe. He isn't

devious. Then maybe you'll believe that I've been writing to my grandmother."

"She reads English?" Hubart picked up the papers and squinted at them.

"Yes. Her father was a businessman with interests in England before the Great War. She was his secretary."

"The censors would never allow letters written in English to enter the Fatherland."

"I won't mail them. I'll give them to her after the war."

From his bunk nearer the stove Lehrmann spoke. "Don't be surprised if we don't believe you, Hofmeyer."

Beside Erich, Nikel snorted. "I've never known Erich to lie."

"What do you know, Nikel? You laugh at everything. What Hofmeyer does best is shirk his duty. It doesn't speak well for his honesty."

Hubart retreated down the aisle, papers in hand. Erich wanted to snatch them back but it would be taken the wrong way. Hubart approached the stove. Erich stretched out his hand, silently pleading, *Don't!* But he did. He flipped the door's catch, swung it open, and tossed the papers in. He left the iron door open so Erich could watch his letters burning. The flames scorched his thoughts, as if these men could read his mind, as if they'd condemn him to the fire too. His scars ached. He couldn't look away as the paper shriveled to filaments of ash and flaked into oblivion.

"You aren't defending yourself, Hofmeyer." Lehrmann's words pulled Erich's attention away from the stove. "Are you admitting to shirking?"

"At what?" Erich snapped. "I work hard."

"At cutting trees, maybe. But you do almost nothing to find out who sabotaged us."

How was he supposed to discover anything when the Canadians weren't talking to them? Erich closed his eyes against nine gazes but still felt their fiery regard. He wanted to hit Hubart for burning his letters. But that would only reap him a beating, as it had in Camp 133, and from his brother before that. *Get out of my head, Gerhard.*

He flattened his hands against his thighs, to stop them quivering. "You're right. I'll tell Henry how we feel and demand answers." Erich grabbed his coat. Anything to escape. Hubart was no better than a book-burning Nazi, but if he told Henry about this then he was the rat Hubart accused him of being. If Hubart learned his grandfather was English the man would latch onto it as more proof of his guilt.

"He won't tell you anything." Hubart clanged the stove door closed.

"Maybe not." Erich tugged up his wool socks and slipped into his boots. He straightened. "But I'd rather be honest with him than ask questions behind his back. He's been fair to us."

Lehrmann inclined his head. Was that agreement? Permission?

Erich closed the door with a firm tug and inhaled the night air. It had been near melting in the afternoon but had cooled off fast. He walked in the light of the moon, two nights past full. His lungs twinged at the cold; his exhalations were steam-engine plumes. The snow crunched. This weather had as many ups and downs as the Bergisches Land forests east of Cologne.

The moon cast the yard into silver relief. At the house, he hesitated on the first step. Was honesty the issue? No, Hubart and the others demanded loyalty. To a flag? A country? A leader?

He could almost feel his grandfather's hand on his shoulder as he recalled standing on the bridge over the Avon River the last night of his visit in 1939. His grandfather's English voice filled his mind: "*Mark my words, my boy. If there is war, Germany will be crushed. No tyrant is ever victorious. They fall to their own hubris, often assisted by an enemy's sword.*"

He deeply loved and admired his grandfather. He could not dismiss the old man's words. Those words had caused him to see things it was safer to ignore over the years. A Jewish grandfather pushed off the sidewalk and beaten in the gutter. Biking past the walls of the camp at Müngersdorf, which he'd been warned away from, and glimpsing a hand sticking through a crack while the voice behind the wall begged for food. The hand had visited his dreams, but he hadn't spoken out. He'd seen what happened to those who had, like their gardener, been arrested twice and never seen again. His tenth-grade history teacher who didn't come to work one day, leaving only whispers of his arrest.

Did *not* speaking make him a coward? He sometimes feared that anger might strip away his shield of silence. So many things were best left unsaid. He could never look at Hubart and say their cause was lost. Just as he couldn't have said it to his father. Gerhard would have knocked him flat for uttering such treason. Hubart would do worse. Or Lehrmann with his knife, snicking wood like an unspoken threat.

Erich studied the door. The people in this house were supposed to be his enemies, but he felt safer with them than with the men in his bunkhouse. Safer than with the other workers. Every look he noticed seemed filled with anger, impatience, or scorn. Here he was everyone's younger brother. Gerhard's spirit whispered through the camp, egging on the men, making him feel...hopeless. He hated that feeling. Even in the Atlantic, swimming toward a British lifeboat, he hadn't felt that.

Cold air ruffled his hair against his ears. Erich expelled frustration in a misty plume, climbed the steps and knocked. When Henry opened the door and Erich stepped inside, the first thing he noticed was Cora sitting on a braided rug with a lap quilt across her shoulders, intent on the console-sized radio. It spilled music reminiscent of Benny Goodman, but with fewer horns, more strings. It was the closest thing to swing he'd heard since the ship, where they'd sometimes played British radio over the intercom. *"Do you like to dance?"* she'd asked. A smile crept over Erich's lips.

"Are you sure that's music?" Alf said.

"Stop teasing the child," Mrs. Lane replied. *"Jolly Miller Time* is a fine show, and Mr. Cable is a fine musician. It's educational to listen to other kinds of music."

Henry's demanding stare pulled Erich's attention from the music. His smile faded. "Could I speak with you for a minute, sir?"

Cora's head swiveled toward them, her surprise obvious. She snapped back to the radio's speakers and smooth wood. "It's past nine thirty, son," Henry said. "A bit late for visiting."

"I apologize, but it's important."

Henry ushered him in. "Join us at the table. Cora, could you turn down your music?"

"No," Erich said. "I mean, I like the music. You needn't turn it down for me."

Chairs scraped against wood as they sat. Cora remained focused on the music, though she did turn it down. Mrs. Lane bustled in the kitchen area to the left.

Erich explained the prisoners' concerns about the sloop accident and about everyone's inaction. "I was chosen to uncover the truth."

Henry drummed his fingers on the table. "They figure they need their own detective, do they? They think I haven't been asking questions? I've pulled aside every one of my local men and asked them about that day. Some of them aren't happy with me."

"Are none of them the least suspicious?"

Henry snorted. "Some of them are upset with me hiring you boys, but most were gone that day, and the ones still here said they were sleeping off hangovers."

"What about the Native boy? He arrived that day. Doesn't that seem odd?"

Cora took the chair beside Henry. "Christmas came from the west, pulling a dead deer on a travois. Jimmy and I met him on the road. He didn't know what Jerries were, never mind that any worked for Henry."

Erich tried not to wince at *Jerries*. He quietly replied, "He could have done the deed and slunk back into the forest to show up later when he'd look innocent."

Cora's chin rose. "And why would he care to attack you?"

"He could easily have been duped by someone from camp or town into doing it."

"Easily?" Cora straightened away from the spindled chair back. "Has he no reasoning ability, then? Is he a dumb animal to be led by the nose by whoever comes along?"

Erich sat back, shocked by her outburst. She was so quick to jump to that boy's defense, yet so ready to always assume the worst about him. Cora breathed deeply as she struggled to control her apparent indignation.

The radio filled the uncomfortable silence with the ten o'clock news. The Red Army had captured Kirovograd on the weekend and continued their advance in Poland. The German High Command was reported as saying that they wouldn't hold Russian territory purely for prestige. And General Sir Henry Maitland Wilson had taken over as the supreme Allied commander in the Mediterranean theater, vowing to continue pressing Germans on their southern front.

Erich schooled his features at the list of German defeats. Henry tapped Cora's wrist and told her to turn off the radio. She complied, folded the quilt she'd left in a puddle, and returned to the table.

Henry drank some tea. "Question Christmas if you want, but do me the favor of believing him. He's as honest as you claim to be, son. Make no mistake."

As you claim to be. Erich's eyebrows curved together as he struggled to hide a twinge of hurt. Alf joined the conversation. "He could talk to the other men, Henry, though he might not get too far. Might even lose a few teeth for his effort."

Did Alf think this was some kind of joke? Erich reached for his tea, gripped it with both hands to stop them from shaking. A lump closed his throat. He wasn't sure he could drink, much less talk. Years of silence weighed down on him, but he knew he needed to find the words to continue. Silence had gotten him nowhere. It was a kind of deceit, just like spying. He lowered his head, forced down a sip of the weak brew, added some milk, then sipped again. No one had spoken while he'd searched for words. He looked up, saw both men studying him with something like concern.

I can do this, Erich thought. He swallowed the lump again. "I don't know what to do." Henry tilted his head forward and raised his brows slightly. Erich exhaled and willed himself to continue. "A few in my bunkhouse will likely beat me if I don't discover anything, and men in the other quarters will beat me if I ask questions."

"Who's giving you grief in your bunkhouse?" Henry's hands flattened to splay beside his mug. He looked ready to go demand answers right then.

Erich extended his hand toward Henry, needing to make him understand. "Please. I've spent my life trying to get along, not cause trouble, and avoid my brother's reach." He closed his eyes. "Where I come from, silence is the best hope of survival."

"So you won't tell me who's stirring the pot, even if he's a Nazi who belongs back in Lethbridge. Even if you'd be safer with him gone. Are you a Nazi, son?"

Erich shook his head. "But I love my country. I hate what's happening to it."

"Did you hate what was happening to your country when a madman came to power?" Cora's tone seethed with condemnation.

Erich started. He'd forgotten she was listening. Both hands cradled his mug and the milky amber liquid quivered. He was so tired of explaining himself, of having to justify every action, to Canadians, to his fellow prisoners. Irritation leaked into his reply. "I was seven in 1933. What do seven-year-olds know of politics? They only care about football and sledding."

"Oh. Of course," Cora replied quietly. After a brief silence, she said, "I heard something." She glanced at Erich, as if offering an apology. "When that fellow was taken to the hospital and Max was here, he told me what he'd seen. How men had flown off the sloop like a tank mine had exploded, bodies flung in every direction. I'm sure he was exaggerating. But he said when he first arrived that day he saw someone walking away from the hill. Only from the back, I'm afraid. The person was in a plaid jacket, but almost every Canadian wears one."

"That's not something I wanted to hear," Henry said. "It's as good as saying one of my men lied to me. I hate it when men lie to me."

Erich cringed under Henry's iron stare, for once glad that he was a terrible liar.

19:

18 JANUARY 1944,
HORLEY (-6°C/21°F)

For half the walk to school, Max thought about playing soccer at the logging camp. He'd gone the last two Sundays and the prisoners had welcomed him. He'd even gotten to sled again and talk with Erich a bit. Well, mostly Erich listened as he talked about the other students and their attacks. The latest game had been to chase Max down and pelt him with snowballs, saying he was a lone German fighter plane and they were the Allied planes. That had happened just after a group of American planes flew overhead on their way to Alaska. Because they lived under a flight path, all the boys could identify the different types of planes. These had been Wildcats.

For the rest of the walk, his imagination relived the sloop accident over and over—*I'm Superman soaring high above. I see the sloop begin to swerve and I dive faster than the wind, grab hold of the sloop and steady it. Everyone cheers.*

Max hadn't been paying attention to how fast he was walking and when he turned into the schoolyard he realized that he was early. Richard and his flock of ravens swooped from behind a snowbank and surrounded him on the lane. Max had read somewhere that a group of ravens was called an unkindness. The boys squawked and flapped their arms. Max was too stunned to move.

Richard stood before him in his knuckle-cracking glory and curled one lip like he was a tough guy from a *Dick Tracy* comic strip. Something about him looked sharper. Meaner. *Click, clack.* His knuckles popped. Max winced.

"What do you want?" Max asked. "I was going inside to knit for a few minutes." Everyone, from kids to old ladies, knitted for the soldiers. If they were good like his mother, they knitted socks. He had gotten good at knitting caps for inside helmets.

"We're going to have a match." Richard's friends chuckled and nodded.

Not wanting an explanation, Max tried to step past Richard, who shoved him back into the circle. "The Nazi against the Ally. Max Schmeling against Joe Louis." Richard grinned. "And since you're a Max, you get to play Max."

"What year is it?" Max couldn't resist asking. In 1936, the first time the two men had boxed, Schmeling had won. But in 1938, Joe Louis had taken the match in the first round.

"Stupid Nazi. It's 1944. This is the tie-breaking match." Richard's fist plowed into Max's left cheekbone and he staggered backward. A push from behind kept him on his feet. He dropped his lunch pail, barely getting his hands up in time to block a second punch.

"Stop it!" Max yelled.

Richard slugged him in the stomach. Once. Twice. Max doubled over and another hammer blow landed beside his right eye. He dropped, drew his knees to his chest, flung his arms over his face.

Above him, the boys cheered. "The Nazi loses! First-round knockout! Louis wins again!" They danced around him, whooped and hollered. The bell clanged and someone kicked him hard, in the middle of the back. They all raced toward the schoolhouse.

Pain spidered along Max's ribs. He stayed on the ground, not moving a muscle until all the students had filed inside. Miss Williams called, "Get off the ground and into class, Max Schmidt."

Max eased onto his hands and knees. His back cricked. He took a few slow breaths then pushed to his feet. Pain swirled out from his back like a whirlpool sucking everything into its depths. Dizziness almost floored him when he picked up his lunch pail.

As Max entered the building, Miss Williams held the door and studied his face, but she didn't ask what had happened. He limped to his chair and slid into it with head down. Sniggers behind him made him sink lower, until Miss Williams ordered him to sit up straight.

Aches and pains and a throbbing face made the morning drag more than usual. At lunch, Max ate in silence and got out his knitting project, the only reason a student was allowed to stay inside. Whispers and giggles flowed around but didn't touch him. He thought of the latest *Johnny Canuck* comic book, recalled each frame in an inner retelling of the story. Brave Johnny has to go to Tibet to rescue General Chang, a Chinese guerilla leader. Johnny would never get beat up, or he'd at least give as good as he got.

School finally ended. Max was stiff from sitting all day. His left eye had a sore, puffy patch below it, and swelling almost closed his right eye. After all the other children left, Miss Williams told him to go.

Outside, a dozen girls, aged ten to thirteen, had formed two lines at the base of the stairs. Max figured the boys had put them up to something, but between those two lines was the only way to get home, so he stepped into the makeshift tunnel, head down.

They started to sing, "Jeepers creepers, where'd you get them peepers? Jeepers creepers, where'd you get those eyes." They kept repeating those two lines of the song, trailing behind Max when he passed the last person. A few of them clanged lunch pails in time. At the road, they stopped following and he turned to look at them.

Two of the youngest girls made faces. "Eww." Spotting no jot of sympathy, he walked away, thankful the boys hadn't been the ones waiting for him. His eyes throbbed.

At home, Mother cleaned his face and gave him cold cloths to soothe the swelling. At supper, Father examined the damage. "I hope the other fellow looks this bad."

Max shook his head.

"Why not?"

"He's way bigger. And his friends surrounded me so I couldn't escape."

"A German doesn't run from a fight."

"I didn't run."

"Nor did you raise your fists, by the look of it. You're supposed to defend our honor, not let it be trampled."

"It's worse if I fight." Max had tried, in the early years, hoping that fighting back would make the boys respect him and leave him alone. Instead they had ganged up on him.

Father hammered his fist onto the table. The cutlery jumped. Max's eye that wasn't swollen shut blinked closed. Father's voice was as sharp as his butcher knife. "You will stand up to them. Understood?"

"Yes, sir." As if he could say anything else.

He planted his elbow on the table and pointed his fork at Max. "I mean it. You will not shame this family again by backing down. We are not cowards. No German is a coward."

"But you let the police search here whenever they want."

"Obeying authorities is not cowardly!" His bellow surprised Max, who pressed himself against his chair's high back. His breathing sped up as his father stood and leaned on his knuckles. His voice was quiet, in the furious range. "Get to your room."

"I'm not finished eating."

"Let your stomach gnaw at your stupidity, then maybe you won't talk back next time."

Max's chair scraped against the floor's wooden planking. He stared longingly at the pork roast, potatoes, and carrots, then turned away, stomach growling its protest. His mother sighed quietly but said nothing. She almost always said nothing.

In his bedroom, Max stood at the window for awhile. He couldn't stand up to Richard and his goons. Why didn't Father understand that? He didn't have a single ally. Not one. Not even here, in his own house. His mother might feel bad for him, but she never defended Max.

Father was the authority, no questions. Obeying authority might not be cowardly, but obeying his father was guaranteed to get Max beaten to a pulp. It wasn't only a group of ravens that was an unkindness.

20:

19 JANUARY 1944, LOGGING CAMP (0°C/32°F)

Delimbing parallel tree trunks turned into a race. Erich balanced on one trunk, facing Nikel, perched on his own tree. Their axes bit into the bases of limbs, and Erich laughed as their pace increased, the rhythmic *thunk-thunk thunk-thunk* resounding like drumbeats.

"I'm going to beat you!" Erich taunted.

Nikel replied, "Keep talking. You've already lost."

Sweat beaded along Erich's hairline. A trickle ran into his eye. He shook his head and missed the limb. Jerked the blade free and arched the ax high. *Swish-thud.* He gaped at the ax head denting his boot's sole, then up at his own ax, which was intact. Had to remember to breathe. Nikel stared at him, eyes wide, headless ax gripped in both hands.

"Are you okay?" Nikel's voice croaked. Erich lowered his ax slowly and nodded as his stomach spun like a butter churn. Freed a second earlier and the ax head could have hit his leg, or any other part of him. Air hitched in his throat.

Nikel jumped off his tree. "Let's gather everything up. Alf will hit the saw blade any minute." His voice trembled. Erich didn't move as Nikel yanked the head out of the wood. "It snipped the sole of your boot but nothing else. *Gott sei Dank.*"

They were halfway to the landing site when Alf gonged the saw blade. They approached him, and Nikel held out the separated ax head and handle. Tension had coiled through Erich as they'd walked, now his tone was sharp. "This is the third one this week, Alf."

Alf's bushy dark eyebrows furrowed into a single caterpillar. "Accidents happen. Take it to the blacksmith shop. Get Sam to fix it."

"Once is an accident."

The other prisoners gathered round as Nikel recounted the incident in rapid German. Alf didn't ask for a translation; he just looked irritated and repeated his insistence that it was an accident. The prisoners' sullen expressions argued with him. Erich's tension turned into jitters. He couldn't stop looking at the nick in his boot. *Scheisse. It could have killed me.*

They rode on the sloop in silence, though the three Canadians were as loud as usual. At the top of the valley, Alf ordered everyone off—Henry's new rule. The men obeyed and waited for Alf to take the team down the slope before they started walking, Germans behind Canadians, and Christmas, who had taken over for the wounded Rudolf, behind everyone.

Erich lagged as he thought about today's mishap—just the latest ax-head incident—and the sloop accident. Unease drifted around him like fog. It started to sprinkle again. He sighed. Second day with rain this week. The snow was soft, hard to trudge through in the forest. Hard to skid logs that lurched and stuck. Everything about this place was hard. And now dangerous. A raven cawed, and for a second Erich thought it was Gerhard laughing.

Ahead, Frank and Chuck reached the valley floor. Chuck had become less friendly as the weeks passed. These days, he avoided the Germans, where he used to at least nod a hello, but he still wasn't as hostile as his younger partner. Jimmy passed the Germans, riding one skid horse and leading the other three. He said something as he passed the Canadians and Chuck scooped up snow and flung it so fast he was almost a brown blur. It hit Jimmy's red plaid shoulder. Laughter rippled back to the trudging Germans. Some hunched their shoulders as if to block the sound.

Why didn't Chuck wear plaid? The red plaid was more visible in the forest than brown. Like the red circle sewn into each prison coat that flashed, "We are the enemy."

Erich's feet hit ice. Flew sideways. He landed in slush. Swore at his clumsiness. Christmas offered a hand. Embarrassed, Erich rolled away and got up. He picked his way downhill, attention on his feet. When the trail sloped up, he glanced back. The Native boy hadn't moved

Christmas. The name bothered Erich. It was as demeaning as when Gerhard called him Little Pianist and told him to "Make love to your piano." When their father had overheard that, he'd laughed and said it wasn't Erich's fault Gerhard stole the heart of every girl around. If a girl blinked in Erich's direction, Gerhard turned on the charm and lured her away.

Erich waited. The boy approached, surefooted as the deer he had seen yesterday, carefully stepping along the trail. When Christmas was almost to him, he asked, "What's your name?"

He squinted past Erich. "I tell my name to my friends."

Erich waited for more, then gave up and was last in line for the cookhouse washbasin. The water was cloudy and cool. He splashed his face, soaped and rinsed his hands. Dried them as best he could on the damp towel.

Cora served the other table. When Christmas entered, she greeted him. Nikel slid a cup of tea toward Erich and gave him a shrug. Cora's gaze flitted past him, as if he were no more interesting than the bench he sat on.

He lingered over dessert until Mrs. Lane chased him away, saying that Henry wanted to talk to the men and he should go to his bunkhouse.

There, Henry talked about a community dance coming in two days. Someone had decided the women needed more partners and Henry should supply them. The men seemed agreeable. Yes, Henry said, there'd be young women there, and some of them might be tickled by the idea of dancing with "the enemy," but if any of them acted like less-than-perfect gentlemen, he promised to deal with them. Nodding answered Henry's gruff, "Do you understand?"

Mrs. Lane was collecting clothing donations so the men could wear something other than denim shirts with red targets, though there might not be enough trousers for everyone to replace their red-striped jeans. It would be worth going, Erich thought, just to get out of his prisoner clothing.

Nikel asked if the Canadians were okay with them going. Henry responded, "They'll be fine with it." Doubt swept a chill into the room. Erich eyed the nick in his boot and frowned.

21:

21 JANUARY 1944,
HORLEY (0°C/32°F)

On Friday, the men quit work early so they could get ready to go dancing. They were boisterous at the thought of seeing women. Some ribald comments made Erich heat with embarrassment, which only made the men tease him about his age and lack of experience.

His clothing had come from Mrs. Lane. Though shorter, her son was a similar build. He used his coat to buff the shoes, half a size too small. Not all the men had shoes, and three of them lacked civilian trousers, but it didn't dim their cheerfulness.

Alf banged on the door. "Wagon's waiting, boys."

The cutter pulled out of the yard when the prisoners piled onto the supply wagon mounted on runners. A lamp tied to a pole on the cutter showed Henry holding the reins, and two heads behind him, one tawny in the light. Cora. There was no point asking her to dance, much as he might want to. Since their exchange at Henry's table she had ignored him completely. He expected tonight would be no different. Beside Alf, Jimmy gripped their wagon's lamppost and smiled at Erich—but he smiled at everyone.

The three-mile ride could have been strained, but Alf got the Canadians and the Germans laughing. Then singing. He taught the Germans a silly ditty about beer on the wall. The words were so simple even Nikel caught on quickly.

Erich rode with coat unbottoned, the week-long warm spell continuing with the temperatures near freezing even after sunset. The town of Horley was smaller than Erich recalled. Most of the dark buildings looked like clapboard structures. Beyond the town, a building was lit by scores of lanterns. Sleighs and horses littered the yard. One truck was parked on the side of the road, Miller's Mercantile painted on the door.

Men lingered on the hall steps. Children played nearby. To the left, a circle of skinny boys tried to hide the telltale glow of cigarettes. Alf had given one to any man who'd asked on the wagon. A lot of them smoked every chance they got. Erich had liked smelling his grandfather's pipe; he didn't enjoy the bitter odor of cigarettes.

Alf led them into the hall, which doubled as schoolhouse by the looks of the blackboard at the far end of the room. Regularly spaced lanterns on wall hooks lit the interior, illuminating a small band in one corner and a refreshment table in the other. Children played under the table. The side walls were lined with filled chairs and more people stood along the back wall. Alf made space for his troop in a back corner. People eyed them curiously.

The music snuffed out when the prisoners entered. The violin player called for everyone's attention. The man was tall, skinny, with a big moustache and a voice to match. He held up his violin in one hand, bow in the other. "Let's welcome Henry's workers in Peace Country style."

A smattering of applause followed. The man invited everyone to dance and began to wheedle a lively song from his violin. The guitar and piano joined in. The piano was mostly in tune; the player had more enthusiasm than skill. The Canadian lumberjacks who hadn't stayed in the yard to talk found partners and whirled them around the floor in a two-step gone mad. It reminded Erich of an obscure Strauss piece he had learned. "What dance is that?" he whispered to Alf.

"A polka."

Nothing like this was played in the dance halls of Cologne. Erich doubted the band would be offering any swing music or even classical waltzes tonight.

He spotted Cora, dancing with someone the same height as her. Max. The poor boy looked miserable. When the song ended, Erich was smiling. Cora looked his way. Her lips pursed, she left the dance floor and joined a group of girls. One touched her shoulder like they were friends. All the girls except Cora glanced toward the Germans. Nikel nudged him. "Someone must go first. Ask one of them to dance." Erich shook his head.

The girl who had touched Cora walked toward the prisoners as another polka started. Dark hair swept into rolls like cresting waves, she wore a plain skirt, white blouse, and a pale blue sweater. She smiled at Erich. Nikel elbowed him again. He stepped forward.

"Do you know how to polka?" she asked. He admitted he didn't. "Would you like me to show you?"

"Yes, if I could know my teacher's name."

Her cheeks blossomed pink. "You *do* speak good English. I'm Elizabeth Williams."

"And I am most pleased to meet you." He inclined his head. "Erich, at your service."

Her lips twitched. "Aren't you cute?" That almost made Erich laugh. She couldn't know he was imitating his brother. He offered his hand. On the edge of the dance floor, they walked through polka steps. The other Germans watched. Another girl asked Conkle to dance.

Elizabeth suggested trying it slowly, then faster to keep time to the music. His natural rhythm kept him from stumbling, but everything felt off-balance. The place was wrong, the music was wrong, the people were wrong. His last dance had been in Cologne, joking with high school friends a few days before he'd joined his ship. The song ended. Flushed and laughing, Elizabeth insisted they dance the next so he could get more practice. When that song ended, Erich thanked her and introduced her to Nikel.

Erich told Alf he was going to step outside. He needed to slow his spinning thoughts and get past the unexpected surge of home-sickness. Once out the door, the cool air immediately penetrated his dress shirt; his coat was piled on Alf's wagon with all the pris-oners' coats.

Some boys raced around wagons. Erich winced at how close they came to the startled horses. There was an unnerving intensity to the game. The boy in the lead charged toward the hall. Max. He looked scared. Would it make things worse for Max to be helped by a German prisoner? Erich didn't have to decide. In a final burst, Max ducked around the closest horse, flung himself up the stairs and into the hall.

He hadn't noticed Erich, but the boys chasing him did. They skidded to a stop near the stairs and glared. One was almost as tall as Erich. His eyes held open hatred.

"Nice weather," Erich said. "Is it always this mild?"

The boys skulked off. A lone snowball winged from the darkness and hit the step by Erich's foot. *At least it's not an ax head.*

He shook his head, descended the stairs, and rounded the cor-ner, looking for the outhouse. As he passed a cutter and a cluster of men, one grabbed him and slammed him against the sleigh's cold side. His shoulder scar prickled as a forearm jammed against his throat. Alcohol fumes filled the air. "This is one of them." The face was shadowed but the voice was Frank's. "He asks lots of questions. Wanna ask my friends any questions, Jerry?"

"No," Erich choked.

"No? How about me? Wanna ask if I tried to hurt you and your kraut pals? You asked Chuck about me yesterday, he said. Ask me to my face like a man."

The pressure on Erich's neck lessened. "I don't want trouble."

Frank cuffed Erich on the side of the head. "Ask me, Jerry."

Erich felt a beating in the air. Like back in Camp 133 whenever Bechtel had cornered him. He should have stayed in the logging camp, or at least in the hall. He exhaled dread. "Frank, did you cut the sloop's chain?"

"Hear that, boys? The police say that broke sloop chain was an accident, but not Jerry here. Jerry thinks our police are damned liars." Frank leaned in again so his arm threatened Erich's air supply. Whatever he'd been drinking, it smelled like turpentine. Air trickled in smaller streams as Erich fought rising panic. Frank's voice vibrated. "I'll tell you this, Jerry. If I come after you, you'll know it. 'Cuz I'll come hard and fast, like your Blitzkrieg attack on Poland. And I'll crush you like they crushed my family, you Nazi son of—"

"Problem here?" Alf's voice cut through the darkness.

Frank dropped his arm, retreated. Erich rubbed his neck and sidestepped away, gulping in air. "No problem, Alf," said Frank. "I was telling him a story."

"Erich?" Alf prompted.

"Just a story," Erich whispered, still breathless.

Alf grunted. "There's coffee perking on the boiler. Switch from the hooch, Frank. And Erich, those girls want to dance. That's why you're here. Get inside."

22:

28 JANUARY 1944,
LOGGING CAMP (-2°C/28°F)

Nikel leaned against Erich's back, legs on either side of the log that served as their bench. "A week ago we were only hours away from going dancing."

Erich grunted. "And now we take up arms against a sea of troubles." Not that he was anything like Shakespeare's Hamlet. Well, he seemed to have collected enemies. He shivered.

"Not troubles. A sea of trees." Nikel laughed.

That made Erich groan. What an awful week, slogging in melting snow that should have been frozen. Alf harassing them to cut closer to the ground so less wood was lost, which meant bending over more with the crosscut saw. Erich's back ached so much he hardly slept at night. The only good thing was that the Canadians were talking to the Germans again. Though when he'd taken advantage of the change to ask again about the sloop accident, the reply had been, "Let sleeping dogs lie."

"Are you listening to me?" Nikel asked.

"What did you say?" Erich bit into the roasted pork sandwich he'd saved from lunch, and craned his neck to see the azure blue sky through a lacework of branches. They were resting briefly after delimbing four downed trees.

"I asked if you regretted coming here. Some days I miss the POW camp. We didn't have to work. We could help with dramas, play games." Nikel used his toque to towel off his brown hair.

"Get pummeled by fanatics." Erich inhaled the sap scent rising from the delimbed log under him. "I don't mind this. Though it's hard work."

"Slave labor."

"We get paid."

"In script we never see. Script they deduct every time we need even a bar of soap. We'll only get what's left when we return to the prison camp or when the war ends and we're released."

"What could we buy out here if we had money? There's no market down the road, no pubs or cafés." Erich missed the cafés, sitting and watching pretty girls stroll down the sidewalks.

"And there's only one available young woman." Nikel grinned.

Not available for him, Erich wanted to say, but he kept silent. All the prisoners liked ribbing him about Cora because they were the same age. He finished the sandwich, now tasteless. "Where is the measuring stick? This tree's crooked. We'll have to cut it."

"Not talking about the girl? Okay." Nikel chuckled. "I forgot the stick at the landing. You get it. I'll attach the skidding tongs to the log."

Erich passed the gray skidding horse, waiting to do its job, and gave it a pat. At the deserted landing the faint chugging of the sawmill steam engine was a low pulse, almost not a sound, a train that never got closer or farther away. Alf must have taken a full sloop to the sawmill to unload. Erich found the measuring stick in its place. The sixteen-foot-long stick had notches at ten, twelve, and fourteen feet, for ease of measuring. He balanced it on his shoulder, clipping a branch. As he swung toward their path, Alf came into sight, returning with the sloop.

Erich was six steps down the trail when pain-drenched cries bounced through the forest. He froze, trying to figure out direction. The undulating cries rippled over his skin. Straight ahead. Nikel.

Erich dropped the stick and raced down the trail, slipping, scrambling. He found the horse trying to skid the log. The yells were spooking it, making it strain at its traces. Erich grabbed the reins under the horse's chin, backed it up. He dropped the reins to the ground, making the horse believe it was tethered. It stood, eyes wild, ears twitching, wanting to run.

Erich's stomach churned as he darted past the horse. The skidding tongs were secured to the end of the log. It had slewed off the trail, trapped Nikel's leg against another tree, and was jammed between the tree and a stump.

Nikel pushed at the log, trying to free himself. "Get it off! It's tearing me apart!" He returned to guttural howls of pain.

No blood. Erich tried to think. He grabbed a stick. "Bite on this. I need to unhitch the horse."

Nikel bit down, his eyes squeezed shut in effort, cheeks stained with tears. Cries became moans that twisted Erich's gut as he backed the horse up, unfastened the chain, moved the horse down the trail. He pressed his forehead against the gray shoulder for a few seconds, wanting someone to come save his friend, someone who knew what to do.

"Erich, don't leave!" Nikel's anguished plea jolted him into action.

He returned to Nikel and tried to lift the end of the log. His muscles strained. It didn't budge. "Help! Someone help!" The heavy snow seemed to trap his words so they sank into nothing. Silence bounced back at him. He circled the tree and tried to help Nikel push, but that just drew louder moans. Erich crouched, eyes squeezed shut as panic rippled through his mind. His pulse raced. Why wasn't anyone coming to help?

Erich jerked his head up as the solution hit him: a lever could pry up the tree. Heart still hammering, he scanned the clump of spruce in which they'd been working. Seeing a spindly poplar, he grabbed his ax, broke through the crust into thigh-deep snow. Fought his way to the tree. His chest heaved. Nikel's moans rose into grating yowls, louder and quieter and louder again. The sounds raked Erich's crumbling control. His hands shook as he raised the ax.

Voices on the trail. He yelled, swung the ax. The poplar vibrated from the glancing blow. Erich wheezed, wiped sweat from his brow. He chopped again and the ax landed near his foot. Huffing, he clenched the handle to stop his hands from shaking and lifted the ax.

A hand grabbed the handle. Alf said, "The crew is here, son. Help us lift the log."

Erich's rubbery arms fell to his side. The ax slipped from his fingers. "No one was coming. I needed leverage."

Alf grabbed his shoulders and swung him around. "Say again, son. In English."

Erich took a breath. Repeated what he'd said. Alf helped him back through the deep snow. "We're here now. Jimmy, Schlenter, take this end. You two take the far end. Erich, you pull him out."

Still trembling, Erich maneuvered behind Nikel and hooked his arms around his friend's chest. Alf counted to three. Everyone strained as they lifted. A moment later, Erich fell back, Nikel in his arms.

"He's free," Alf yelled, and the men released the log with a chorus of grunts.

Erich didn't move. His eyes ached from unshed tears. Without Nikel, he'd go crazy out here. He had to be okay.

Alf squatted beside him. "You can let go now, son. He's free."

Free, perhaps, but Nikel was limp in Erich's arms. "Is he...?"

"Unconscious. Can't tell how bad his leg is. We'll get him back to camp."

The image of carrying Rudolf up the hill came to mind. "Y-you have a blanket?"

Alf shook his head. Christmas squatted beside Alf. "I can make a travois faster than running for blankets."

"Do it." Alf ordered the other men to help, then moved away. Erich could hear him rustling in the bush, but he didn't have the energy to turn and look. He concentrated on holding his friend, and ignoring the cold that was seeping through his denim. Moments later, Alf tapped his shoulder. "Move back. I've got a fire going. You both need to keep warm."

They settled by Alf's smoky little fire. Nikel woke, face gray and crumpled. He gripped Erich's arm, spoke in quiet German. "I tried to speed things up. Thought if the horse was hitched, we'd cut the log and go." He cringed, hissed.

"You left the reins over the horse's neck, Johann. The horse thought it was time to skid."

Nikel shuddered and shook his head. "I left the reins down."

"Are you sure?" Nikel nodded. Erich swore quietly and watched Alf feed twigs to the fire.

A few minutes later, Erich pulled Alf aside while the men moved Nikel to a bed of spruce boughs woven onto a triangular frame and fastened to the traces. Erich kept his voice low. "I want to look around, Alf."

"I thought you'd want to go with your friend."

"To sit and watch him suffer? I need to do something."

"Do what? It was an accident. They happen in logging, more than I like."

"He said he tethered the horse. When I arrived, the reins were over its neck."

Alf shook his head. "He's crazy with pain. Isn't remembering right." Erich clenched his jaw, struggling to keep angry words in his head. Had the sloop incident been an accident too? And what about all the loose ax heads? How long before an "accident" did more than injure a prisoner? How long before someone was killed?

Something in his expression must have spoken to Alf. He looked up at the bright blue sky and then back at Erich, reaching out to grip his shoulder. "Suit yourself. Just get back to camp before dark. You heard those wolves a few nights ago? In deep winter they can get hungry. That makes them brave."

The men left, trailing behind the stretcher contraption they called a travois. Nikel had passed out again. Perhaps that was for the best. When the rescue party was nearly out of sight, Erich stooped where he'd found the horse. Too many tracks, horse and human.

He sank to his knees and clamped a hand over his eyes as panic belatedly swamped him. His breathing became rapid, shallow. He undid the top button of his coat and pulled the thick material over his nose and mouth. Counted his breaths to slow them down. Nausea rose. He doubled over, vomited the remains of his pork sandwich. His stomach slowed to a lazy churn.

Shaky legs barely held him when he stood. They gained strength as he gathered the mess from lunch, the crosscut saw, the two axes. He found Nikel's gloves on a stump and pocketed them, then looked around, trying to shake the feeling of hopelessness that had settled in his chest. What had he hoped to find? Maybe Alf was right. Maybe he should have gone with Nikel, stayed with his friend instead of wandering around in the woods. It was time to head back.

Erich walked slowly toward the camp, pausing at the first crossing of skid paths. The forest was a maze of them. He looked back the way he'd come. From here he couldn't see where Nikel had been pinned, nor could he see the landing. Someone could easily have come along this path unnoticed.

Leaving the axes and saw in a pile, he examined the south trail. Horse tracks, boot prints. All the Germans would have the same print since their boots were identical. He could pick out some prints that definitely belonged to the prisoners. Others didn't.

Frank and Chuck had used the north path last week, but Alf had moved them west. No one was using it now, yet some prints looked fresh. Went both ways. He memorized one clear print pattern, like a stained-glass window, with a central panel and lines radiating out to form smaller panels.

Erich brushed off a stump and sat, imagined sneaking down that skid path, seeing the horse hitched to the skid tongs, throwing the reins over the horse's head and urging it into action, possibly backward to make the log lurch and trap Nikel, who hadn't seen anyone approach, then forward to wedge the log and man in place. But who would do it?

He returned the axes and saw to the landing, retrieved the measuring stick and stowed it, then returned to the north skid path. He studied the tracks, and hesitated. Answers or a dead end? His eyes flinched closed as Nikel's screams echoed in his mind. He needed to do this, and not just for Nikel. He took a single step beside the tracks. Head down, his own stink overpowered the fresh spruce scent. He took another step and glanced around. The shadows were lengthening, shading from blue to gray. He wouldn't have light for long.

Erich increased his pace, footsteps alternately crunching and squelching in the dappled light. Behind him, cawing echoed and faded. He passed two more skid paths, paused to examine each one, but the stained-glass tracks continued in a clear line. He scanned the path as he walked, the silence growing heavier as the shadows deepened. The tracks dipped into a hollow. Intent on the prints in the shady dip, he slipped on the incline, then skirted around a clump of skinny spruce. He caught the scent of stale sweat. Paused.

A swoosh. Pain cracked his head. The trail rushed up. Crashed into him.

23:

28 JANUARY 1944,
LOGGING CAMP (-6°C/21°F)

Max kept Gertie to a walk, like Mother wanted. He shifted on the gray horse's broad back and checked behind to make sure the oversized toboggan was still running true. They used it for hauling wood, but Mother needed it now that she had agreed to help Mrs. Lane by doing the German prisoners' laundry. Two crates, tied down and lined with oilcloth, hadn't moved.

The sun was almost below the treeline, but Max had assured his mother he didn't mind riding home in the dark. She had strapped a lantern to the front of the toboggan in case he wanted his path lit. He wouldn't use it. Darkness always seemed like a comforting blanket, warm even on a chilly night. Safe.

A good place to hide.

The logging camp's yard came into view. He'd been hearing the chugging of the steam engine that ran the sawmill for half a mile. Now it cut off. The silence plugged his ears like thick wax. The horse snorted and shook its head, making the bridle jingle.

He followed the path to the front of the Lanes' house to ask where Mrs. Lane wanted the clothing delivered. The men from the sawmill walked out from the trees that formed a wall between the yard and mill. All of them were watching the house more than where they were walking. Max waved, but no one waved back.

Gertie pulled the toboggan around the last corner. Henry Lane and several lumberjacks were gathered by the steps, Canadians and Germans. Mrs. Lane and Cora stood shoulder to shoulder on the top step. Max dropped to the ground and left the reins hanging to tether Gertie. He trotted over and wedged himself into the circle of men. Half of them had rifles slung over their shoulders. Had a wolf attacked? Were they going to hunt it down?

"We'll fan out to search every trail between here and the landing. I'll get the sawmill boys to search the yard in case he's just hunkered down somewhere having an old-fashioned worry over his friend."

That didn't sound like a wolf hunt. Max's shoulders drooped slightly.

Christmas cleared his throat. "I will start at the accident spot, work this way."

Accident? Max perked up again. What had happened? He clamped his mouth shut to keep from blurting his curiosity.

Henry crossed his arms. "I don't want anyone out there alone. It's getting dark. Everyone should have a partner and a lantern."

"I track better alone." A surprising stubbornness settled onto Christmas's face, making it look carved from wood.

Tracking? Was someone lost? Excitement bubbling up, Max asked, "Who are you looking for?"

"Your damned fool sledding friend," Chuck replied.

"Erich?" It came out more like a squeak than a word.

Henry clamped his hand on Max's shoulder. "You should get home, son."

"No! If Erich's missing, I want to help look. I'm old enough."

"You won't be any help out there."

"I'll be more help than the prison—" He cut off, scuffed the snow, looked back up. "I mean, I know the countryside. I won't get lost." Henry shook his head. Max took a deep breath, then spoke again. "I'll go out by myself as soon as you're gone." He bit the inside of his cheek, amazed at his sudden courage.

"I'll take him with me," Christmas said.

"Thought you liked tracking alone, Chief." Chuck curled his lip.

Christmas's only reaction was a narrowing of his eyes. "It is good for a man to help a friend who needs it."

"Man?" scoffed Chuck. "That runt?"

Max scooted over to Christmas's side. "I can hold the lantern so he can track better."

Henry looked as if he were about to say something, but he just lifted his cap and scratched his bald head. "Fine. But you damned well listen to Christmas. Don't go running off or I'll see to it you're too sore to ride that horse home."

Max grinned at the hollow threat. "Yes, sir."

He backed out of the circle to ask Mrs. Lane about unloading the clothes, but she was already hanging onto Gertie's reins. "I'll deal with your horse, Max, and I'll get word to your parents. If the search goes too late, you can sleep on our couch."

"Thank you." He tagged along behind Christmas. The Native boy was the same age as Erich and had his own rifle, but Max's dad couldn't keep his because he was German. That was so unfair. He shook his head to clear the thought. "Where is Alf?"

"Taking the laughing German to the doctor."

"Johann?" Christmas shrugged, so Max tried again, "John Nikel?" That got a nod. "What happened?"

"Leg crushed."

"Geez. Will he be okay?" Christmas lifted one shoulder. Max continued, "Why is Erich missing?" Another shrug. "Do you think he's hurt?" When all he got was another shrug, Max fell silent. They got a lantern from the cookhouse and backtracked past the house, through the valley, and into the forest.

The sun dipped below the treeline as they walked. The blue shadows, which already stretched across the sloop trail, deepened toward indigo. Max had to jog every few minutes to match Christmas's pace. Fifteen minutes later, they arrived at the landing where logs were loaded onto the sloop. Huffing, Max leaned against the wooden platform.

Christmas set the lantern beside him and lit it. "Rest, Little Mouse. I will look around here first."

While Max caught his breath, Christmas used the lantern to sweep the area, stopping at an open shed that faced south, a shelter if they needed it, Max guessed. Christmas spent long minutes studying the ground, sidestepping, studying some more. He returned to Max's side. His face was golden in the lantern light. "His measuring stick, ax, and saw are here. He was here. He went back to the bush." Christmas pointed at a trail.

"How do you know?"

"Tracks from the measuring pole are newest. On top of others. They go that way."

"How do you know it's his measuring pole?"

"Team number carved on each. Me on team four. He on team three."

Max straightened, excitement filling him. They were like Dick Tracy, following clues. If they found Erich, they would be heroes for sure. "Can I take the lantern now?"

Christmas handed it to him and waved for him to follow. Max whisked to his side and held the lantern out so it bathed the trail with light. There were so many footprints and marks. The logs dragged to the landing left scooped out hollows, horses left sideways Cs, but men's boot prints were more varied, with some deep and clear, some shallow, some smeared.

When they left the clearing, trees leaned in to peer over their shoulders. Max stopped. "What are those marks?" He pointed to two evenly spaced lines created by something dragged through the snow.

"Travois. Laughing—John carried out on it." He crouched. Max joined him, catching a whiff of woodsmoke. Christmas indicated the mess of markings. "See tracks on top of travois going into bush? All the men left bush with John. Not your friend."

"Erich."

"He returned tools, returned stick. It was beside this trail when we left with travois."

Max hung onto Christmas's words. He was talking as if Max were an adult. No one did that. "So Erich went back into the bush, but for what?"

Christmas turned toward Max. "If we find him we will ask him, Little Mouse."

"Why do you call me that?"

A smile twitched across thin lips. "You scurry in where you want to be. You hurry from place to place, watching for hunter owls and hungry coyotes. Always you smell for danger."

Max bit his lip. Was his fear really so easy to see? The air was cooling quickly in the growing darkness. Max tugged his toque down over his ears. "Thanks for explaining the tracks." He also wanted to say thanks for talking, because Christmas rarely talked. Maybe it was because they were alone out here. Maybe Christmas felt uncomfortable around adults too.

As they moved deeper into the forest, the path closed in behind them. Max's frosty breath turned yellow in the light. Pine and kerosene tinted the air. *Whoo, who, who.* Max tensed. *I'm not a mouse, not really. The owl isn't hunting me.* "Can an owl see mice at night?"

"Not a hunting call. It only watches. Waits."

"It's really dark."

"New moon three nights past." Christmas stopped at an intersection of paths, crouched, and indicated Max should join him.

Max set the lantern down and they both studied the clutter of tracks. Except Max couldn't figure out what they were looking at, or looking for. *Superman would know. I want to be Superman, zooming overhead until I find Erich. Is he in danger? Did he run away?* Max thought about running away, ususally when he was at school, but where would he go?

He eyed Christmas. "Where do you live when you aren't here in Horley?"

"You squeak much for a mouse."

Max lowered his head and squinted at the travois skid marks, tried to count how many tracks were over top. He stuck out his hand. The marks were almost three fingers wide. "Do you live with...with a tribe? On a reserve? Or..."

A quiet snort was his only answer. A moment later, Christmas said, "I stay some days at my aunt's home in the bush. I stay some days at a trapping cabin north of the Peace. I stay some days here."

"That sounds lonely."

"Your friend needs help."

Max squinted at his Cree friend—they were talking so they must be friends—but Christmas's attention had never left the tracks. He was being politely told to be quiet.

He looked around. The lantern created a ten-foot circle of light. Beyond that the trees were gray, then black silhouettes. The burning wick sent flickers of shadow and light rippling outward, the way a dropped stone sends out tiny waves in water. The edges of boot tracks seemed to grow and shrink with the cast shadows.

Beyond this trail, another, older trail stretched north. Snow had wiped out tracks like an eraser cleans a blackboard. Except the snow seemed to have fallen in little ripples too. Would the wind do that? You didn't usually feel much wind in the bush. Max squinted. He rose, moved the lantern closer to the path. He went down on all fours, head close to the ground and studied it.

"What do you see, Little Mouse?"

Max sat back on his boots. He swished his hand back and forth. "The snow on that path looks strange. Like ripples, not smooth like the snow under the trees."

Christmas turned his attention away from the confusion of tracks. He swung around to the other side of the lantern and frowned at the trail. His eyes widened slightly and he surged to his feet.

Max popped up too. "You saw something."

"*You* saw it, Little Mouse. The path was swept with pine branches."

Max's heartbeat began to gallop. "That means someone hid their tracks."

Christmas nodded. He motioned for Max to pick up the lantern, then unslung his rifle, checked the chamber, and pushed the bolt forward. "Walk behind. Hold light to the side so it falls ahead." He cradled the rifle so it pointed forward.

Christmas was serious, focused—the intensity rolled off him like heat off a stove. Mouth dry, Max swallowed, nodded. Three steps down the swept path, a single set of tracks suddenly appeared. Christmas halted and stared.

"Where did they come from?"

"Someone covered them up at first. From here, only covered a second track on the left." He pointed, and sure enough, Max could see that half the trail was swept.

"So they changed their mind about this track?"

Christmas shrugged and started out again. Max had gone only a few more steps when a wolf's howl froze him. A second, closer howl undulated through the darkness. The sound shivered over Max's skin.

He startled when Christmas appeared back by his side. "They do not hunt us, Little Mouse. But we must find your friend."

Were wolves hunting Erich? Max searched Christmas's face, looking for reassurance, but found only urgency. He lurched into motion, his heartbeat speeding from a gallop to a thundering run.

They advanced slowly, with Christmas occasionally raising his hand for Max to stop before continuing on. He was listening, but Max couldn't hear anything except his thudding pulse. The path rose, curved. At the top of a dip, they paused. The wolves howled again and Max shivered.

The lantern pushed back the shadows. Up ahead, something dark blocked the path. Two steps revealed the form, low and long, dark. Then Max spotted the shape of a circle on the dark form. A circle, like the ones on the backs of the prisoners' coats.

"Erich!" Max dropped the lantern, bolted forward.

"Wait," Christmas called.

Max stumbled, sprawled in the path near Erich's boots. Scrambled toward his head.

As Christmas caught up with the lantern, Max recoiled at the halo of red in the snow around Erich's head. "Is he dead?" *No! Please not dead. Please not dead.*

Christmas nudged him out of the way and rolled Erich onto his back. His head lolled to the side. His face was smeared with blood, and pale as the snow beyond the red stain.

Air stuttered in and out of Max's lungs. His vision blurred.

A single rifle shot fractured the night.

29 JANUARY 1944, LOGGING CAMP (-8°C/18°F)

Erich blinked. Then again. His eyes wouldn't focus. Someone pale hovered above him. "Gran?" he rasped.

"No, it's Max." The face came closer. "We were really scared when we found you."

Erich's eyes closed. When he opened them again, he realized he wasn't in his bunk. Too warm. In the dim, waivering light he could see a brick column beside him and the back of a stove. He turned his head slowly, for it pounded like the steam engine that ran the sawmill. A radio seemed to lean toward him. Other than a dream about his grandmother and Max, the last he remembered was the forest, a path...

"Johann?" he whispered, voice creaking.

Max appeared in his line of vision. "You're awake? Really awake."

"I think... Where...?"

"You're in the Lanes' house, on the floor by the stove."

"Johann was hurt. Is he...?" Erich continued to whisper; it hurt to even do that.

"Alf took him to the hospital in Spirit River. Everyone is upset. All the lumberjacks like Johann." Max wiped his brow with a warm cloth. "What were you doing out there, Erich?"

A mantle clock ticked as Erich considered the question. "Not sure."

"You don't remember?"

"It's...cloudy."

"They think you hit your head out there."

"I did? I...was looking for something I think." He squinted as pain bounced in his head.

"Mrs. Lane said I'm supposed to make you rest if you woke up."

He gave a small smile that was more wince. "Why are you here?"

"I stayed over and have been sleeping on the couch. Well, I guess I haven't slept much. I was really, really worried."

Erich could see the lingering concern. It curdled his stomach. Of all people, Max shouldn't have more worries piled on him. "Sorry," he whispered. "I'll be fine." He licked his lips. Max lifted his head and held a cup for him so he could sip some water. He lay back with a groan.

"You should go to sleep."

"First...tell me."

"What happened?"

Erich nodded, which set waves of pain sloshing around his head. He shut his eyes.

Max touched his shoulder briefly. "Don't move. Here's what I know. I used Gertie, our horse, to haul the big toboggan filled with clean laundry to camp. When I got here Henry was ready to send out search teams because no one had seen you since they'd brought Johann back to camp. I told him I wanted to help and he wasn't going to send me but I made him and I went with Christmas, who's really good in the bush. He was teaching me to track, but I saw the clean path. And he took his rifle off his shoulder like we were hunting an animal, but he was just being careful. And wolves were howling. And we found you. And Christmas fired his rifle to bring everyone else there. We brought you back by travois, the one they'd made for Johann. Henry and Chuck carried you inside, we made a pallet on the floor, and here you are."

It was hard to stay focused on the river of words. Max stopped.

"I need to thank you." Erich gave a weak smile.

"And Christmas. We were a team."

The smile faded. It wasn't likely the standoffish fellow would even accept his thanks, and he knew his own attitude was part of the problem. Erich gave a tiny nod.

"Mrs. Lane made us take off your wet clothes and she gave you a warm sponge bath to heat you up. I helped. Mrs. Lane said you were lucky it was so warm or you would've had frostbite. It got a lot colder after dark." He pressed the damp cloth against Erich's cheek. "This spot was the worst. Where you were face down in the snow. But Mrs. Lane said it should be okay. I thought they should've taken you to the doctor, but Henry refused."

"Why?"

Max's eyes widened and his voice dropped. "He said you're too hardheaded to be bothered by a bump on the head."

Erich snorted, which set off a fresh clamor of pain. He winced, and wished he could remember what had happened.

25:

31 JANUARY 1944,
LOGGING CAMP (-4°C/25°F)

Erich scooped tea from the pot on the bunkhouse stove. He added sugar and delivered it to Nikel, who was propped up on his bed, leg on one pillow and three others behind his back. A smile stretched across his white-edged lips; pain rippled across his brow with any movement.

The doctor didn't know why Nikel's leg wasn't broken. It was scraped raw in places, bruised from mid-thigh down, so swollen that they'd had to cut away the right trouser leg. He needed crutches for at least a week, probably longer.

Erich was going to sit on Nikel's bed but thought better of it. The men wanted a meeting. They had waited three days for Nikel to be able to sit up and take part.

Hubart stood. He eyed Nikel's leg, traced his own scar from cheek to chin, then turned to face Erich. "Nikel's your partner. Do you think this was an accident?"

"No." Erich explained about the horse's reins not being as Nikel had left them. "Alf thought maybe Nikel wasn't remembering right, but he seemed sure. I believe him."

"And your fall?"

"Sometimes I almost remember, then it slips away. Henry's doubtful about Max's claim that some other tracks had been covered up." He shrugged. "I'm not sure. Maybe Max saw what he wanted to see." Erich had only managed two-thirds of the work day before he had become nauseated. If he hadn't been trying to keep up with Christmas, his temporary partner, he might've rested sooner. He'd felt kitten-weak when he finally buckled.

Lehrmann whittled a horse, its wooden features emerging with each cut. "We should assume it wasn't an accident, even if everyone else disagrees."

"And do what?" Nikel asked.

"Don't go anywhere alone. Your mishap happened when you were alone. So did Hofmeyer's. Even if it's getting a measuring stick, go together."

"What about the latrine?" Nikel asked.

"That should be safe when we're all in camp," Erich said. Others nodded.

Hubart glared at Erich. "You never uncovered anything about the sloop accident. You are young, but I didn't think you were stupid."

"No one wants to talk."

"You didn't try very hard."

"You're right," Erich straightened. "I should've pushed until someone stuck a knife in my ribs. That would uncover our saboteur." He headed for the door. "I'm going to the cookhouse to check for leftover dessert. Do I need an escort?"

"You need to stop this insolence or I'll make it stop," Hubart said.

"Then I'm glad you aren't the one wielding a knife." Erich grabbed his coat and walked out. Somewhere to the west, a wolf howled. He inhaled deeply to calm down. That was stupid—like backtalking Bechtel in Camp 133. A wolf lived in the German bunkhouse, one he needed to fear, not mouth off at. He'd sometimes baited Gerhard too, but only when he could escape. Here, there was nowhere to go.

He had lied to the men about not remembering anything, but what he remembered puzzled him. He kicked at the snow as he walked to the cookhouse. There had been boot prints on the skid path where Max and Christmas found him. He remembered thinking they might belong to whoever had caused Nikel's accident. He had believed Max about that path being swept clean of tracks. Someone had covered them up. Maybe Henry didn't want to believe one of his men was responsible. It was too easy to dismiss the word of someone who was twelve, or seventeen—especially if they happened to be German. But if he told the other prisoners about the tracks, tensions would increase between them and the Canadians again. Worse, they might turn their anger toward Henry. He didn't want either thing.

Erich stomped the snow off his boots and crossed the dining area, glad Alf left two lanterns burning in this room until at least ten o'clock. Mrs. Lane set leftovers available for snacking on the window counter looking into the kitchen. Tonight's dessert had been a kind of bread pudding. With raisins in it. This was rationing?

Someone had beaten him to it. The pan was there, but had been scraped clean. He heaved a sigh. No deliciousness melting on his tongue.

"That's a long face."

Erich startled. "Hello, Mrs. Lane. I didn't see you." He picked up the pan and slipped into the kitchen to lean against the work table in the middle of the room. A lantern hung on a hook above it, throwing a circular shadow onto its plaid oilcloth table covering. He picked at a plump raisin wedged in a corner of the pan.

Cora walked in the side door with an armload of towels. She paused when she saw Erich. "Are you the mouse sneaking desserts?"

Was this teasing note because of Mrs. Lane's presence? Relieved he didn't have to face more hostility, he allowed himself to snicker in response. "Sadly, a rat beat me to it. I'm brokenhearted."

She lifted her shoulder in an unconcerned manner, put the towels in a low cupboard, then snatched the pan away just as Erich was reaching for the last half raisin someone had missed.

"This is the last pan, Mrs. Lane. I'll wash it if you want to rest your back."

"You make me sound ancient." Mrs. Lane wiped her hands on a towel. "But I'll accept your offer." She put on her navy coat. "I'm glad to see you looking better, Erich. You were awfully gray this afternoon."

"Your bread pudding revived me." Erich gave her a smile.

She patted him on the cheek. "Save it for the girls, son." She thanked Cora and left.

Cora's back was to him as she scrubbed the pan in a tub of water. He took a step to see if he could start a conversation but stopped short as a wave of dizziness hit him. He leaned over, bracing his forearms on the table.

"Are you okay?" Cora asked from behind him. He hadn't realized she'd moved. Something scraped across the floor. "Sit. Mrs. Lane said you have a huge goose egg on your head. You must have really walloped a branch."

"I think the branch walloped me." He sank onto the chair. Fainting in front of the only girl in camp wouldn't win him any admiration.

"Are you feeling dizzy? You're very pale."

"I overdid it today, that's all."

Cora gave a short nod and returned to washing. She'd never been so civil. Maybe playing the invalid could win her friendship. Not that he had to play.

Erich thought over what he knew. Nikel insisted he had left the horse's reins down. Footprints on the path that had been swept away by someone. He closed his eyes, working to recall those prints. He remembered memorizing the shape of one.

"Do you need help back to your bunkhouse?" Cora's worry almost made him smile. Of course, her concern might be more about trying to move him if he keeled over.

"I was trying to remember something. A footprint."

"Could you draw it?"

"I think so. If I had a pencil and paper."

"Not out here…Hang on." She dried the pan and her hands, went to a bin beside the cupboard, and returned with a cup of flour. She sprinkled some on the table. "Draw it now."

Erich stood and leaned over the flour. He stared until he could imagine the print imposed on the white surface, then traced it. "Like a stained-glass window." Now he recalled thinking that. "I followed tracks like this." Cora leaned over his arm and studied his work. She smelled of dishsoap and lavender.

"Max insists tracks were swept away where he and Christmas found you. If you were following someone, do you really think you slipped and fell, or was it something else?"

"I can't remember. But I woke up the last two mornings feeling that the pain came *before* I fell. When I try to grasp the idea, it disappears like fog."

"Have you told Henry?"

"He doesn't believe Max. Or doesn't want to. Why would he believe me? I'm the outsider." He inhaled slowly, reveling in Cora's nearness. She had never stood so close to him or talked to him like this. "No adult believes a seventeen-year-old, no matter how smart."

Cora's eyes widened briefly. "Only seventeen? I thought… If you're smart why didn't you finish high school?"

"I graduated at sixteen. I'm good at school. Not very good at life."

She moved away and brushed her floury hands on her apron. Her brown and yellow dress turned her eyes tiger-like. "Not if people are knocking you unconscious. If that's what happened. Couldn't another prisoner help you find out?"

Erich shook his head. "They push me to do any talking with the Canadians. None of them are confident with English. Even if they asked, it would only turn them into targets too." He tapped the flour by the heel of the print he'd drawn. "Maybe I won't be a target if my attacker believes I can't remember." He glanced up, raised his eyebrows in a question.

Cora returned and swept her palm over the flour. "I won't tell if that's what you want, though you really should make Henry believe you."

Somewhere outside of the kitchen, a door closed.

Cora started and retreated, while Erich's heart flapped like a bird trapped in a house. The echo pounded in his head. He pressed against the corners of his eyes to stop the rising dizziness. When he looked up, Cora was bustling around the kitchen, putting on her coat, saying she needed to get to the house, that she'd clean up tomorrow. In a blink she was gone.

A door had closed. But no one had come in. Who had been in the building? And what had they heard?

26:

2 FEBRUARY 1944,
ON THE ROAD TO HORLEY (-4°C/25°F)

Henry ordered Erich to remain in camp and help him, which meant a trip for supplies. Henry usually went by himself. Erich was happy to rest his aching head but wondered if the other Germans saw it as favoritism. He rode on the wagon's bench beside Henry, too worried to enjoy his first time seeing this road by daylight, hating how often worry consumed him.

Erich squinted at the cloudy horizon. A scattering of snowflakes drifted from a pale sky. Gray like his mood. He wished he knew who had entered the cookhouse Monday night. He wished Nikel were back in the forest, laughing and making the drudgery bearable. He wished his Cree partner's silence wasn't so unnerving. Mostly, he wished his battles had ended with his capture by the British. Everything he did seemed to end in disaster.

February days were noticeably longer, but still short. Beyond lamplight, the overcast nights were as dark as blackout conditions in Cologne, Erich thought, but howling wolves were worse than air raid sirens. With sirens he knew what to expect. The Canadians enjoyed teasing the prisoners about ravenous wolves snatching people on their way to the outhouse.

Henry cleared his throat. "You're determined to find trouble, aren't you, son?" He kept his attention on the pair of brown horses clopping along at a steady clip.

Erich clutched the edge of the bench. "What do you mean?"

Henry's brows beetled together. "Monday night, the missus sent me to the cookhouse to fetch Cora. Met one of the men in the yard. Said he saw you cozying up to her. Right then, Cora burst outside like her tail was on fire." Which man? Erich wanted to ask, but Henry harumphed. "Mildred and I need the extra help Cora gives. I'll hog-tie and beat you if you take advantage of her."

Erich was tired. Tired of fighting. Tired of every day being a grind. Tired of being treated like a child. "We were talking. It's maybe the second time she's spoken to me in two months." He didn't count New Year's Eve; she had spoken to him then, but only to spew venom at him.

Henry cleared his throat and squinted forward.

They rode in silence until Erich asked, "You said she's helping you. Is she getting paid?"

"She will be."

"In script?"

"She'll be paid in lumber like every one of us, at the end of the season."

Like every Canadian. Erich glanced at the forested hills. "Lumber? That'll buy a nice dress."

"I know she can't use lumber directly. I'll sell it for her and she'll get the cash." He scowled. "I do not take advantage of my staff. You being paid in script isn't my rule. I've tried everything I know to treat you boys fair and square, like regular workers. Did you repay that by seducing Cora in my cookhouse?"

"How did you jump from talking to seducing? I didn't touch her."

"Did you kiss her?"

"No. I said I didn't touch her. I swear."

Henry launched into a lecture about Erich respecting Cora and keeping his distance. Be darned if he was going to let that girl get hurt. Erich only half listened. He wondered what it would be like to have a father, or father-figure, this determined to protect his child. His father wasn't. Neither was Max's, from the sounds of it.

When Henry took a breath, Erich interrupted. "No matter what one of your men suggested, I won't harm Cora. I'm just glad she can now say two words to me without telling me how much she hates my being German." Henry gave him a long look, then inclined his head. Erich asked, "That was Monday night. Why did you wait two days to lecture me?"

Henry cleared his throat. "Waited until you felt better. In case I had to tan your hide."

"Did you think you'd need to?"

"Hell, no, but a man has to be prepared."

Erich looked away to hide his smile. A comfortable silence filled the space between them. "Tan your hide" sounded more like something Henry might say to his son, not one of his workers. Either way, Erich liked being spoken to as a person instead of an enemy. Henry had treated him fairly from the first day. Was that just his personality, or did something else make him want to treat his enemies "fair and square"?

The horses sped to a brisk walk. As they swooshed into town, the smell of woodsmoke masked the horses' musk and Henry's wool-and-wood-chip aroma. Erich's fingers traced the red stripe on his denim trousers as far as his knee. He didn't feel self-conscious in camp wearing his POW garb, but in this village the stripe and the circle on his jacket's back felt like marquee lights. A woman who had been beating a rug on her clothesline ceased her rhythmic thumping and scowled as they passed. Henry greeted her; she pursed her lips but gave him a terse nod. Moisture fled Erich's mouth.

Henry steered the team around a corner, then down a back alley. They stopped behind a clapboard building with a single door and a loading dock with a wide rolling door. Henry said, "The store's back entry. Our goods are inside. Let's go tell George we're here to load up." He hopped down without looking to see if Erich was following.

He reluctantly followed Henry through the storeroom into the store, wishing he could wait with the wagon but not wanting to stay alone.

Erich pulled the toque off his head and twisted it in his hands as he scanned the small store, amazed by the amount of goods crammed into three aisles. Groceries, dry goods, farm supplies, the selection boggled the mind. He noticed a stack of white and blue wrapped Ivory Soap and immediately thought of Cora catching him fresh from the bath. His mouth went dry again. *Don't think about it. Be happy she finally talked to you.*

"What are you doing here?"

Erich blinked out of his reverie. A broad-shouldered man peered at him from under the brim of a red plaid hat. He was three inches shorter than Erich but with chest and chin stuck out and fists clenched. Erich slid half a step backward.

The man's face reddened. "My boy is missing in action fighting the likes of you. Might be captured. Might be dead. Yet here you stand, bold as brass, when my Walter—"

"Is there a problem, Bill?" Henry stood behind the man, arms crossed, light reflecting off his bald pate. Behind him, a man as tall and thin as a sapling watched with a concerned frown—the violinist from the dance. He wore a grocer's apron.

Bill spun to face Henry. "Did you know a W.I. lady came and collected some of Walter's clothes? I'll support the Women's Institute, but not so these damned Jerries can dance with our women. And the missus gave 'em stuff. They're wearing his clothes while our boy is missing, or dead, or in some prisoner-of-war camp." He waved over his shoulder. "You're treating these Jerries a damn sight better than your boy's being treated over there, and you know it. Why should—"

Anger slashed across Henry's face. "That's enough, Bill. Unless you figure on helping load my supplies, you'd best go home."

The man deflated under Henry's ferocious gaze. After the man slunk away, Erich followed Henry into the back, silent in case his wrath still needed a target. As Henry's jerky movements smoothed out, the band constricting Erich's chest loosened.

They were over a mile out of town before Henry spoke again. "Is Bill right? Do they treat their prisoners of war poorly?"

Erich considered the harshness of his basic training for the navy. Hitler had said he wanted his young men to be as hard and sharp as Krupps steel. The Nazis hated weakness and used every means possible to eliminate it in their own people. He had never considered it before, but that likely meant enemies of the Reich would be treated badly. The Canadian government must know that, yet they pampered their German prisoners, especially in the big camps. And in this remote forest, Henry strove to treat them with respect, something he was certain Canadian prisoners of war wouldn't experience.

Henry sighed. "Not answering is an answer too, you know."

"I'm sorry," Erich whispered.

"So am I, son," Henry replied. "So am I."

27:

9 FEBRUARY 1944,
LOGGING CAMP (-18°C/-1°F)

In the week following the trip into town, temperatures dropped nearly twenty degrees. Working in the forest became exhausting, bearable only because Alf kept a fire buring, in front of the shed-turned-shelter by the landing, so they could warm up at regular intervals.

Dreary clouds showered daily traces of snow. Erich had become used to the shocking blue skies of the northern Alberta winter, which made it feel as if he were living in a crystal world of white and blue. The gray afflicted everyone and reminded Erich of grim Cologne winters.

The Germans trudged into the cookhouse. The Canadians were already huddled around the potbellied stove near the door. Erich cast a wistful glance at the stove. He hung up his coat, washed, and lingered nearby, hoping some warmth would reach him and penetrate the ice encasing his bones. When Nikel hobbled inside on crutches, the prisoners encircled him, forming a blue-shirted fence, red circles facing out. A silent declaration of their distrust. Their fence opened when Alf entered the room.

"Hey, Alf," Jimmy called out. "Full moon tonight. Weather going to get colder?"

The eight men around the stove laughed. Alf gave an exaggerated shrug. "Don't know, but it's gonna change. You watch. Let's hope not for the worse. Metal gets brittle when it's really cold. Your head, being wooden, won't be bothered at all." More laughter.

Erich suppressed a shudder. As if this wasn't *really* cold. But Alf insisted January had been the mildest in years. It wasn't unusual to get down to minus forty. *Impossible,* Erich protested silently.

Alf led the line to dish up his stew. The Canadians fell in behind him, and the Germans behind them. Chuck barred the way of the first German, Conkle, from the sawmill. Loudly, he said, "Christmas, get in line with us where you belong."

Erich helped Nikel settle at the table as tension spiraled through the room. Some men fisted their hands. Hubart's scar stood out as a white gash as he stepped up to face Chuck. "There is a natural order. He's where he belongs."

"Wrong, Jerry," Chuck said.

Frank joined him. "The natural order is for us to wipe kraut scum off the bottom of our boots. You're where *you* belong, Jerry. Back of the line."

At the other table, Alf set down his bowl. "Damned full moon. Makes people crazy." He stomped toward the men. Frank shoved Hubart. Before he could react, Alf stepped between them and yelled for everyone to sit. When they didn't move, he started to swear, then glanced at the women and apologized. He shoved men in the direction of their tables.

Alf strutted between the tables and lectured about behaving like men, not boys in a schoolyard scrap. Chuck's shoulders hunched as he glared at the table. Frank looked as belligerent as ever, and beside him, Sam the blacksmith, ham fists on the table, looked ready to flatten whoever stepped too close. Like all the Germans, Erich sat ramrod straight with eyes front—standard procedure when a superior ranted. From the corner of his eye he saw Mrs. Lane double over and Cora help her to a chair.

Alf ended his spiel and entered the kitchen. His voice rumbled through the building. "I'm serving the stew at the tables. I need help." While he served the Canadians, pausing to whisper in each man's ear, Cora served Nikel first, giving him a brimming bowl of stew and three slabs of bread. His wide smile lit up his broad face. From him, she went clockwise around the table, which put Erich last. She kept flitting glances his way, her expression wavering between unsure and irritated. Did she regret promising to not tell anyone his suspicions?

As he waited, Erich studied the feet of the Canadians, like he had all week. But he was no closer to discovering Nikel's attacker. Cora set a plate and bowl in front of him and he jerked his head up, then noticed all the prisoners were bouncing glances from her to him.

She lifted her chin. "Who wants tea?" All their hands went up. Erich rose. "I'll help." A few prisoners snickered.

At the tea urn, Cora picked up a cup and narrowed her eyes. "I don't need help. Your stew will get cold."

Erich offered a shrug. "It's fine." He nodded at the Canadian table. "Why did Chuck have to start something? Our system worked."

Cora poured the first cup. "Mrs. Lane told me Chuck got bad news today. His only sister lost her second boy to the Nazis. The first went missing near New Year's. Now they're both dead and he's upset. He knew it would insult the *Aryans* to have Christmas ahead of you in line. I thought you, at least, might defend him. If not for Christmas, you could've frozen in the bush. You should want him at the front of the line. Do you think he's less important than you?"

"It's not... You can't know. In Germany..." Erich deflated. "It's easier to not cause waves."

Cora handed him the cup. "No matter who it hurts?" She walked away.

28:

10 FEBRUARY 1944,
HORLEY (-2°C/28°F)

Max's bladder was bursting. He stashed his knitting in his knapsack and put on his outerwear. The girls who had stayed inside to knit after lunch ignored him, as always. Recess was in full swing so he scouted the schoolyard through a cracked-open door. No boys in sight. He closed the door and imagined his route to the outhouse. He was Captain Canuck, sneaking through enemy territory to a command post.

After a quick peek to make sure it was still clear, he snuck outside and plastered himself against the side of the building as he crept along. At the corner he hesitated, pulse drumming. He dared a glance. *All clear, Captain.* The outhouse's door was ajar. *It's broad daylight, Captain. You'll have to charge the post.* Max dashed across the open space and locked himself inside, huffing relief. He leaned against the door until he calmed down.

He was buttoning his fly when something hit the wall. He flinched. *Thunk. Thunk.* A pause, then a full barrage, hammering the door and one side of the outhouse. *Don't let them break in, Captain!* He bit his lip and wedged his shoulder against the door. Each hit vibrated down his arm. How much ammo did they have? They had to be running out. Maybe they'd get bored and leave. He shifted and pressed both hands against the rough wood slats with his thumb under the hook and eye latch, ready to pop it up if he needed to run.

What would Captain Canuck do? *Fight them!* Max rested his forehead on the back of his hand. Why couldn't he be brave? Why couldn't he get them to stop?

After countless strikes, he heard a wail, "Stop it! I need to pee!" That caused a lull in the bombardment. Air caught in Max's lungs as he tried to decide what to do. Then, a voice: "Get out of there, Hitler. Mel needs the biffy." Max's breath whooshed out. Of course his attacker was Richard. It always was.

Another minute passed before a timid knock made Max step back. "Please?" a voice floated through the quarter moon carved in the top of the door to let in light. "I hafta go real bad."

Max clenched his jaw for a moment. "Step to the side, out of my way." He silently counted to three, then flipped up the latch and burst outside. The little boy who just a moment before had been desperate to pee, stuck out his foot and tripped Max. He landed with an, "Oof!"

Richard and his friends whooped their glee. "Good one, Mel!"

As Mel locked himself in the outhouse, Richard made his move. He pounced on Max and dragged him off the trail, straddling Max's stomach. Max covered his face with both arms. Hands grabbed his wrists and pinned his arms above his head. The boys gave him savage grins.

Max struggled to get free. He tried to buck Richard off, but now hands grabbed his ankles too. Alarm thrummed through him. Not again. *Why?* Desperate to understand, he wailed, "What did I do?"

But Richard didn't answer. He just mashed a handful of snow against Max's face. He whipped his head back and forth, trying to avoid the cold grit. Another handful of snow. Richard ground it against his cheeks like icy sandpaper. Snow packed against his nose. He opened his mouth to breathe and Richard shoved snow into it.

Max thrashed and writhed and managed to spit it out. Water trickled down his throat, making him cough. He gasped. "Why are you doing this?"

"Because you're a bastard Nazi." Richard slapped him, snapped his head to the side. "Walter is missing and might be dead because of bastard Nazis." Another slap.

"I didn't do that! I'm not a Nazi!"

"You should've stayed where you belonged." Richard hauled back his fist.

The school bell rang, signaling the end of noon recess. Richard narrowed his eyes and a grimace twisted his mouth. He struck. Max jerked his head aside and took the blow on his ear.

Richard jumped up, kicked his thigh, then ran off with his friends.

One hand on his ear, Max sat up, struggling not to cry from the pain. All the students would laugh at him. Again. Like always. Max wanted to crawl into a hole.

Richard's brother was missing. That's why his attacks had gotten so vicious this last week. Max pulled his knees up and wrapped his arms around his legs.

His face ached from the scrubbing, his thigh throbbed from the kick, his ear buzzed from the hit, and he could feel a headache starting. He didn't know how much more he could take.

Miss Williams yelled at him to get inside. Max didn't move.

Max rode Gertie up the lane to the logging camp's barn. He let her plod slowly. After the awful day he'd had at school, the last thing he wanted was to help in the camp's kitchen, but Mother had insisted. She was up to her elbows in camp laundry, Mrs. Lane was sick, and Henry had ridden into town for medicine. He hadn't argued about it only because he really liked Mrs. Lane.

At least he didn't have to listen to another lecture by Father about wonderful Germany and how proud he should be of his heritage. Today he might have said something back—always a mistake with his father. All afternoon he'd felt like a tightly wound yo-yo.

It wasn't *his* fault Richard's brother was missing. Why did *he* have to pay for what was happening on the other side of the world?

He left Gertie in the first stall with some hay and water, then angled toward the cookhouse, wondering what he'd be expected to do. Not much, he hoped.

Max stopped two steps into the kitchen and gaped. Bowls and spills were scattered across the big work table. Over by the stove, Cora stood with a teatowel over her shoulder, hands hanging by her side like dead things, dismay stamped her face. She gave him a forlorn look.

Before either of them spoke, hissing from the stove claimed her attention. She opened the oven door. Max dropped his coat on the chair and peered over her shoulder. "The biscuits look kinda white."

She slammed the door, stepped back. Max opened the firebox and heat washed his face. A few stubs of wood glowed red in their bed of gray ashes. Behind him, Cora sobbed, "Not again."

She's having a bad day too. Max tried to smile. "I can get the fire going again."

Cora collapsed onto a chair. "How do women do it? Mum only showed me a few basics on our stove, never how to cook for so many." She slipped her shoes off, rubbed each foot. After a moment's rest, she groaned, gathered the plates and carried them into the dining room. Max restarted the fire.

A door slammed, and when Cora returned, Henry followed her into the kitchen. His eyebrows rose. "The boys are sharpening their axes for tomorrow. Roast not sliced?" he asked. "I could do that."

"Oh, thank you." Cora lifted a pot lid and poked a potato. "These need to cook more before I mash them."

"Serve 'em boiled. Max, help her dish everything up." Henry used two tea towels as pot holders and pulled the huge roaster out of the oven. "Biscuits are looking mighty brown."

Cora stopped draining potatoes and rescued the biscuits. "Oh no." She dropped the baking sheet on the counter. One side of the biscuits were more black than brown.

"They can cut the burned parts off. Get 'em into bowls."

"I'll do that." Max found two bowls and tossed half of the piping-hot biscuits in each.

While Cora dealt with the carrots, Max finished draining the potatoes. He was used to helping Mother do this kind of work. In each pot, a layer of scorched potatoes stuck to the bottom as if welded there. Half the potatoes were mush. Max dumped them into big metal serving bowls.

"Cora?" Henry asked. "When did you put the roasts in the oven?"

"When Mrs. Lane told me to." Cora and Max peered over his shoulder. Both roasts leaked blood from red centers.

Cora gulped loudly. "The...the fire went out a few times..."

"Get out the frying pans. I'll slice these and add a bit of color to them." Henry had eight slabs braised when men started filing in. Alf had them wash up and sit down. He came into the kitchen. "Food ready?"

"The food," Cora replied, sniffing, "might not be edible."

"Then I'll tell the men that whoever complains gets double portions."

Max covered his mouth to stop a laugh. Cora gaped at Alf. "Y-you wouldn't."

He winked. "Hungry men will eat most anything. I already told them Mildred's sick and you're doing your level best to get something on the table."

Henry handed Alf a platter with the cooked outer slices of the roasts and the raw ones he had browned. "Divy these up. More coming. Max, you get the other food on the tables. Cora, put out some butter since the potatoes didn't get mashed."

Cora delivered biscuits to each table. Max was carrying a bowl of potatoes to the prisoners' table when Erich, biscuit in hand, spoke in German. The men laughed. Nikel almost tipped off the bench by Max, who nudged him upright and set his bowl down on the table. What Erich said hadn't been nice—and hearing the words brought Richard's hateful face to mind, the way he'd sworn about the Nazis who had captured or killed his brother. Any of the men at this table might have done the killing if they'd still been in Germany. Even Erich. For a second Max saw them through Richard's eyes. The enemy. His throat closed.

Cora set carrots beside the potatoes. The men turned sheepish. She glanced around, looked at Max, Erich, then back to Max. "What did he say?"

Max pressed his lips together for a second. "Nothing." He scowled at Erich as irritation bubbled inside.

Cora flushed. "Tell me."

Max bit his lip. Erich raised his hand. "I didn't mean anything. I said...you cook like my grandmother."

"That wouldn't make them laugh. What else did you say?" Her fists parked on her hips.

Erich squinted one eye. "That luckily she had a cook."

Cora sputtered. Her face turned a darker shade of red. "How dare you insult me like that. How...dare—" She ran from the room, crying.

Hearing Erich's words again, in English this time, curdled Max's irriation. It tasted sour. Erich raised his eyebrows and made a little "foof" noise. He sounded like someone who didn't care that he'd just hurt someone.

The same way Richard didn't care if he hurt Max. And how no one cared if he got hurt, just because his father was German. How everyone laughed at him.

It wasn't fair.

Mixed-up feelings of hurt and anger and confusion and shame churned and seethed and surged to the surface. He gripped the edge of the table, tried to swallow them, trembled with the effort. But all he could think was how much he hated being German. Hated being beat up, despised, ridiculed, just because he was German. And now the one German he really liked had insulted Cora in the same smug way Richard always insulted him. He took a deep breath, trying to calm himself, but it was too late. Everything boiled into dizzying rage.

Max seized the biscuit bowl, fired a biscuit at Erich. "You numbskull! She worked hard all day." Max shot another biscuit at him. He ducked and fell backward off the bench. The prisoners started laughing.

Max barely heard them over the roar in his ears. He stepped around the table and hurled another biscuit. "You think this is funny? None of it's funny!" Erich curled into a ball as Max pelted him. "You're rude. You think you're better than everyone. You deserve to lose!" A biscuit flew with each word. " ...fat-head, creep, booger."

A hand grabbed Max's wrist, throwing cold water on his sizzling anger. Alf looked ready to laugh. "Your ammo is running low, and I'm pretty sure Erich got the message. Maybe Cora isn't the only one who had a hard day. Why don't you head into the kitchen and have some rhubarb crisp?"

Max dropped the bowl on the table and stomped to the kitchen. He found the crisp in two big cake pans on the warming shelf above the stove's cast iron surface. He dished some up for himself, found a spoon, sat down, then glared at the closed serving window, feeling worse every second. Erich was his friend...as much as someone five years older could be a twelve-year-old's friend. What he said might've been a bit funny, if Cora hadn't looked so frazzled.

Max knew how she felt, knew what it was like to be teased in a mean way. He replayed the scene in his head, saw himself hurling biscuits and screaming. That must have been what had made him go crazy. No, it was more than that. All the teasing, all the cruelty, all the hate, had given force to every biscuit he'd thrown. Years of holding it all in. Max sniffed. Blinked and sniffed again. The crisp smelled good. He squinted at the rhubarb, pieces like pink and red jewels in the golden brown setting. It looked good too. Way better than the half-blackened biscuits. His stomach gurgled.

Henry entered the kitchen, closing the door behind him. He nodded at Max. "How's the crisp?"

"I haven't tried it." Max took a bite. The sourness puckered his lips and wrinkled his nose. "Needs sugar."

"That's all?"

Max licked his lips. "I think so."

"Sugar coming up." Henry got down a cannister from a cupboard and set it beside Max. "Let's keep this our secret. Sprinkle a bunch on the dessert for me and no one will know better. We'll tell Cora her rhubarb crisp was perfect." Henry winked.

That wink felt like forgiveness. Max smiled. "Yes, sir."

29:
11 FEBRUARY 1944,
LOGGING CAMP (-5°C/23°F)

Another Friday, another dance. This one apparently had a reason, being that it was the closest Friday to St. Valentine's Day. Dancing seemed an odd way to celebrate a martyred saint, but Alf explained about it being a celebration for people in love. That sounded vaguely familiar. Had Erich's grandparents mentioned the holiday?

Whether dancing made sense or not, the work day ended early because of it, so Erich was grateful. Jimmy sprinted to the outhouse the moment they reached the yard, and Erich volunteered to lead the skid horses to the barn. To his surprise, Nikel was there. "Henry said I could help with the horses," he explained as he took the reins of one and hobbled into the barn on one crutch.

As they worked, Nikel told him that he'd also helped in the kitchen. "Mrs. Lane is feeling well enough to supervise. I apologized to Cora for our rudeness yesterday, but..."

"Yes, I'll apologize." The memory of last night's dinner had haunted Erich all day. Cora had been right to be angry, and Max... well, Erich had tried to talk to him after dinner, but he'd been gone by the time the men had polished off their dessert.

With no chance to apologize to Cora during the day, Erich had tried a different approach. He'd hoped to be able to impress her by saying he'd gotten to know Christmas a bit, but that had failed. He'd tried to start a conversation, hinting he should finally learn Christmas's real name, since they'd been working together for two weeks. The only reply had been, "I like that you can work without words." Erich had never been told to be quiet so politely.

He undid harness straps, removed traces, collar, and bridle, and draped it all over the top plank of the stall fence. Swearing turned him around. Nikel was dragging a harness across the floor to the row of oversized hooks at the back. With every step it became more tangled.

Erich laughed. "Alf will whip you for messing up his harness."

"Come help, *Dummkopf.*"

Erich stepped forward as Nikel yanked, and the next instant, he was sprawled facedown on the snarl of leather, a strap twisted around his heel. Now it was Erich's turn to swear—his head narrowly missed one of the posts supporting the wide bench under the hooks. He lay, catching his breath, eyeing burlap sacks stuffed under one end of the bench. The pile struck him as odd. The top sacks were roughly folded, but the bottom ones looked different—as if they were bundled around something. He tugged and lifted the corner of one sack, glimpsed rounded metal. Raised the sack higher. Bolt cutters. Heart clogging his throat, he snatched his hand back.

Behind him, someone started laughing. He rolled over to see a boot propped on the lowest plank of the closest stall. In his mind, he saw the prints in the snow from the day of Nikel's accident. This boot sole had the same pattern.

He raised his gaze. "You're one clumsy boy!" Alf grinned down at him. "I'm amazed you lived long enough to get captured. Get ready for the dance, though I don't know who'd want to dance with such a bumbling oaf. John, leave that and help me get the other horses stabled."

Erich inhaled a shuddering breath as Alf walked away, still laughing. Nikel limped after him, the single crutch counting off. *Tap. Tap. Tap.*

Alf. The missing bolt cutters. The boots.

It couldn't be.

Erich was shaking when he got to his feet.

30:

11 FEBRUARY 1944,
HORLEY (-5°C/23°F)

Erich ate supper mechanically. He didn't notice what was served
or how it tasted. His thoughts swirled with black possibilities.
Could Alf—one of the few who had won the Germans' trust—be
their attacker? Could he be so calculating? It was hard, very hard
to imagine.

After the meal, he dressed for the dance, then picked his way
across the sloppy yard. Cora answered his knock on the door. She
wore a fitted dress with a red floral pattern, and red shoes. With hair
swept up and lipstick highlighting the curve of her lips, she looked
stunning. He tried to not stare at the dress's sweetheart neckline.
He couldn't recall why he'd come.

"Yes, Erich, what is it?" Mrs. Lane asked from behind Cora.

"I..." *Think, Dummkopf.* "I came to apologize for my behavior
yesterday. I'm..." He swallowed. "There are no words for how rude
I was."

Cora blushed. She muttered a hasty acceptance of his apology
and retreated, her swaying skirt and shaply calves drying out his
mouth again.

Transformation from schoolhouse to dance hall was again complete.
Tables had to be outside, for there was only one tiny back room
housing the coal-fueled boiler that provided heat. The same trio of
piano, guitar, and violin warmed up in one corner. Women set out
cakes, cookies, and juice in the other. With the dance not begun,
children used the floor space to play a noisy game that someone
nearby called Duck, Duck, Goose.

Talking and laughter rippled through the room. Erich felt detached from it all, cold when the room was warm, alone in a friendly gathering. He studied Cora, talking with a blond girl. The neckline of her dress now covered by a demure white sweater, waist-length and closed by a row of pearly buttons. She no longer wore lipstick, but nibbled at her bottom lip in a way that darkened it anyway. Was that because of his foolish reaction earlier? Drooling like a love-struck idiot.

Jimmy burst into the hall. Everyone looked. He turned redder than his hair, spotted the blond girl, and pulled her onto the dance floor. The music started and a few older couples joined in a waltz. Frank asked Cora for the second dance. For the next hour she had a succession of partners, including a few prisoners. Rudolf asked her for a second dance and they stumbled through a polka. Wedged into a corner, Erich only watched, too numbed by his earlier discovery to dredge up enthusiasm. The only person he wanted to dance with would probably rather slap him. Numbness gave way to queasiness, as if he were on a ship in storm-tossed waters.

A nearby talkative matron pointed out that Frances, the blond, had danced every dance with Jimmy, but now she charged up to Cora and dark-haired Elizabeth, who had taught him to polka at the last dance. Face stormy, Frances turned on Cora. Erich couldn't hear, but he saw Cora flush as Frances railed. Erich tensed, wanting to rush to Cora's aid. Would she welcome it? Erich inched forward. Maybe she would. Maybe she'd appreciate being rescued and would finally see him as a friend. His pulse tripped.

Before he could think himself out of it, Erich approached the girls. Elizabeth's knitted brows confirmed their topic was serious. He swallowed hard, tugged at each cuff of his borrowed dress shirt, more nervous than he'd been at his first piano recital when he was ten. Erich stopped behind Cora, catching a whiff of her lavender scent. His pulse increased to a rapid tempo. He touched her shoulder. "Might I have the pleasure of this dance."

Cora pirouetted on those elegant shoes, relief on her face. At the sight of Erich, however, she froze, and his courage withered under her stare. Moments ticked by in awkward silence. The color in her cheeks heightened, but still she only stared.

Elizabeth sidestepped toward Erich. "I'll dance with you." He wanted to smile at her, to thank her for breaking the tension, but he couldn't respond. Cora's reaction turned his insides into a barren icefield. She still saw him as a dirty German. Maybe he deserved it after his impolite gawking, but it felt like needles under his fingernails. He lurched away, leaving Cora's scowl and Elizabeth's shocked expression, and edged around the dance floor. He parked by the piano, as far away from Cora as he could get without leaving the hall. He should have left, but she was near the door.

Now his stomach roiled. He'd been a fool to think Cora might see him as a friend. He hid his clenched fists under folded arms, tried to strike a casual pose. He needed a distraction from his humiliation. She had danced with other prisoners, and with Rudolf twice. But not with him. Rudolf would never let him live it down. The piano player banged out a vaguely Bavarian tune that had dancers doing another frantic polka.

Uncurling one fist, he laid his hand on the top of the piano, felt the strings' vibrations through the wood, tried to slow his breathing, but the music was too brisk. Did Cora hate him that much? The thoughts tumbled through his mind, a confusion of churning emotions—over her reaction, over Alf's guilt. It was engulfing him, filling his lungs, making it hard to breathe. The vibrations stopped and the violinist announced a break. The piano player paused by Erich, spoke. He shook himself. "I'm sorry?"

"I asked if you played," the middle-aged woman said. Sweat

added a sheen to her lean face. "I'd love for someone else to play awhile."

"I play, but not dance music."

"Classical stuff?" He nodded. She exchanged quiet words with the violinist. "Mr. Miller suggested you entertain the folks during our break. If you want." She headed to the exit.

The white and black of the piano keys beckoned. He'd last played over a year ago, the night before he'd enlisted. He had avoided the piano in the hall at the prison camp, hadn't wanted to entertain anyone there.

Erich slipped onto the piano stool. It rocked but he couldn't see any way to adjust it other than raising it by turning the seat. He rested his fingers on the keys. Closed his eyes. He shut out the hum of voices, let his fingers decide what to play. The *poco moto* opening of Beethoven's "Für Elise" trilled from the instument, flowed as if he'd played it yesterday. His fingers danced through the second, lighter section. When it moved into the more agitated theme, he poured all of his remorse into the music, giving the return to the main theme a layer of sadness that blocked his throat.

When the final note faded, a smattering of applause made Erich look up. The piano player stood where he had earlier, amazement widening her eyes. "I never knew music could be so filled with feelings, happy and sad and... I don't know whether to laugh or cry."

Erich wanted to ask what was the point of music if not to evoke emotion, but he was too overawed by his own emotions to trust his voice. Instead, he offered a slight shrug.

"Would you play another?" the woman asked. "Please? Anything at all."

Erich gave a terse nod. He stared at the keys but could summon nothing that suited a celebration of love. All he felt was overwhelming sorrow. Cora's rejection, Alf's possible betrayal, the worry of more accidents, the pressure by Lehrmann and Hubart to uncover the saboteur—each one an added weight that together threatened to crush him. He rested his fingers on the keyboard. "Tristesse," a solo piece by Chopin, intoned its mournful melody under his fingertips. Ninety seconds into the solo, when the tempo was supposed to pick up, Erich stopped playing. Sad music was suffocating right now. He apologized to the piano player and strode to the exit.

Elizabeth captured his arm at the door. He frowned, wanting nothing more than release. She poked him in the chest. "You made Cora cry with that first song." He blinked. She jabbed again. "Get outside. Find her. Apologize." She planted her hands on her hips. "Boys are idiots. You and Jimmy both."

When Erich only stood, trying to make sense of what she had said, she pushed him out the open door. A man coming in stopped him from falling. He stumbled down the stairs, stood in the mild cold and peered at the stars. He had made Cora cry? It seemed fitting, since she'd almost done the same thing to him.

Instead of Cora, Erich found Max sitting on an upside-down table that was stacked on another table. Over his left shoulder, light shone from the window nearest the piano. The dance had resumed and the two-step music was a jaunty counterpoint to what Erich had played. He inhaled the crisp air to clear his mind.

"Just the man I was looking for." Erich braced a hand on an upturned table leg. "I've apologized to Cora and wanted to apologize to you too. I was rude yesterday." No answer. Erich raised his eyebrows and tried to sound upbeat. "Could you at least tell me what a booger is?"

Max sniffed. "It's the stuff that comes out of your nose. And it's a not nice person."

Erich wrinkled his nose. "Was your biscuit bombardment only about me saying something stupid for a laugh?"

Max fiddled with the top button of his coat. "You play piano real good."

"Thanks. What else upset you yesterday, Max?" No answer. "My big brother used to do that to me. He'd be angry about something that happened at school, then he'd come home and beat me up. My father laughed. He said I needed to stand up to Gerhard."

"That's what my father says too."

Erich nodded. Here was something much less confusing than figuring out Cora. "It's hard standing up to a big brother. Are the boys causing trouble at school bigger than you?"

"Way bigger. And they gang up on me. I never have anyone on my side."

The air settled through the cotton shirt and clung to Erich's skin. He shifted and propped his backside against the table so he could cross his arms. He unconsciously slipped into German. "Sometimes it feels like that for me too."

Max replied in German. "But you have friends here."

"Johann Nikel is sort of a friend, but he's nine years older. He was with me in the camp by Lethbridge. He adopted me as, I don't know, a younger cousin."

"Like you did with me."

"A little. You're a smart kid. I like that."

"You see me as a kid."

Erich rolled his eyes. "That's how adults see me."

Max's smile flashed momentarily in the dim light.

"Will Johann be okay?"

"Yes. He's already hobbling around, helping Alf with the horses." Erich frowned, remembering what he'd discovered in the barn. *Have you betrayed us, Alf? Please, no.*

"Do you ever wish you'd stayed in the big camp? I heard the men saying it has electricity and all kinds of things. Then you and Nikel wouldn't have gotten hurt."

"That camp wasn't safe for me, Max. The only thing I miss is a hot shower." His fingers raked through his hair. "I do miss Cologne though, like it was before the war. Coffee shops, plays, football games and concerts and ski trips. And this one dance hall near the university that played swing music, even though it was forbidden." The memories coaxed a smile.

Max's voice dropped. "Who do you want to win the war?"

Erich glanced around to make sure no one was near, and pivoted to face him. "Honestly? I want the Allies to win."

"Really?" Awe filled Max's voice. "But you're German."

"Yes, but our government is bad, Max. I've seen some of the things they're doing. They arrest people who speak out; they beat up people they don't like or even kill them; they get children to spy on their parents. They use fear to control everyone. That first song I played on the piano? That's German, and it's a good part of our history, a part my grandfather told me to be proud of. Maybe that's what your father's talking about when he tells you to be proud. There are a lot of things about Germany to like."

"But not the Nazis?"

"Right. It's dangerous for me to admit this, so you can't tell anyone."

Max bit his lip, then whispered, "I won't. I promise."

"Good, because you and Nikel—Johann—are like my lifelines here on the edge of the world. That's what friends are: lifelines."

"I need one of those."

"We all do." Erich tapped Max's shoulder. "And now, I need to find the outhouse."

11 FEBRUARY 1944, HORLEY (-8°C/18°F)

Max pondered Erich's light punch, and what friendship meant, until shouting began in front of the building. Max raced toward the sound, expecting to see two teenagers fighting.

He jostled his way up the steps, already crowded with onlookers. In a circle of men ten feet from the steps, Sam the blacksmith held Erich in a chokehold and gripped his one arm. Frances stood in the circle as well. She looked around, as if surprised at the gathering, then narrowed her eyes as she caught sight of someone in the crowd. Max followed her gaze to the person standing next to him: Cora.

"Is Frances mad at you?" he asked.

"She thinks it's my fault that Jimmy is enlisting, because I talked to him about London and my aunt and uncle who were killed. She said she was going to get me back."

"By being mean to Erich?"

She gave him a startled look, as if it hadn't occurred to her that this event was related to the look Frances had given her. But Max had seen those "now you'll pay" looks before. Everyone knew Jimmy had been sweet on Frances for years, and Frances now liked him too. Why would hurting Erich get back at Cora? Max whispered, "Does Frances think you like Erich?"

Cora squinted at him with a wrinkled up face. "Of course not!" She hesitated. "Well, she did get me to admit that he's cute. But that's not—"

An older man in the circle spoke above the murmurs. "You sure this is who attacked you, Miss Miller?" Cora and several others gasped.

"Yes. I was returning from the biffy and he—" Frances covered her mouth, as if too upset to continue.

Max was about to say she was a terrible actor when a voice shouted from the darkness, "Find some rope, boys. We'll show these damned Jerries what happens when they touch our women."

The voice sounded vaguely familiar. Frances winged another glance Cora's way. This was definitely to get back at her. Max scrunched his brow. Frances couldn't really want Erich to get hurt...

The mutterings got uglier. Louder. Henry pushed between Cora and Max, and forced a path through the crowd. Nerves jumping, Max followed in his wake and slipped to the front of the circle when Henry stepped inside it. "What's the meaning of this?" he demanded. "Sam, let him go."

"No, sir." The man's beefy arm tightened across Erich's neck, turning his face crimson. "Not if Miss Miller's telling the truth."

Henry turned to her. "What truth?" The girl stammered out her story, less confident now that she was faced with Henry's skepticism. He turned from her to Erich. "You were outside a long time, son. Explain that."

"I just did," Frances cried.

Erich's gaze found Max. He couldn't talk with Sam's log of an arm squashed against his throat. Max bit his lip. He knew he should speak up, but everyone sounded so angry. And they'd be more angry if they knew Max was friends with a real German.

"Found some rope!" came the voice from the darkness.

"Let's use it," someone else said. A few agreed.

The rope sailed into the circle and landed on Henry's toe. He picked it up. "This is what you want?" he shouted. "No law. No court. Just lynch him up?"

In the momentary hush it felt as if the night and cold were squeezing Max's chest. Erich hadn't stopped looking at him.

"Yeah," someone replied. "Damned Jerries deserve it. Every one of 'em."

"And if we do this, Lars, how are we any better than them?" Henry asked.

A stranger grabbed the rope. "Get inside with the women if you're too squeamish, Henry."

They were really going to do it. They were going to hang Max's only friend. For something he didn't do. Max's throat closed. He couldn't let that happen. He started to step forward, then hesitated as fear lassoed him. *I have to do this.* He met Erich's gaze. *He needs me. Someone needs me. Not someone. My friend.*

"No!" Max joined Henry in the circle.

"You get inside too," the man said. "This is nothing a boy should watch."

"Stop it! He didn't do anything." He stamped his foot. The silence was so big Max thought he could hear stars rustling.

Henry said, "Max? You're calling Frances a liar?"

"I... I'm not saying someone didn't try to hurt her. But it wasn't Erich." Max gulped cold air. These men would hate him for being friends with a German, but what difference did it make? Everyone at school already hated him. And a lot of Father's friends now hated him too. He couldn't let something bad happen to Erich. Henry set a hand on his shoulder, as if to encourage him. Max braced himself and blurted, "It couldn't have been Erich. He was with me."

The man with the rope lowered his hands so the line dangled. He looked furious. "What in hell were you doing with a rotten Jerry?"

"N-nothing. We were talking. Outside by the window near the piano."

"What the hell would you have to say to a Jerry other than get lost?" The man's digust branded his face.

Max lifted his chin. "We were talking about brothers, and music, and stuff."

Henry cleared his throat. "Max is an honest boy. I believe him. Miss Miller was likely mistaken in who approached her. Instead of stringing up Erich, maybe you should focus on finding whoever did bother her. If she still insists one of my men acted badly, she can make her claims to the police and I'll cooperate with them." His grip on Max's shoulder tightened. "Sam, release him. Round the others up. We're going home."

Henry turned Max around to face the door. "Go find your parents, son. They might want to take you home too. And tell Mrs. Lane we're leaving."

Max's legs wobbled as he walked toward the hall. He moved like a sleepwalker. Those gathered stepped back to give him a clear aisle. Like they didn't want to touch him. Like he was diseased.

No one looked him in the face. No one except Richard Anderson, who glared with hatred that blasted him like heat from an open firebox. He had done the worst thing possible. He had sided with the enemy.

32:

11 FEBRUARY 1944,
LOGGING CAMP (-14°C/7°F)

Hubart slapped Erich. He rocked but remained standing at attention. As ordered. Blood trickled over his lips. His tongue touched the familiar metallic taste. This was the sixth, no, seventh time he'd been hit or attacked by fellow prisoners. So much for being comrades-in-arms. He pressed his lips together. Oh to be back in school where the worst injuries he faced were on the soccer pitch. And there, a person knocked down was helped up, patted on the back. Not threatened. Not beaten into submission. Erich wished, for the fiftieth time, that he'd kept talking with Max so he could have avoided Miss Miller and her accusations.

Hubart's scar was a savage line. "Bringing trouble down on your head brings it down on us all. They should have hanged you." He slapped Erich again. Fresh blood warmed his lip.

"Enough," Lehrmann said as he whittled. Hubart retreated and watched Lehrmann. He waited with hands clasped behind his back, as if yielding to someone of higher rank. But that made no sense. As a sergeant, Unterfeldwebel Hubart was the highest-ranking soldier in the room. Erich stole a glance, waited for the man's next move. Still Hubart waited. Erich almost gasped when it hit him: Lehrmann had higher standing in the Nazi party. But no Nazi should've been allowed to volunteer for this camp. Unless he'd lied.

Lehrmann's bed was to Erich's left. From the corner of his eye, Erich saw he was carving a swastika—and not even bothering to hide it. Erich snapped his eyes forward. Being treated like a soldier again when they'd been casual for weeks filled him with dread. And having a known Nazi in the room solidified the dread, made it a living thing that snaked through his insides and up his throat. Erich's hand twitched with the need to rake his hair, but he didn't dare move. He'd been made to stand by the stove and his left side was hot, scars painful. Sweat dotted his hairline and ran down his neck.

Lehrmann spoke quietly. "Your carelessness concerns us, Hofmeyer. Are you thinking with only your *Schwanz*?"

Nervous laughter trickled around the room. Erich clenched his jaw to keep silent when Rudolf said, "Hofmeyer's just a foolish boy who will chase anyone in a skirt. We all did it at that age. But that skinny girl was mean. Better stick to wooing *Fräulein* Cora." He grinned.

Lehrmann flicked at his carving. "That's what I don't want. Is Cora luring you away from us, Hofmeyer? Whispering lies, drawing you from devotion to the Fatherland." He pointed his knife at Erich. "Whether we're in this shabby camp in the forest, or in the prison camp in Lethbridge, or in our glorious Fatherland, loyalty is what matters, Hofmeyer. Do you have any left? Or are you more concerned with cutting logs for the enemy and flirting with girls?"

Beside Erich, Hubart chimed in. "He works like a dog trying to please his master. He should be like us, working as slow as possible without getting into trouble."

Lehrmann continued whittling. "That's the real question: Who is your master, Hofmeyer?"

Erich clenched his jaw as unease mauled his stomach. Lehrmann carved the swastika deeper into the wood. No one spoke. "No answer, Hofmeyer?" Lehrmann said.

How could he answer? There was no right answer. To say he loved Germany wouldn't satisfy them. To lie was to risk discovery and punishment. Any answer was trouble; no answer was trouble. All he could do was try to withstand the beating. Hubart raised his fist; Erich tensed. In the stove, something popped and shifted. Heat radiated from the black surface like Hubart's eagerness to thump Erich.

The door swung open. Hubart spun as Alf stepped in. "Why're your lamps burning so late? Got to get an early—" He planted his hands on his hips, took in Hubart, fists still clenched, then Erich. "What's going on?"

Erich thought about telling, wanted to tell. *A dog trying to please his master.* "Nothing."

"That's mighty red nothing on your face and shirt."

Erich touched his nose. "I was stoking the stove and fell. You know how clumsy I am."

"Lucky you didn't fall on the stove." Alf faced Hubart. "Everyone better show up for work tomorrow looking no worse for wear. Not one bruise." He marched down the aisle, grabbed Lehrmann's whittling project, and grimaced at the swastika. "I'm not blind. No Nazi shit happens on my watch." He stuffed the wood into the stove. "Remember what you were told when you were sent here. Nazi shit of any kind gets you shipped back to the prison camp. If you want to go back, just say so."

Hubart spoke in stilted English. "You haf no right to step in our matters."

Alf stopped by the door. "I have every right. This bunkhouse isn't a piece of Germany. It's part of my brother's operation. I'm in charge of the men, including all of you. I've looked after two of you when you got hurt. I take it personal when something happens to one of my men. I won't have you fighting with my local boys, or with each other. So drop it."

Alf left. Erich backed away from the stove, thoughts swirling and colliding like snowflakes in a storm. No one stopped him from retreating to his cot. He stared at the door, wishing things made sense. One thing he knew: Alf didn't sound like someone who'd cause an accident, even if the injured person was his enemy.

33:

12 FEBRUARY 1944,
LOGGING CAMP (-14°C/7°F)

Found some rope! Erich woke, sweat dampening his pillow. He lay in the dark and listened to the others sleeping as the cool air in the bunkhouse chilled his sweat. The dream had seemed so real. Men dragging him to a tree, slinging the rope over a branch and around his neck. Lehrmann holding the other end. The cord strangling...

A violent shiver rippled across his shoulders. He crept down the aisle to the stove, opened the metal door, stirred embers to life, and added logs from the storage bin behind the stove. He watched to make sure the logs caught fire. Satisfied, he started to close the door. On his bunk, Lehrmann propped himself up on one elbow. They stared at each other until a pop from the fire startled Erich. He latched the door as Lehrmann whispered, "We're watching you."

Erich knew sleep wouldn't return, so dressed and went to the cookhouse. Someone was rustling in the kitchen behind the closed window. Jimmy sat at the table near the potbellied stove, hunched over a cup of coffee. His freckles stood out like black dots on a map. Erich lifted the blue enamel coffeepot off the stove, topped up Jimmy's cup and filled one from the stack on the table.

Jimmy half smiled. "Sure will miss Mrs. Lane's coffee. I doubt the army makes it so good."

"At least you get real coffee. Mostly we drank *Ersatz* coffee." Jimmy looked puzzled. Erich said, "*Ersatz* means fake, artificial. It tastes like sludge."

"Things are pretty tough over there?"

"On both sides, I think." Looking weary, Jimmy sipped his

steaming brew. Would enlisting cause such sleeplessness? "You are volunteering?" Erich asked. "Why? You aren't old enough, are you?"

"Are you?" Jimmy flung back. Erich shrugged. Jimmy sipped his coffee. "I'll be eighteen end of this week. I've wanted my folks to sign permission papers for months. As for why? There's a war on, in case you hadn't noticed. I'm not gonna miss it."

Erich had been peering into his cup. Now he raised his face. "Look at me." When Jimmy did, he said, "We're the same age. I will be eighteen on the twenty-third of February. I'm the face of your enemy, Jimmy. Could you shoot me?"

"Geez. You're not my enemy, Erich. I mean, not no more. You're okay for a Jerry. Quit trying to scare me. Won't work. No one's gonna call me a coward."

"I'd never call you that, but you will be scared. I was terrified when my ship was sinking..." Erich scowled at the tabletop. The unfinished sentence swirled with memories.

"Hey, I was gonna look for you later and tell you something. Well, two things."

Erich shrugged without looking up. He hoped Jimmy made it through alive, but that meant hoping he killed whomever he faced. He hated knowing people from both sides. That had been his problem from the start. If he didn't have an English grandfather maybe he'd be as loyal to the Fatherland as Lehrmann. But he couldn't change who or what he knew. Couldn't change his mixed feelings, or the sense that he didn't fit in anywhere.

"Remember the New Year's Day accident?" Jimmy's finger traced the rim of his cup, round and round. "I remembered something. It's probably nothing but I wanted to tell you, 'cause, well, I don't want anyone else to get hurt."

Erich peered from under his eyebrows but didn't raise his head. Jimmy gave an apologetic smile. "I remembered waking up that morning and seeing Chuck's brown jacket on its hook, but he was gone. Probably snagged another coat to go to the john."

"Was he gone long?"

Jimmy's smile turned sheepish. "Don't know. I left right after to ride with Cora into town."

Erich took a drink, watched Jimmy's finger circle his rim.

"Geez," Jimmy sighed. "And about that stuff at the dance. Franny was really mad. She blamed Cora for me enlisting, just 'cuz I asked her lots about England. She lived there, years back. Soon as I heard what happened—Franny saying you hurt her—I knew she was getting even with Cora. Kind of... 'you mess with my guy, I'll mess with yours.'"

Erich stared, mind blank. He shook himself. "You mean to say that girl wanted to hurt Cora so she accused me of... *Scheisse. Sie ist verrückt.* Sorry. That's crazy. Cora and I aren't even friends! We've only talked a few times."

"Yeah, you know how rumors go. Pretty girl. Handsome prisoner." He reddened. "So the girls say. Franny told me Cora admitted you were cute, so I guess she thought... But geez, you could've gotten lynched." Erich gave him a wry look. Jimmy returned another sheepish smile. "Yeah, I guess you knew that. I didn't see it. I was inside dancing with Elizabeth." The smile died. "Good thing Max spoke up, though some folks are mad at him for that."

Frown lowering his brows, Erich took a long drink of his cooling coffee. A girl he didn't know thought he and Cora were a couple? He could only wish. *She thinks I'm cute? Then why does she avoid me?*

"I would've liked to have left on Monday knowing Frances was waiting for my letters..." Jimmy sighed again.

"You aren't going to write to her? Didn't you dance with her almost all night?"

"I think I'll send her one letter, telling her that she shouldn't wait for me after all. What she did was so mean, it downright bamboozles me."

Erich gave a nod, though he didn't know what the word meant. "Cora and you talk a lot. Maybe she would write to you, as a friend."

Jimmy brightened. "You think so? I'll go see if she's up yet and ask." He left his coffee half finished and ran out of the cookhouse.

Erich slumped over his cup. Jimmy was so happy over such a simple thing. But he felt like a discarded husk, too empty to hold any joy. Even that one shining star—*Cora thinks I'm cute*—was hidden by storm clouds. Known enemies in his bunkhouse. Unknown enemies in the camp.

And they all seemed to be closing in.

34:

15 FEBRUARY 1944,
HORLEY (1°C/34°F)

The schoolroom emptied more quickly than usual. Max stayed seated and breathed in the silence. Miss Williams swished the brush over the blackboard in rhythmic strokes, humming "Somewhere Over the Rainbow" as she worked. The low sun filtered through fingerprinted windows, bathing her left side in warmth, streaking her dark hair with red. Dust motes waltzed in the light in time to her song.

She set the brush on its ledge and turned. She startled. "Max, why are you still here?"

If he said anything, she'd call him a liar. At least that's what it felt like she was doing when he told her the other students were picking on him and she ignored him. It was no use. "I like the quiet," he said.

"Well, scat, so I can finish up without getting the heebie jeebies." She crossed her arms and pursed her lips.

With a sigh, Max shoved his books into his knapsack. He rolled out each step to prolong the walk to the coat hooks. When he finally pulled on his second boot, the clacking of Miss Williams' shoes chased him onto the outside step.

"Goodbye, miss."

She closed and locked the door.

Children were still trickling out of the yard, a few on horses, and in one case three on one horse. Max searched for any sign of the older boys but found none. As he considered whether he should be running for dear life because they were waiting around the corner to ambush him, a smell wafted into his notice.

He set his lunch pail on the wooden rail and peered under the tea towel his mother always tucked around wax paper–wrapped sandwiches. Three horse turds clustered in the bottom of the pail. He squinted at them and almost smiled. Was this all they were going to do to him today? Max dumped them onto the snow and headed out.

Yesterday he had pretended to be sick and had stayed home so he didn't have to face Richard after the dance on the weekend. That ruse had only fooled his mother for one heavenly comic-book day.

The jitters overtook Max when he reached the road. He turned a full circle, searching for the enemy. They weren't soldiers with winter camouflage. Their plaid jackets, like Max's, would stand out against the white blankets covering the fields.

The blue vastness above stretched to the northern horizon and leaked into the far hills, turning them royal blue. His father had told him that those hills bordered the far side of the Peace River. Hidden in an indigo valley in the blue hills was the trapping cabin Christmas had told him about. *Hey, Superman, fly me there. Just for a day. Or until the war ends.*

From near the village, the calls of children reached back like birdsong on the breeze. Max's footsteps crackled and smooshed on the half-frozen roadway. His pail hit his leg with muffled thuds. He came across some horse turds and kicked one like a soccer ball. It wasn't frozen. Lip curled, he turned his ankle in and rubbed the edge of his boot in snow.

He took three steps and stopped, frozen by dread. Holding his breath, he scanned the lane going into the Anderson farm yard, but there were no signs of Richard and his friends there either. He exhaled relief. They must've had chores that made them head straight home.

But a dozen steps later Max spotted Roy, Richard's friend. He sat on an overturned rain barrel beside the Millers' house on the corner. Roy faced the main street so hadn't spotted Max, who stopped again. Was Roy alone? Were his pals preparing an ambush on Main Street?

His father always wanted him to fight, to stand up to what he called a "gang of ruffians." He didn't understand what it was like to be surrounded by bigger, stronger boys. How fear gripped him when there was no escape. Max's breathing sped up. If he got any closer Roy would hear him and give chase. There had to be another way. He glanced behind him, hoping to see an adult coming along. With an adult beside him they wouldn't do anything. The road was empty. He peered down the alley that ran behind the house and general store. Also empty, except for Mr. Miller's truck, parked with its tailgate butting up to the loading dock. If he ran that direction, and kept running until he was completely out of town, he might make it.

Might. Seconds of fear humming low, then louder like an approaching airplane, held Max stock still as Roy shifted on the barrel. When he didn't turn, Max finally convinced his feet to move. He edged down the alley with careful, silent steps. When Roy was no longer in sight, Max broke into a trot. Then a jog. His boots mushed the soft snow. It sucked at them, slowing him down.

Max glanced back, expecting to see Roy. He slipped, found traction, tried to run as his heart chugged like a train. He passed the truck with arms pumping.

A stick shot out, caught his shin. Max yelped as he sprawled onto the ground. His lunch pail clanged, bounced, and rolled away. The snow injected him with cold that wrapped around his limbs. He lay unmoving, arms and legs splayed, as terror battered him. This was different than their usual attacks. Sneakier. A shrill whistle made him winch. Something nudged his ribs. He squeezed his eyes closed, wanting it to be a dream. A harder nudge and he rolled onto his back.

Richard rested the butt of a hockey stick on Max's chest. "Look what fell into our trap, boys." Three faces leered down at Max. *Trap*? Max's mouth dried up; he couldn't swallow.

Running footsteps slapped the snow, then Roy's face joined the circle. "Ha! He tried to slip around me, just like you said he would. How about that?"

Save me, Superman. Please. "What do you want?" Max's voice cracked.

Richard half snorted, half laughed. "That's a stupid question. We've caught ourselves a Jerry. What do you *think* we want, Hitler?"

Max scrambled up and tried to push past Roy, who spun him around and locked his arm around Max's neck. He pulled at the arm with both hands but Roy's hold only tightened. Fear scratched like a mouse in the walls. He searched Richard's face, looking for a clue to what he was thinking. All he saw was hate. He struggled harder, tried to hit Roy in the face, stomp on his boots. Fear writhed inside him.

At Richard's signal, Hank pulled twine out of his school bag. Tom helped him tie Max's hands behind his back. Richard leaned close, and mustard breath clogged Max's nose. "So, what should we do with someone who defends the enemy?"

"Hang 'em!" the three replied.

"No!" cried Max. He started shouting for help.

Richard grabbed the tea towel from Max's pail and wadded it into his mouth. Max shook his head and tried to spit it out, certain he tasted horse turds. It wouldn't budge. Richard pointed to a bag on the truck's running board and Tom looked inside. "Hey, look! I found some rope!" They all chuckled, like they'd known it was there.

A low moan rumbled in Max's throat as understanding punched its way through fear. They were reenacting what had happened at the dance with Erich—only with a different ending. *They're going to kill me!* His legs trembled. His eyes bulged as his gaze flashed from one boy to another and another—and saw only eagerness.

He struggled to get air into his lungs. *This can't be happening.* His legs collapsed.

Roy hauled Max to his feet. He jerked and struggled, heart crashing. *No! Nononono!* The boys dragged him across the alley. A poplar towered over three wooden apple crates. Piled like steps. Waiting. Stones dropped into his stomach and his legs buckled again. Roy held him up. *Can't be happening. Can't.*

Richard nodded to Tom, who threw the end of the rope over a limb ten feet above the ground. The end swung back and forth, a noose already tied and waiting. Max couldn't take his eyes from the noose. *Oh, God. OhGodOhGod. They're going to do it. They're really going to do it.* He bucked and heaved until a hard slap temporarily stunned him.

Richard fixed the noose around Max's neck and Roy released him. Max's legs shook and his breath huffed. The rope fibers scratched his neck. Tom and Hank both held the other end of the rope. They stepped back so the rope was taut. Terror clogged Max's throat. His breathing sped up.

"Step onto the box, Hitler," Richard ordered.

I can't! No! Please! Tom and Hank inched backward and the rope tugged on Max's neck. It started to cut off his air. He made a strangled noise. Stretched onto his toes. Couldn't breathe. Stepped onto the first box. His trembling rattled the boxes. He twisted his hands. Strained to loosen the knots. *Please, no. Please, no.*

"Step onto the top box, Hitler." Richard sneered.

The words made no sense. Again Tom and Hank backed up. Forced Max to take another step up. *Don't want to die.* His tormentors leered at him.

Richard said, "Tie it off." Max stared, eyes wide. His breaths came in rapid snorts. Behind him, mutterings. "Like that?" "This way." "Got it."

The rope tugged, had no slack. The fibers dug at his neck.

His vision blurred, cleared. Panic ate his thoughts. He twisted his hands and pain shot up his arms.

Tom laughed. "His knees are knocking!"

Richard poked the top box with his hockey stick, making it wobble. "Take your punishment like a man, Hitler." He planted his stick in the snow. "Someone will find you sooner or later. But tell them who did this and we'll make sure it's real next time."

Real? This wasn't real? Max clung to that thought. They weren't actually going to hang him. They only wanted to scare him. He tried to breathe deep. To find calm. He shifted his weight.

Beneath him, the apple crate caved in.

Max's body jerked down, and in an instant the noose clamped against his neck. He flailed and kicked, but the movement only tightened the noose. Spots danced in his vision. Through them, he saw Richard and his friends retreat, eyes wide. They scattered like dandelion seeds.

Max continued thrashing. He jolted down a notch. Kicked and writhed. His lungs caved in. Blue sky faded to gray.

A crash. Something dug into Max's back, his side. It took him a moment to realize he was on the ground, on wooden slats. Air trickled into his lungs. *I'm not dead.* He inhaled as deeply as possible. The noose let him. He flopped off the broken crates.

The terror gradually retreated, allowing him to think again. He tucked his legs up to his chest and slipped his tied arms past his backside and legs to his front, yanked the towel from his mouth, gnawed the knot loose and released his hands. He lay still for a moment, exhausted from the effort, from the fear. Then he scratched at the noose, got it off and curled into a ball, wheezing and hiccupping.

Superman hadn't come. No one had come. Max's bones ached with the knowledge that Richard wanted him dead, or at least very, very hurt. And there was no one to help him.

Max sat up. The rope dangled above him. He traced its length, saw that the knot at the fence had given way. Saved by a poorly tied knot. He shifted to get up, bumped the rope. It hissed as it snaked off the branch and landed in a heap on his back. He turned away from the tree and threw up.

35:

15 FEBRUARY 1944,
LOGGING CAMP (-3°C/27°F)

Erich sat on the bunkhouse steps. Snow drifted through the lamp-light, each flake painted gold. He inhaled, hoping to smell the fresh-ness of the white blanket shrouding the yard, but all he got was a noseful of stink. Sweat and grime and sawdust. It was only Tuesday. Five more days until he could soak off the layers of filth. The week was already a brutally hard struggle. Exhaustion weighed him down, made it hard to even think.

At Henry's house yellow rectangles of light decorated the fresh snow, making it look like an idyllic winter scene. The saying was true: looks *were* deceiving. There was nothing romantic about lan-tern light when you were half-asleep, slapping the wall to locate the light switch, and wondering why you couldn't find it. Smell, however, was always truthful. Hot showers were a distant memory, making him wish he could sluice away the pain and stink. Between the two, it was no wonder he hadn't been sleeping well.

Darkness cooled things off quickly and the cold wooden slats felt like marble. Erich stretched and massaged his neck, then entered the bunkhouse. He had just started to close the door when Lehrmann appeared out of the gloom and slammed him against the wall. His head smacked between two coat pegs. Dizziness spun the room.

"Where is my knife?" Lehrmann growled.

Scheisse. Erich had picked it up when it had slipped out of Leh-rmann's pocket at breakfast, then completely forgot about it. If he admitted he had it, Lehrmann would punish him. He choked out that he didn't know. The man buried his fist in Erich's stomach. His coffee breath puffed over Erich's face. "I want my knife."

"I don't—" Another fist to the stomach. Erich gasped for breath. Could Lehrmann tell he was lying? His brother always could, but maybe that was familiarity. Turtling had often worked with Gerhard, and with the army; you never fought someone of higher rank. In the POW camp they'd almost killed him for one clumsy swing. He strove to stay limp. No resistance. Nothing to make Lehrmann angrier.

Two more demands, punctuated with Lehrmann's fist, produced nothing except Erich's conviction his stomach was shattering. Could anyone see the lie behind the pain that constricted his chest and bled into trembling legs that no longer wanted to hold him up?

"He must be telling the truth, Lehrmann. Look at him," Nikel said from his bed. "Another punch and you'll be wearing his dinner."

Some of the men chuckled, cutting off when Lehrmann threw them heated looks. He glared at Nikel. "Then where is it? Did you take it?"

Nikel laughed. "I'm so graceful with this crutch, I'm sure I could snitch it without you noticing. I wake up half the men if I get up in the night. Clunk around like a granny." He gave an exaggerated shrug. "Maybe it fell out of your pocket. It's probably in the forest and a raven is cackling over its shiny new treasure."

Lehrmann huffed, then flung Erich onto his cot. He retreated to his own bed and scowled at the stove. Coat still on, Erich curled up, back to the room, arms cradling his stomach. Why hadn't he thought to throw the knife away in the forest? The deep pocket of his jacket had kept its secret. Now it dug into his hip. If Lehrmann calmed down and started thinking, he might return and do a search. Where could he hide it that it wouldn't be found? Erich squeezed his eyes shut, trying to fight rising panic.

Half an hour later, Nikel thumped around his bed and swore at the crutch. He tapped Erich's foot. "Carry my lantern to the latrine.

The last time I tried I almost set myself on fire."

The pain in Erich's midsection had retreated, but he still hunched slightly, one arm shielding his waist. Dread shivered over him, a certainty that when he stood up they'd all see his guilt. He pressed his lips together and kept his focus on the lantern that dangled from the ceiling over the foot of Nikel's bed. He pushed up the lantern base to lift it off its hook and followed his lurching friend outside. At the outhouse, Nikel opened the door and stepped half in. The odor of human waste rolled from the cubicle-sized building. Nikel looked over Erich's shoulder and Erich followed his gaze. From here, no bunkhouse windows were visible.

Nikel said, "I saw you pick up the knife this morning. You should have left it. Tell me you dropped it somewhere in the forest."

Erich whispered, "It's in my pocket. I forgot about it."

"Stupid boy. He would have found it if he'd been using his brain."

Nikel had never sounded more like an older cousin, lecturing his foolish young relative. "I know. I don't know what I was thinking. I...feel safer knowing he doesn't have a knife." Erich ran his fingers through his hair, sending his toque into the snow. He bent over to retrieve it. "I thought it would be better here, that I wouldn't have to worry about hatred, or beatings."

"Hatred is everywhere. In the camp, the town. You need to keep your head down. Haven't you figured that out yet? You may be young but you don't usually do stupid things."

"No, usually I'm too worried to do anything." Erich took the knife from his pocket. "Do you want it?"

Nikel shot another glance over Erich's shoulder and snatched the knife. "Of course I don't want it." He dropped it down the toilet hole. "But maybe now you'll sleep better. I hope so. I'm tired of your groans waking me up. Don't be a *Dummkopf*. Stay out of trouble." He took the lantern from Erich's unresisting grip and closed the door.

Light leaked out of the crescent moon cut into the door. If only it was so easy. Wherever Erich went, versions of his brother followed him, tormented him. He leaned against the outhouse to wait. Even that slight movement made his stomach clench.

He walked Nikel back to the bunkhouse but left him at the door; he wasn't ready to face everyone just yet. He handed Nikel the lantern and claimed he wanted to check for leftover dessert. Which wasn't a bad idea. The rhubarb pie had been tasty. And maybe Cora would still be cleaning up. He wanted to apologize for whatever had upset her at the dance. He'd do almost anything to win her friendship, anything for a friend his own age.

He had barely cracked open the cookhouse door when a booming voice turned him into a statue—a voice he could never forget. *Found some rope!* For a moment, his lungs wouldn't work. He managed to close the door without a sound. Laughter seeped through the wood. He crept down the steps, to the nearest window, and peered in.

Four laughing men sat at a table playing a card game the Canadians called cribbage. Alf, Frank, Chuck, and Sam. That voice didn't belong to any of them normally. Someone had dropped his voice into a different register to deliver a punch line, maybe.

Erich ducked into a crouch and leaned with his back against the log wall. His breaths puffed out in alarm as he held his stomach and considered the possibilities. Not Sam; his arm had been crushing Erich's neck. Surely not Alf, even if his boots had the right pattern of tread. Frank seemed the logical candidate. His anger was always close at hand.

Enemies surrounded him—in the bunkhouse, in the cookhouse, in the town. Erich could almost hear Gerhard's laughter in the breeze. Elbows braced on his knees, he burrowed his fingers into his hair.

Why can't things be easy? Why can't they ever be easy?

Voices across the yard pulled Erich from his uneasy thoughts. He pushed away from the wall and walked toward the bunkhouse, stopping halfway to watch the shadowed forms of a horse and rider leave the yard and rejoin the darkness. Henry got the occasional visitor, but eight o'clock at night seemed an odd time given the dropping temperatures.

Erich shivered. It was going to be at least as cold as last night, which meant frosted bedcovers again. Would anyone back home even believe him if he told them he woke up some mornings with frost on his blankets? All the men kept their boots covered or turned upside down at night to keep them dry inside.

Henry was still on the outside steps, as if listening to the horse and rider retreat. He pulled a hat from his pocket and put it on, turned up his collar and started across the yard. He moved from faintly lit steps into darkness, becoming a silhouette until light from the cookhouse touched him. He spotted Erich and motioned him over.

Glad to have a reason to not return to the bunkhouse, Erich joined his boss. Henry pushed his hat back, revealing his high forehead and a concerned expression. "Do me a favor?"

"Of course," Erich replied.

"Go to the barn and rouse Christmas. You saw that rider leaving?" Erich nodded. Henry's worry waves etched deeper into his forehead. "Max didn't come home after school. When they went looking, they found his school bag and lunch pail behind the store. They searched everywhere they could think and couldn't find him. I told Helmut we'd search the camp. The boy likes coming up here on weekends to play soccer and sled, so maybe..."

"Christmas is in the barn?"

"He still won't move into the bunkhouse with the other men; he's in the hayloft. Tell him to meet me in the cookhouse." He paused. "Max isn't in your bunkhouse, is he?"

"No."

Giving a single nod, Henry marched toward the cookhouse. Erich sprinted to the barn, visible by the glow of a lantern hanging outside the door. Above, a crack of light showed through shutters of the small loft door. Erich slipped inside into warm semi-darkness and clutched his nagging stomach.

The horse and manure smell wrapped around him, sweet, tangy, and dusty. "Hello?" he called. Several of the horses shifted and a few turned heads to eye the intruder. Erich paused as his gaze searched the darkness for the bench that hid the bolt cutters. Alf couldn't have caused that accident. He was straight-forward and helpful. With everyone. And he'd never do *anything* to risk one of his horses. So, Chuck or Frank? Chuck used to be a bit friendly. Now he was as surly as Frank.

His thoughts jumped back to Max when a square of light in the ceiling at the back of the barn fell over a ladder nailed to the wall. Feet appeared in the light, blocking it off. Erich advanced as Christmas reached the bottom of the ladder. They met between the last stalls.

Christmas crossed his arms. Erich cleared his throat. "Henry wants you in the cookhouse. Max is missing and Henry is organizing a search of the camp."

"Little Mouse?"

Erich could barely see the other teen's features in the dim light. "What? I said Max."

Christmas nodded. "I name him Little Mouse." He pointed at the ceiling. "He did not say he was missing."

Erich's breath caught. "He's here?"

Christmas nodded. "I will tell Henry. You bring him down. He likes you." He motioned toward the ladder, then grabbed Erich's arm. "He's hurt. He didn't say, but I saw a mark."

Uneasy, Erich watched him leave, then clambered up and swung off the ladder. An area cleared of hay featured a wooden crate with a lantern on top of it. Max sat cross-legged near it, hands outstretched, as if warming himself at a campfire. His eyes grew wide when he spotted Erich. He scrambled backward onto a bed of hay covered with several blankets. The space was suprisingly warm given that frost touched some of the boards between rafters.

"Hi, Max." Erich joined him on the prickly bed. "Henry said your parents are looking for you." *What mark?* he wondered.

Agony filled the boy's face. "I couldn't go home. Father would tell me to...to stand up to them, and—" He pressed his face to his raised knees and shuddered.

"What happened?" Erich rested his hand on Max's back and felt trembling.

"I... I can't tell."

"What if I promise to keep quiet?"

Max raised his face. The naked longing made him look much younger than twelve. "Promise? Really, really promise?"

Erich nodded. Sometimes he almost felt like a big brother to Max, and he was determined to be the kind he wished he had. "Whatever it is, you can tell me."

Instead of speaking, Max arched his neck and unbottoned the snug collar. Lantern light played over a mark two inches below his jaw. Erich lifted the lantern and examined the red line that circled Max's neck like a garrish smile. Erich set the lantern back on its crate. "*Scheisse.* Is that what it looks like?" Max nodded. "Someone tried to hang you?" Max nodded again.

Horror skimmed over Erich's scalp, raising his hair. "You can't keep this secret, Max. This is... It's..."

Max grabbed his forearm. "I can't tell. They said they'd do it for real if I told. This was supposed to only scare me, but the box broke. And—" He pressed the heels of his palms into his eyes.

"You're scared. I understand that. I'm scared a lot too, Max. But—"

Max's head jerked up. Eyes dry, he spoke through clenched teeth. "I'm not scared, not anymore. I'm mad. No one ever helps me. No one ever rescues me or stands up for me. I have to do something. Father says fight. Maybe he's right. I've tried and tried to stay out of trouble, stay away from Richard and his goons. It's not working. I'm the only one who can help me, Erich. No one else even wants to try."

Erich leaned back, startled by the venom in Max's voice. He opened his mouth to offer his help. Snapped it shut. What could he do, stuck in the camp? And even if he could do something, would it really help, or would it make things worse for Max? "What will you do?"

"I can't fight them straight on. I'll get even. Somehow."

"Revenge isn't a good idea Max. I tried it with my brother, played a prank on him once. He paid me back twice over."

Below, someone stomped into the barn. Henry called, "Max? Get down here, right now. Your folks are worried sick. Frank'll take you home."

Max buttoned up his coat, concealing the rope burn. He kept his voice low. "Richard's gotten way meaner since his brother went missing in the war. I have to do something before they kill me. I came here to think 'cuz I knew Christmas wouldn't say anything. You promised. You can't break your promise, Erich."

Henry called out again. Max crossed to the ladder and held Erich's gaze for a moment, looking equal parts angry and determined. He climbed out of sight.

Shocked, Erich peered at the lantern, vaguely registering its glow. Max could be in serious danger from those hooligans. But he'd promised. Henry had once insisted a handshake was a binding contract. What was a promise worth in this remote, primitive place?

Chirstmas sat beside him, jolting Erich from his reverie, and his closed expression suggested he didn't like Erich being in his room, such as it was.

"What should we do?" Erich asked.

"Go to sleep." Christmas pointed at the ladder.

Two steps past the lantern, Erich froze as he spotted a coil of rope in a shadowed recess by the ladder. Max's from the near hanging? He swallowed. *Found some rope!* Had this happened because Max defended him at the dance? He looked back at Christmas. "How do you sleep when you're surrounded by enemies?"

Christmas only stared until Erich retreated out of the hayloft. Outside he squinted up at the sky where hungry clouds swallowed the stars. *Be careful, Max.*

36:

23 FEBRUARY 1944, LOGGING CAMP (-2°C/28°F)

Snow had fallen so hard and fast that their tracks from an hour earlier were almost filled in. Alf called it a "dump" as he walked Erich to Henry's office. Erich kicked at the snow cloaking the path. "He didn't tell you what it was about?" If it was about the accidents, Erich was relieved he could face Henry knowing he didn't suspect Alf. Why hadn't he realized when he'd found the bolt cutters that Alf would always put his horses' safety first?

"Nope." Alf tromped along beside him.

A second worry hit Erich. "Is it Max? Is he okay?" He hadn't come to camp on Sunday. Was his neck healed? Had he tried to fight back?

"Don't know. If he was my son, his backside would still be sore from last week."

Alf gave him a small shove, stamped up the stairs, and entered the main part of the house. Erich continued on and knocked on the office door, nerves quivering.

The gruff command to enter didn't sound encouraging. Inside, Erich brushed snow from his shoulders. Toque in hand, he felt like a boy called into the headmaster's office. Henry leaned back in his chair, reading a letter. He motioned for Erich to sit. "Leave your boots on." Erich sat, twisting the toque until he realized what he was doing.

Henry asked how things were, got a noncommittal answer, then said, "Alf wasn't happy to interrupt what looked like an interrogation after that danged dance. He's been keeping his ears open since. Heard some whispers that Hubart and Lehrmann are trouble."

Erich blinked. Could another prisoner have spoken?

"You're mighty close-mouthed about your German pals. Nothing you say will leave this room."

"It doesn't matter. If you do anything, I will be named the rat."

"Is that so? Then I'll get my information elsewhere."

Erich gave a small nod. "Could I ask *you* something?" Henry raised his bushy eyebrows and inclined his head. "Did you...ever find out anything about...about the sloop or Nikel's accident? I've been trying but...the Canadians brush me off like I'm a fly."

"Make sure you don't get swatted." Henry clasped his hands on his desk. "I haven't found anything new. And I'm still not convinced that John's accident was caused by someone, no matter how much you insist. But I'll tell you this: if anything else happens, I'm done. I'll shut down the whole damn operation for the season."

The heat drained from Erich, leaving him feeling like he'd been thrown into an icy lake. He stared at Henry, but all he could see was Bechtel.

"Are you okay, son? You're white as a sheet."

"I... I can't go back." His breaths shortened. "I can't."

"You might not have a choice."

Erich jerked to his feet. "If that's all..." Henry motioned Erich back down. He raked his hair and sat with a sigh, then twisted his toque until a measure of calm returned. Long moments later he looked up.

Henry eyed him with concern, then tossed an unopened letter onto the desk. "I didn't want to give this to you in front of the men in case it caused trouble, but I'd like to know why you got a letter from England."

The prospect of mail had excited the prisoners at dinner. When his name hadn't been called it felt like being chosen last for the soccer team at school. Erich picked up the letter, ran his thumb over the Stratford-upon-Avon address, surprised the censors hadn't blacked it out. The words were an indigo link with the summer home he loved. The sight of it soothed his jangled thoughts. Erich said, "It's from my grandparents."

"How'd they end up in England?"

Erich hesitated. "After the Nazis came to power, my grandparents left Cologne and retired to my grandfather's family home."

Henry drummed his fingers. "You're telling me your grandfather's English? That explains why you speak like an Englishman."

"Some would say I was a spy if they knew. Since becoming a prisoner of war, I've kept it to myself."

"So I should keep my trap shut." Henry drummed his fingers again. "Would Lehrmann assume that?" Erich lifted a shoulder. "Damn. You never make things easy. I think I have it figured out and you throw something else at me." Henry narrowed his eyes. "Why haven't you told Cora? It might make her like you a little." Erich started to protest and Henry cut him off. "You're seventeen and she's the only girl around. I see you watching her. You'd be sweet on her for sure if she showed any interest."

Alarmed, Erich shook his head. "I'm not trying to, to...take advantage of her."

"We already had that talk. But I was seventeen once too, son."

Erich's shoulder's sagged. "I'd like to even be her friend. But I want her to like me for me, not because my grandfather is English."

"You've set yourself a hard task then. That girl sure is touchy about Germans. I'm surprised she's lasted this long with us. But how you handle things is your business."

"Thank you."

"Take the letter. That's all I wanted to know."

"Could I read it here and leave it with you?" Henry's question-mark eyebrow made Erich explain. "Someone took away letters I'd been writing to my grandmother. I'd written in English, thinking it would give me privacy, but it only made them suspicious. They burned the letters."

A shadow fell over Henry's face. "Who?"

"It doesn't matter." By his expression, Henry disagreed. They faced off in silence, Henry obviously wanting a name. Finally, he relented, told Erich to leave the letter when he was done, his heavy tread a comment as he went into the house. The door banged shut.

Erich pulled the letter from its envelope, loving the sight of his grandmother's spidery handwriting. His parents might be too disappointed in him to write, his brother too full of hate, but so long as he kept getting these letters, he had one anchor to stop him from feeling adrift.

He opened the letter. *Dearest Erich. I hope this reaches you before your birthday.* He turned to scan the calendar hanging from a nail beside the door. His birthday was February twenty-third—today. He snorted quietly. *Thanks for remembering, Gran. At least one of us did.*

37:

25 FEBRUARY 1944,
HORLEY (3°C/37°F)

On Thursday during lunch, when Max had stayed inside and let his mind wander while he knitted another cap, Miss Williams had written out the next day's list of chores. He had been assigned blackboard duty. Roy had to bring in coal from the lean-to shed built onto the back of the building. The idea had hit him with the force of a snowball thrown by Richard.

So here he was, at school early while Miss Williams got the furnace running with the last of yesterday's coal. He'd offered to wash the blackboard since it was looking so cloudy. She emerged from the back room, toweling off her hands.

"I'm almost done," Max said. "I have to use the biffy, then I'll finish."

"That's fine, Max. It looks much better."

Max darted across the room, stepped into his boots and put on his coat as he went outside. But instead of going to the outhouse, he veered to the lean-to shed. Inside he used the miniature coal shovel to scrape coal dust into an empty pail. He got it half full and laid aside the shovel. He didn't want to get messy.

The door swung open to the inside, so the next step was tricky. He spent several minutes propping the door open to exactly the right angle, with the pail balanced on top so it leaned just so. Finally satisfied with his efforts, he examined his clothes. Seeing no telltale black smudges, he returned to the classroom to finish the last two feet of blackboard, all except the chore list in the top corner with its rectangular border.

He was sitting at his table, knitting, when children started to arrive. No one paid him any attention. Good. If no one noticed him, no one could say when he arrived.

Roy came in with the rest of the goons, loud and laughing. Miss Williams bawled him out for being tardy and ordered him to the coal shed. He muttered an apology and disappeared.

Miss Williams had just armed herself with the bell to summon latecomers when a tremendous clang and a shout rang out. The whole classroom seemed to freeze, mouths open, like they were drawings in a comic book. Then a sooty monster appeared in the door. Several girls and smaller children screamed.

Max stared, afraid to laugh, or smile, or react in any way. Roy's hair and face and jacket were covered with soot. His eyes glowed white in the grime.

"Goodness," Miss Williams said. "What did you do, Roy? Dive into the coal bin?"

Several children giggled, then others started laughing. Fear walloped Max as he imagined what would happen if Roy blamed him. He continued to stare, not even blinking, refusing to let any emotion show in case it was the wrong one.

"Someone set a trap!" Roy waved his arms as his friends hooted with laughter. This seemed to upset him more than the coal dust he wore like paint. "Shut up! It's not funny. I'm going home."

He stomped out and slammed the door, which made his friends laugh harder. A few children ran to the window to watch him cross to the stable. Miss Williams stood in the middle of the room. "Sit down children!" No one listened. She sighed and returned to her desk, seeming to realize that she wouldn't have any control until Roy was gone.

A girl in grade three said, "Here he comes. Oh. His horse looks scared."

More children crowded around the windows. "It's dancing!" "He's up." A collective gasp rose as the smallest boy cried, "It bucked him off."

Max wished for a superpower that would turn him invisible. He watched the backs of his classmates' heads bobbing and weaving, and now leaning to the side to track Roy's progress. Despite the fear still squeezing his stomach, a slice of satisfaction lodged in his thoughts. He'd caused this hullabaloo. "I guess he's walking home," the same little boy said. "His horse sure runs fast."

That started Richard and his friends laughing again. Finally everyone settled into their seats, though whispers flitted through the room. Behind Max, someone murmured, "You did that, right, Richard? You always have the best ideas."

"No! I thought it was you!"

Fighting the warmth that inched up his neck, Max opened his math book, glad for the high collar that hid his nearly faded rope burn and his guilt. The page blurred. *Richard* had the best ideas. *Richard* had come up with the hanging scare. Why was Max wasting time targeting Richard's goons? It was time go after the biggest bad guy.

38:

27 FEBRUARY 1944,
LOGGING CAMP (-12°C/10°F)

Eager to tell Erich how well his prank had gone, Max hiked to the logging camp early Sunday morning. Temperatures had dropped in the last two days, so he walked as fast as possible to keep warm. Despite the cold, he was in a good mood. Other than a round of yelling by Father, his parents had been quiet since his disappearance after the near hanging. They both seemed to be waiting for Max to explain more than, "I was tired of being bugged by the bigger boys and wanted to be alone for awhile," but neither had ever pressed him for details.

That suited Max. What was the point of telling them what had happened? Mother would get upset; Father would bluster like a summer storm. But nothing would happen. Even if they went to the police, which Mother might want to do. They'd expect him to tell who had done it, and he could *never* do that.

Max found some lumberjacks in the cookhouse. Nikel said Erich was still sleeping, so Max left them to their coffee. He caught a whiff of pancakes and sighed in time to his stomach's rumble. When he stepped outside, Alf, who was coming out of the barn, called to him. "You're here mighty early. Eaten yet?"

Max shook his head, though he'd had a piece of bread with jam.

"Come to the house with me. Pancakes are waiting and there's always extra."

Minutes later, Max was tucking into a stack of four pancakes slathered with syrup. He couldn't help but listen to Alf and Henry as he ate, though they seemed to have forgotten he was there. He learned from Alf that Sam was a widower and couldn't read, so Alf read his letters from his daughter aloud. Sam's son-in-law had been taken prisoner by the Germans. Then Alf talked about Frank, who understood Chuck was upset over losing his nephews, but was fed up because he often wandered off when it was time to delimb trees and left Frank to work alone. Henry reported that the boys in the sawmill figured it was time for re-bearing the babbitts again. Max wanted to ask what babbitts were, but instead stuffed another forkful of pancakes into his mouth. Sam had asked Henry what the Germans were doing to their axes because three more heads had come loose this week.

As he was wiping up the last of the syrup with the last piece of pancake, Henry said, "Max, I'll give you a nickel if you help Cora clean up. She's cooking pancakes by herself across the yard."

Max agreed. If she was cooking by herself she must have gotten over the roast-beef dinner disaster. Maybe it was easier to cook when it was just one thing and not a whole bunch of things at once.

At the cookhouse, Max had started washing dishes when Erich carried an empty plate into the kitchen. "Hello, Max. So you're the reason Cora is sitting with the Canadians, enjoying her pancakes instead of working. Let me help."

He snapped open a folded tea towel and picked up a plate to dry it. They worked in companionable silence, the hum of voices from the next room sounding almost musical. Max smiled as he scrubbed. After a few minutes, two voices grew louder—Cora's and Frank's. They stopped beyond the edge of the open window between the kitchen and dining room. By the table with the extra cups and a teapot, Max guessed.

Frank offered to pour her a tea. *Bingo.* Max noticed Erich listening hard, so he did the same, knowing Mother would box his ears if she caught him.

Cora asked Frank about his family. After a pause, he spoke about his Polish grandparents, driven from their home so it could be used by Germans. About two uncles and a cousin killed or captured (the family still didn't know which) in the first days of war. About two cousins raped, one shunned by the village because a Nazi had left her pregnant. When Cora asked how he knew so much, he explained that another cousin had written after he'd escaped to Sweden and had joined other Polish fighters in England.

When he asked about her family in return, Cora told him about her widowed mother in Grande Prairie, how she learned about this job from her cousin the schoolteacher, and about her relatives in England who had survived the Blitz then died in a random bombing raid.

Erich had stopped drying and held a cup in his hand as he stared in the direction of their voices. They chatted for a few more minutes. Frank mentioned Chuck and his grief over losing two nephews. Cora said she understood that grief completely.

Erich scowled at the cup as he furiously dried it, shoving his hand in so hard that it flew out of his hands and shattered on the floor. Cora and Frank both appeared in the window.

"Oh dear," Cora said. "I'll get the broom and dustpan. Don't move, Max. You don't want to get cut."

Frank glared at them both, but especially at Erich, then marched out of the cookhouse.

"I forgot you were here, Max," Cora said as she swept up. "I shouldn't have left you to do my work." She nodded at Erich, but didn't meet his gaze. "Thank you for helping."

"Thanks are hardly needed when I'm the one breaking things."

She turned red and kept sweeping without comment.

Max set the big mixing bowl in the water to soak and grabbed another towel to dry his hands. "When did your relatives get bombed?"

She halted mid-sweep. "You shouldn't eavesdrop, Max."

"Sorry. But you were talking kind of loud."

Cora half smiled, shrugged, then finished sweeping and held the dustpan in front of her, as if serving the broken pieces to him. "They died almost a year ago."

"And you're still sad?" She nodded. Max considered that. "I guess a year isn't so long. Alf said this morning that Chuck is so sad he wanders away during work and leaves Frank alone. His nephews died a few weeks ago, so I guess he'll be sad for a long time yet."

"Very likely."

It seemed odd how she was only looking at him, almost pretending Erich wasn't there. Was this a boy-girl thing like with Jimmy and Frances, or something else? What had Erich called Cora? Strangely alluring? Or had he meant all girls? They were all strange as far as Max was concerned. But at least girls didn't beat him up. They just ignored him, like Cora was ignoring Erich.

Erich cleared his throat and set his tea towel aside. "I'll see if the soccer game is starting soon. Max, will you play?"

Max gave an enthusiastic yes, then noticed Cora watching Erich leave. "He really is nice, you know."

Her cheeks turned pink. "Maybe, but I have a hard time seeing past his uniform."

"His prisoner's clothing?"

"I suppose. Though I'm very relieved none of them are wearing their German uniforms." She shuddered.

Max bit his lip and thought. "Erich didn't want to wear a uniform at all. He's a prisoner because his father made him join the war. Did you know that?"

Cora hesitated. "I...don't recall." She got a twisty look on her face, then seemed surprised to be holding the dustpan. She dumped the broken cup in the garbage.

Max sighed. "Sometimes I feel like a prisoner too."

"How's that?"

"I'm trapped in a town where all the kids hate me and I'm too young to leave."

"Surely they don't *all* hate you." She folded the used tea towel and smoothed it.

"They do. All they see is that my father is German. The same way you only see Erich's uniform." Max gripped the edge of the wash bowl. "Maybe you're a prisoner too."

She tilted her head and curved her eyebrows. "What do you mean?"

Max's eyes widened as his thoughts came together. "You can't see that Erich's nice...because you're trapped in your sadness for your relatives. Being trapped is like being in prison."

"I've never thought about it like that. I don't feel like a prisoner."

Max shrugged, then brightened. "Maybe we need to break out of jail, like Captain Canuck always does. We'll escape and run away into the forest."

Cora ruffled his hair and laughed. "Oh, I don't think that would be a good idea, Max."

Max clamped his mouth shut. It sounded like a good idea to him. In fact, it sounded like a great idea.

39:

27 FEBRUARY 1944,
LOGGING CAMP (-10°C/14°F)

Erich's mind wasn't in the soccer game at all. He kept hearing Frank describe his family's suffering during the German attack and occupation—*killed, raped, shunned*—and it was reeling something from the depths, something Frank had said once. Erich stopped dead when the memory surfaced. Frank at the first dance, pinning Erich against a sleigh. *"If I come after you, you'll know it. 'Cuz I'll come hard and fast, like your Blitzkrieg attack on Poland."*

Frank's tone had been thick with hatred, but not deception. *Hard and fast, like your Blitzkrieg.* Erich shuddered. Someone yelled at him and he bobbled a pass, then chased after the ball. But his thoughts continued to range away from the game. Frank had mentioned that Chuck was grieving over two nephews. Now it was Jimmy's voice whispering in his mind, about *"seeing Chuck's brown jacket on its hook, but he was gone. Probably snagged another coat to go to the john."* But why would you grab someone else's jacket? It made no sense. Habit would make you reach for your coat on your peg. Unless... Unless you wanted to disguise yourself by wearing what every other lumberjack wore: a red plaid jacket. You'd want to disguise yourself so you wouldn't get caught. Which meant...

A snowball caught Erich on the back of the head. "Thanks for nothing," Schlenter said. "You missed a dozen easy passes and lost us the game."

Erich waved him off and left the pitch. Max followed and sat with him on the top of the hill, the snow cold and unforgiving, but not melting, which was worse. Max related his triumphant prank, which Erich had to admit was funny. But foolish, given those boys' inventiveness in finding ways to harass Max.

"Leave it at one prank, Max. I've told you about my brother. Mean boys don't suddenly become nice when you get them back."

"For the first time in four years I feel good about something, Erich. Don't spoil it by sounding like a grown-up."

"Maybe I'm more grown-up than I know. I sometimes feel like I haven't had the chance to be young. I was barely fourteen when Cologne was bombed for the first time. Living in a war..."

"I know about living in war, how awful it is."

"You know one part of it. Being hassled or beat up isn't the same as having bombs falling on your home."

"I guess." Max looked away, obviously displeased with what even to Erich's ears was sounding like a lecture.

Christmas approached with his rifle slung over his shoulder. "Little Mouse, Alf thinks you should go home soon. Walk with me. I am going hunting for a few days. We will share the path down the hill." So Max left, features stamped with irritation.

40:
4 MARCH 1944,
LOGGING CAMP (-20°C/-4°F)

On Monday, temperatures plunged. Days were colder than anything they'd experienced, and the nights were brutal. Erich's lungs
ached and his nose seemed to freeze, hairs and all. Frost as thick
as his pinkie caked the windows and dusted his blankets each
morning.

Henry made sure everyone had a balaclava or scarf to protect his
face. Erich's days shrank to surviving work in the forest, shoveling
hot food into his stomach, and huddling by the stove to keep warm
until it was time to dive under the covers and sleep. He couldn't
even rejoice in having Nikel back as his partner. He was too busy
freezing, and he lived in dread that it might get colder. Alf insisted
that it could, that it had in other winters.

Nightly they checked fingers and toes for signs of frostbite. How
could anyone survive this weather without shelter, like the soldiers
who'd tried to take Moscow? Erich's bones ached from the cold;
he longed for Cologne's mild winters.

Afternoons improved toward week's end, though nighttime
temperatures dove deep. On Saturday, Erich relished his stew at
dinner. Its warmth seeped through him like hot chocolate. But even
stew didn't stop a chill from gripping him when Henry announced
that Max was missing again.

After the meal, all the men searched the sawmill, yard, and
every building, but found nothing. Erich wrapped blankets around
him to keep warm. *Verdammt, Max! Where are you? It's too cold out
there.* He stood and blew a porthole in the window frost. When he
peered outside, the frost crept inward in seconds and closed off the

sight of the Lanes' house. *They don't even have a telephone to learn if Max is found.* Erich blew at the spot to clear it again and watched the frost aggresively cover the glass. No wonder Alf wasn't letting anyone take one of his horses out in this ice box.

Near ten o'clock, Erich bundled up for a trek to the outhouse. The cold slapped him in the face and punched his lungs with every breath. Even through gloves, the metal lantern handle felt cold. On his return he stopped for a moment. Footsteps crunched so loudly over the brittle snow that the sudden silence pressed on him. Tree branches cracked. He walked into the middle of the yard. Only the bunkhouses and main house shone any light. The night was smothered by clouds, the dark heavy and threatening.

Max was out in that. What had driven him to run away this time? Had his father chided him for not defying his tormentors? Erich groaned with remembered despair. He had always wanted his father's approval and had never gotten it. Though his father had never raised a hand to him, he had also never stopped Gerhard from harassing him. If he were Max, he'd go where he felt safe. Erich faced the barn. Three men had searched it. But...

Erich trudged through the cold, cursing himself for leaving his scarf on his coat peg. His cheeks stung from the air's icy touch. It was warmer in the barn, thanks to the horses' heat. Erich stood at the bottom of the ladder and peered at the black hole above. He hung the lantern on a nail and climbed into the hayloft, then reached down and drew up the lantern. The hay acted like a layer of insulation, holding heat from below. The air higher in the loft was frosty.

"Max?" Erich felt foolish speaking into the silence. "Please come out if you're here. It's too cold. My joints are freezing and soon I won't be able to move." The smell of hay tickled his nostrils. He squeezed his nose to keep from sneezing.

From somewhere nearby, a quiet voice spoke. "Then go inside."

Erich dropped his hand. Swallowed an excited shout. "I can't. You're my friend. If you're staying here, then I am too."

"But you'll freeze."

"Probably."

Silence. Below, horses shifted. One nickered. Behind Erich, hay rustled and Max spoke again. "I don't want you to freeze."

Erich turned. "So let me take you to Henry's and I'll crawl into my warm bunk." A small lie. It would take at least a half hour of shivering to create a warm cave under the covers.

"They'll be mad at me. So will Father. Madder than last time."

"No. They'll be happy you're safe and warm by their stove." Erich removed a glove and wiped at some dust itching his neck. "Three men looked here. Why didn't you come out?"

"Mother sent me to town and I didn't want to go, so I came here." More rustling. Max rose from a pile of hay looking like a scarecrow losing its stuffing. "This is a good thinking spot. I need to figure things out. Richard and his friends beat me up every day this week. And they don't even know I did the coal-dust prank. There has to be a way to get them back so they'll stop."

"Trust me. There isn't, not without an adult stepping in. The police might help if you reported the near hanging."

"No!" Max brushed at the hay. "You don't understand. A policeman told me if I caused trouble he'd arrest Father and me both." His hands dropped to his side. "Richard can talk his way out of anything. He'd convince the police it was my fault. Then Father and I'd get arrested. And we'd lose the farm because Mother couldn't run it alone."

Erich motioned him toward the ladder. "It can't be that bad."

"It *is* that bad." Stubbornness curved his eyebrows and he crossed his arms. "I thought you'd understand. Aren't you trying to find out who caused the sloop accident and who hurt Johann so you can get even?"

"No. If we know who did those things, maybe the accidents will stop. That's all. I'm not...brave enough to get even, Max. Any time I tried, bad things happened."

At the bottom of the ladder, Erich gripped Max's shoulder and steered him toward the doors. It was noticeably warmer down here, if thick with the smell of animals. The two nearest horses pricked their ears and snorted.

A shadowed figure swung the door open. Erich hesitated, then started forward with Max.

His lantern threw swaths of light back and forth, revealing an angry Chuck. When he noticed Max, his brow smoothed. "Good to see you're okay, boy. Lotta people looking for you." He stepped aside, but grabbed Erich's arm and whispered, "Stop spying on my friends, Jerry. Their business, my business, it's none of yours. Wouldn't want you to get hurt. And stay away from the girl. I know you're trying to sweeten her up."

Erich pulled free and walked toward the house with Max, eager to get out of the cold and away from Chuck's frosty menace. He entered with the briefest of knocks. Henry started to rise, scowl in place, then spotted Erich's companion. He smiled, and invited Erich to warm up.

All three Lanes fussed over Max, who looked both embarrassed and pleased over the attention. Cora was stoking the stove, so Erich moved to help. He squatted and opened the firebox, sighing when the heat hit him. Cora passed him some wood.

She whispered, "Chuck warned me to stay away from you."

"He told me the same thing."

"What is it about? The accidents? I do hope they find out who caused them."

"That won't happen. No one wants justice. The victims were only prisoners. Enemies. They don't care."

The color drained from Cora's face, but she didn't correct him.

Erich straightened and returned to the table. He gently swatted Max on the back of his head. "If you run away again, Max, I will kick you in the behind."

Max grinned like they'd shared a joke. He was still planning something, Erich could tell, but he could hardly accuse him of that without revealing what had happened to Max. Not for the first time, he regretted having made that promise.

"I mean it, Max." Erich squinted one eye and rubbed his neck. "Think about it," he continued, raising his eyebrows, hoping to encourage Max. "Do what's right."

He left behind the Lanes' quizzical looks and stole warily across the yard, scanning the shadows in case someone was lying in wait. Frank might've said he'd attack in full view, but Erich didn't feel like he could count him out as a suspect. If Chuck was prone to wandering off when grief overtook him, Frank could have used that time to cause Johann's accident, or to loosen all those ax heads. But Chuck could have done the same.

Frank or Chuck? Or both?

41:

10 MARCH 1944,
LOGGING CAMP (-2°C/28°F)

Sunday had been spent sledding with Max. When Cora came to watch for awhile, Erich noticed Lehrmann's regard and kept his distance. He was sick of it. Sick of needling comments every time Lehrmann or Hubart walked by. Sick of being reminded they didn't trust him and would pounce if he misstepped. They had ordered him to get close to the Lanes, yet every time he went near them, they accused him of betrayal.

Frank watched him too, with an unsettling wrath curving his brow. He'd been worse since the day in the cookhouse, when Max and Erich had overheard his conversation with Cora. Each night before going to sleep, Erich checked that the big red circle on his jacket hadn't changed into an actual target. It only felt like it had.

The weather swung from too cold to too warm. The snow started melting again, which made Alf swear creatively. The week had been hard slogging, but as upset as Alf was by the warmth, Erich was glad it no longer felt like he was trapped in Niflheim, the Norse frost giants' land of ice.

Friday arrived and the local men quit work early to get ready for another dance. None of the prisoners wanted to go after the disastrous events of the last one. Erich longed to play the piano again, but—*Found some rope!* The mere mention of the dance revived visions of the circle of enraged faces, of the thrown rope landing on Henry's foot. Nothing had come of Miss Miller's accusations—the police had never come to the camp—but Erich knew he and the other prisoners would still be targets. It was no surprise that everyone refused to go.

Alf stayed in the forest with the prisoners and worked until their usual time. After dinner, the prisoners pitched in to clean up, then started a poker tournament. Alf joined in. Erich liked poker well enough, but people always knew he was bluffing.

After a few hands—and down by more than a few chips—he slipped outside. It had snowed a trace earlier but now clouds scudded across a moonlit sky, turning into soft halos as they passed in front of the full moon, reverting to pale ghosts as they floated away. The yard was cast in steel gray. Erich walked to the edge of the valley and toyed with the idea of taking a sled ride. The idea held no appeal.

The house was dark. Erich had heard Cora tell Mrs. Lane she didn't want to dance but would visit a friend. He hadn't caught the rest, something about this friend hearing news about Wally. Could Wally be short for Walter? Could that be the son of the man in the store, the son who had gone missing in the war? In such a small community it was likely.

He wandered behind the house and drank in the sight of silvery snow mounded on black silhouettes of evergreens. He'd never been interested in art other than music, but sometimes these winter landscapes made his fingers itch with wanting to capture them on paper. If only he could draw more than stick men.

Erich paused to face the barn. He entered, felt along the right-hand shelf, found a lantern and matches. The yellow light threw long shadows. Horses whinnied as he passed. He greeted his skid horse, a gentle gray named Molly. He hung the lantern by the ladder, stood in the aisle and eyed the spot where the bolt cutters were hidden. If he'd thought it through, he'd have realized their presence in the barn meant Alf hadn't hidden them. He was smarter than that.

Shuffling footsteps turned him around. Expecting Alf, Erich smiled. It choked off when a hand grabbed his collar. Chuck yanked him, almost off his feet, and breathed the smell of stale cigarettes into his face. "What're you doing? Figuring on stealing a horse?"

"No." A whisper was all Erich could manage. "You...aren't dancing."

"You Jerries'd like that. Overpower Alf and all escape." His eyes were black marbles in his shadowed face. "Too bad for you my knee got banged up today. Slept through supper but saw you come in here."

Erich pulled at the man's wrist to loosen his grip. "None of us would risk the freedom we have here. Henry and Alf treat us fairly."

"Treat you too damned good. Better than you deserve."

"So are you giving us what *you* think we deserve? None of us here killed your nephews. We were already prison—"

Chuck shoved Erich and he slammed into a post separating two stalls. A horse kicked, brushing Erich's pantleg. He stumbled away, landed on one knee, jumped up.

"You need to stay outta other people's business." Chuck spat. "Did you sweet talk Cora into siding with you? She watched me all week, squinty-eyed like *I* was the enemy."

"Maybe she doesn't like being told what to do."

"Maybe she needs to be taught how Jerries should be treated."

"Leave her alone." Erich balled his fists.

"Take a swing, Jerry. I'll gladly tune you in. But first you're gonna tell me what you've learned, snooping around so much." Chuck's gaze flicked toward the end of the barn.

Erich straightened. So Chuck knew where the bolt cutters were. Maybe he'd hidden them there; maybe Frank had told him. Either way, Erich needed to tell Alf. He sidestepped toward the door, but Chuck cut him off. There was another, smaller door in the back corner, to access the corral. Erich shot away from Chuck, rammed his shoulder against the rear door. Yanked the top bolt down and open. Reached for the bottom bolt.

Hands grabbed his shoulders. Threw him onto the floor. Erich grunted and rolled onto his side, three feet from the hidden bolt cutters. Boots edged into his line of sight. Of course. "Want to show me your boot print, Chuck?"

"Gladly." The man stepped forward, raised his foot to flatten Erich's face, but Erich twisted away, reached under the bench. The boot slammed between his shoulder blades, pinning him.

"Evening, boys. I've gotten so I worry when I see Erich wander off on his own, given how trouble follows him. But I'm sure you're just having a wrestling match." Alf spoke from six feet away, between the stalls. Chuck curled his lip and glared at Erich, who twisted his neck to glare back. "You win, Chuck," Alf said. "Let him up."

Chuck shifted his weight onto Erich, then stepped back. Seeing his chance—a chance to tell Alf, to finally end this—Erich reached under the burlap sacks and tossed the bolt cutters so they landed near Alf's feet. "Ask Chuck how those got under your bench, Alf."

Chuck kicked him in the stomach. "You're not gonna blame me for your dirty tricks, you lying Jerry prick."

Curled into a ball, Erich tried to inhale so he could speak. Spots gave the barn a kaleidoscope look. "I caught this bugger stashing the cutters, Alf," Chuck said. "I figure he musta hid them somewhere else and decided to move them. Was probably gonna blame you, except I caught him red-handed."

Erich shook his head, which made the spots dance like frantic lightning bugs.

"That so?" Alf said. "Next I suppose you'll tell me this boy hurt his own partner out in the bush. What for, Chuck?"

"Hell, to stir up trouble, make you think we were guilty. He's been getting cozy with you from the start, using his fancy English and pretending to be like us. Now he's trying to fool that poor girl. Crock of Nazi shit."

Erich saw the boot swinging back again. Air flooded his lungs as he rolled away, and sirens clanged in his ears. He gulped more air. The kick never landed. Erich could only guess Alf had stopped it. He croaked, started to rise, eyes on Alf's face, his own features contorted with trying to speak.

"Damn but I hate full moons." Alf stood over Erich. "Save your breath, son. I figure you're going to accuse Chuck of the same thing he laid at your feet. Seems it's your word against his."

Chuck snarled. "You can't mean you're giving his words the same weight as mine."

"I'm not discussing this tonight, Chuck. You're both going to your bunkhouses, and you're staying there, and you're not mentioning this to anyone. I'll sit up with a shotgun all night if I need to."

Alf grabbed the lantern, marched to the door and held it open. Chuck didn't move as Erich struggled to his feet. His breath was still rattling into his lungs, but he heard Chuck whisper, "You shut your trap, Jerry, or I'll hurt that boy who worships you like a hero, and you'll get blamed. Then see how fast rope is strung from a tree."

42:

11 MARCH 1944,
LOGGING CAMP (-12°C/10°F)

The minute Erich stepped into the cookhouse for breakfast Alf turned him around. Lehrmann's narrowed regard tracked his progress as he followed Alf back to the bunkhouse. Inside, Alf motioned him to sit. He perched on the edge of his cot and squinted at the caulking between two logs, dreading what was coming. Alf was going to send him back to Camp 133. He knew it in his bones. Hadn't slept for knowing.

Alf planted a snowy boot on Erich's bed and leaned on his raised knee. "Did you talk to anyone?"

Erich shook his head vigorously.

"So no one knows what you suspect?"

For a second he was tempted to lie. *I'm a terrible liar.* Erich swallowed. "Nikel knows something is wrong. I...didn't sleep well." He squeezed his eyes shut. *Don't send me back. Please. Please.*

"Do you understand why I want you to keep quiet?"

Brow wrinkled, Erich raised his head and searched Alf's face. "No. We need to get this into the open. The prisoners need to know we've solved this."

"That's just it, son. Chuck is looking mighty suspicioius, but it's still mostly his word against yours."

"But—"

"No. We've got to find a way to prove his guilt, or his innocence. In the meantime, you have to keep quiet."

"But they always push me to find out what I've learned."

"Lehrmann and Hubart?"

Erich dropped his gaze back to the logs. "Mostly, but the others want to know too."

"Can you keep mum on this?"

"I still don't understand why I need to."

"What happens if we accuse Chuck? Those two troublemakers of yours will try to get revenge, won't they?"

Fingers raked Erich's shaggy hair. He lowered his hand, clamped onto his knee and nodded. Henry's words returned to him. *I'll tell you this: if anything else happens, I'm done. I'll shut down the whole damn operation for the season.* Fear chilled him.

Chuck wanted to kill him. Lehrmann would kill him for not reporting this. And back in Camp 133, Bechtel waited for his return.

"I'll try to say nothing, but will Chuck?" Erich searched Alf's face again. "You have to find out the truth. I can't keep something this big quiet for long."

Alf's boot clumped to the floor as he straightened. "I'll do my best. And I'll keep an eye on Chuck. Now, I'll send someone back with your breakfast. You're having a sick day. Get some rest." He squinted. "You are looking a bit pale."

A bit? He'd be looking a lot paler if Lehrmann got wind of this. *Deathly pale.*

43:

12 MARCH 1944,
LOGGING CAMP (-12°C/10°F)

When Max arrived at the logging camp for the Sunday soccer game, it had already started. Erich wasn't playing, so Max checked the cookhouse. He wanted to tell Erich he had thought of a great prank. One step inside and Max stopped. The Canadians were gathered around a table. At his entrance, they all stared. A few of them looked really angry.

The air in the room made Max remember the day the police took away Father's guns. He had fumed like a banked fire about to burst into flames. Max scraped his boot backward, the noise loud in the stuffy silence.

He backed outside and jumped off the steps. When he turned toward the German bunkhouse, Alf called to him. They met halfway between the cookhouse and barn. "Not a great day to be here, son." He tipped his hat back on his head the same way Henry always did.

"I wanted to see Erich. Is he sick?"

"No." That was such a grown-up reply. No explanation. Worry wormed its way under Max's skin.

"I don't understand. Can I see him?"

Alf studied the wall of trees separating the yard from the mill. "You need to go home, Max. There's nothing to worry about."

That made Max worry more. Possibilities rattled around his brain: Henry sending Erich back to the POW camp. The police taking him away. A lynch mob arriving. If he was Superman, Alf wouldn't tell him to go home. Even Johnny Canuck would be able to find out what was going on—why the men in the cookhouse looked angry, why Erich wasn't playing soccer.

"What's going on?" It came out more childish than Max intended, whiny.

Alf laid a hand on Max's shoulder and peered into his face. "It's not your business." He gripped Max's chin and turned his face side to side. Firmness gave way to a gentle tone. "Who's been thumping you, son?"

"What do you care?" Max pulled away from Alf. "Nobody cares. Not even Erich, and he was supposed to be my friend. I could disappear and no one would care."

"You know that's not true."

"It *is* true. I'm just a big bother to everyone." Max stalked toward the road. He could hear Alf calling him back, but he broke into a jog. Around the corner of the house, one of the Germans leaned against a tree by the road. He took a long draw on his cigarette as he watched Max approach.

Max slowed to a walk, then stopped and studied him. Other than Nikel and Erich, he hadn't talked to the other prisoners much. This one was lean and narrow, face ruddy from working outside. The name came to him: Lehrmann.

He blew out cigarette smoke and spoke in German. "You are Hofmeyer's little friend. I'm surprised to see you today."

It took Max a second to realize the man was talking about Erich. He kept his distance. Something about the man felt oily.

"Hofmeyer is double-minded. He's hiding something. He'll get what's coming to him, from the Canadians, or from me." He dropped the cigarette in the snow and advanced.

Mouth dry, Max jolted into motion. He stuffed his hands in his pockets and crunched down the road with rapid strides. He strained to listen but no footsteps followed him. When he glanced back, the man was still watching him.

What did he mean, "double-minded"? A person couldn't have two minds, could he? Or maybe he could. Maybe it was like how his father made him feel pulled in two directions by wanting him to love Germany when everyone hated it. He wanted more than anything to fit in, to feel like he belonged, but how? He didn't belong. Not really. Did Erich feel like that too?

In the trees a raven squawked. Tiny dry flakes sifted down from a dull sky. His red plaid jacket was the only splash of color in a world turned gray. It made Max feel like a target.

44:

15 MARCH 1944,
HORLEY (-1°C/30°F)

Tonight Richard would finally get what was coming to him. When Max had overheard Richard, at the end of the day, telling Roy that his gut was ripping him apart and he'd probably spend all night on the biffy, Max had known it was time to act.

He blew out his bedroom lantern and crawled outside, then lowered the window. Water dripping off the roof, splashing unseen in the darkness, made it feel like spring. He squelched across the yard.

In the barn, the musty smell of hay tickled his nostrils. He called quietly to Gertie across well-deep darkness. A snort from the gray horse and a faint meow answered him. He felt his way to the stall when something rubbed against his leg. He jumped. Released his breath, picked up the barn cat, and scatched behind its ears. "You scared me," he whispered. His eyes adjusted and he could see the horse's rump a few feet away. He found Gertie's lead rope and a longer rope that his father used for any number of things. He thought of the one he'd left in Christmas's loft and hoped Richard had gotten in trouble for losing it.

Max expected the tricky part to be leaving the yard. With the extra rope slung diagonally across his chest, he led the horse out of the barn and past the house. After going through the motions of a normal night—homework, dishes, saying he was going to read before bed—he'd made a human-shaped lump under his covers. Now he watched the curtains for movement, hoping no one heard him. But even some snorts from Gertie didn't draw anyone to the window.

On the road, Max looped the lead rope around Gertie's neck and fastened it to the halter's tie ring. It took him three tries to jump high enough to wriggle onto Gertie's back and swing his leg over. She was used to him practicing this and didn't move.

Mounted it only took fifteen minutes to reach Horley. He rode through the village, half the houses already dark and the rest with only one window still lit. This was the town at its best, quiet and everyone minding their own business. The inside of Max's legs were warm against Gertie's thick coat and her horse smell filled his nose with a tang of sweat and hay. Pleasure filled him like darkness filled the sky. This was freedom—no one knowing where he was or caring, feeling he wasn't tied to this small cruel place, that he could go anywhere, be anything, do anything.

At the far edge of the village, Max slid off Gertie's broad back. His destination was less than a quarter mile away: the Anderson farm. They had a dog, but it knew Max and usually came to get a pat when he passed. He led Gertie forward, going over the plan.

He knew the layout of the farmyard from walking by it five days a week. The outhouse was about twenty yards behind the house, to the left near a line of trees. Between it and the barn was a large storage shed.

At the end of the farm lane, the shaggy dog greeted him with wagging tail. He patted it for a few minutes. Three windows were still lit up, but like at home, all the curtains were drawn. Mother claimed it kept the heat inside. Knowing he was wasting time, Max started forward, slowly to reduce noise.

Cloud cover muted the moonlight, but everything was visible to night-adjusted eyes, though dark and hulking like monsters from a comic. Max's heart thundered. If anyone stepped outside right now he was done. Gertie plodded along behind him, head high, ears perked with curiosity. The dog trotted beside Max.

He led Gertie behind the shed. From here he could see the outhouse and its V-shaped path, one arm leading to the house and one to the barn. He scratched the dog's ears for a few more minutes then whispered for it to go lie down. He had to repeat it four times before the dog whined and left.

A manure pile was nearby, and the warm weather had started to thaw it. The smell was sweet and sickly. Max leaned against the back of the shed and held his mitten against his mouth and nose, though this cow manure didn't smell nearly as bad as the pig manure at home. He wondered how long he should wait.

What if Richard had already used the biffy and was in bed? His throat closed.

No. He'd come this far. He was going to get ready. He tethered Gertie, snuck to the outhouse and wrapped the rope around the building, snugging it against the base at the front. At the back he used a stick to keep the rope waist high. He left the extra off to one side and covered it with snow then returned to waiting with jittery impatience.

Thirty minutes later a door slammed. Max pressed himself against the shed and peered around the corner. Wally's wife, Emily, appeared, lantern held high. She picked her way down the path in shoes instead of boots. They'd found out Wally had been taken prisoner. He'd been injured and had been in a German hospital, so the Red Cross didn't have his name for a few weeks. Max had overheard Richard telling his friends all about it on Monday. Maybe he wouldn't be so mean now that he knew his brother was alive.

But this still had to happen. If not tonight, then another night. Memories of the near hanging flashed through his mind. Anger rekindled. How they treated him wasn't fair. He had to take a stand, and Richard had to know that he wasn't safe either. Richard *would* know what it was like to live in fear.

The outhouse door banged, startling Max back to attention. Emily tiptoed like a cat back across the yard. Tension faded to boredom as Max continued to wait. He leaned against the shed and wished he had something to sit on. The ground squished. Beyond the outhouse, an owl hooted, flew across the night sky. The flapping silhouette disappeared. Gertie nuzzled his arm. He leaned against her, rubbed her neck, reviewed the plan. Wished it was done. He played out comic-book stories in his head.

Twenty minutes later the door across the yard opened then closed. Max stiffened and again peered around the corner. Richard. An icy vise clamped Max's chest. He bit his lip as his enemy sploshed down the trail, lantern in one hand and the other pressed against his stomach.

For half a second, Max wondered if he should come back when Richard wasn't sick. *Doesn't matter where you hide, Hitler. Step onto the box, Hitler.* Max's jaw clenched. No, this was happening tonight.

The minute the outhouse door closed behind Richard, Max leaped into action. He nudged Gertie forward and flung the tether rope off her neck, then quick-stepped to the outhouse, trying to be quiet. Like all outhouses, this one had a latch on the outside as well as the inside so the door didn't swing open when not in use. Pulse rat-a-tat-tatting, Max silently twisted the wooden latch and brushed the snow off the rope. Inside the outhouse, Richard groaned.

Max took both ends of rope and flipped them up as if playing Double Dutch with skipping ropes. The cords slapped against the wooden walls. Max pulled them taut and started tying his knot.

"Who's there?" Richard's voice was angry, impatient. "If that's you, Clem, I'm going to kick your ass. I don't care what Mom says."

Max tightened the rope as much as possible, securing the knot in front of the door.

"Clem? You fat-head. This isn't funny." He moaned as his business claimed his attention.

Gertie had stopped halfway down the path from the shed. Max backed her close enough to harness her to the rope tied around the outhouse. His father had taught him all sorts of knots, so he didn't need light to loop the rope around Gertie's neck and tie an easy-release mooring knot. *Look, Father, all those lessons are finally coming in handy.* Max smiled grimly.

He took the tether rope and led Gertie forward until the rope went taut. Gertie's ears perked forward. She pulled things for Father, logs and wagons, so she knew what to do. Max made a double clicking sound. "Come on, Gertie."

She leaned into the crude harness and started forward. Behind her, the outhouse rocked, and Richard yelled his surprise. Then he started cussing. Max urged Gertie forward, anxious to finish the job. He hadn't considered that Richard might raise the alarm.

The shifting outhouse creaked and cracked, and Richard yelled louder. The dog started barking. Then, a thud as the outhouse toppled. Snapping wood as it struck something. Richard's yells turned to cries of pain.

Gertie started snorting and sidestepping as the dog's barks sharpened. The back door slammed. Lantern held high, Mr. Anderson hollered, "What in hell is going on?"

No, no, no! This wasn't how it was supposed to go. Max yanked the dangling rope end to release the knot. He reached for his horse's mane, to mount. To escape. But Gertie bunny-hopped out of reach and galloped past the house, through the circle of lantern light and down the lane.

"I know that horse!" Mr. Anderson exclaimed. "That's Helmut Schmidt's mare."

Max pelted away from the mayhem. He could barely breathe for the fear squeezing his ribs and pressing up from his stomach. His boots pounded the slushy lane. He slipped at the turn onto the road, rolled through a half-melted puddle, scrambled up and raced toward home.

He ran all the way and stumbled into the barn, panting and wheezing. Gertie was already in her stall, snorting her displeasure. Max squeezed in beside her and draped his arms around her neck. "What now, Gertie? What am I going to do?" He hid his face against the horse's mane. *Think, Max! Oh, God. Think.*

To keep from panicking, Max gave the horse oats and fresh water. He felt around for the brush and began grooming Gertie by feel. The motion was soothing. He stroked with one hand, patted with the other. The smell of hay and horse wrapped around him like a hug.

As panic receded, a memory surfaced: Corporal Mason saying that if Max got into trouble he would arrest both Max and his father.

He dropped the brush and plastered himself against the broad boards of the stall. Corporal Mason was going to arrest him. And his father. All because Max had wanted to get even. He bit his lip.

"What have I done?" Max whispered. More importantly, how could he make it right?

Eyes wide, Max searched the darkness for answers, for a way out, for a new plan. Erich had warned him revenge always went wrong. Why hadn't he listened? The horse snorted, content now. Max couldn't ever imagine feeling content again—not here, in a town where everyone hated him.

That was it. He could leave. Get away from everyone.

He couldn't take Gertie. Father used her on the farm. But he could leave. No one could blame his family if he wasn't there.

45:
16 MARCH 1944,
LOGGING CAMP (5°C/41°F)

Across the table from Erich, Lehrmann sat beside Nikel. Between every spoon of oatmeal, he glared with undisguised fury. Fed up with it, Erich set down his spoon and returned what he hoped was a calm look. Lehrmann whispered, "I'll find out what you're hiding. You and your master, Alf."

Heat crept up Erich's neck. He lowered his head and globbed jam on his oatmeal, then focused on stirring it into the steaming cereal. Five days of silence. Erich wasn't sure how much more he could stand. Alf needed to find out something, because Lehrmann's needling was going to get a response. Soon.

Henry marched into the cookhouse. "Finish up. Max is missing again. We need to search the camp."

Several men groaned. Erich shoveled three spoonfuls of oatmeal into his mouth. He was first out and angled to the barn. He called and called, but got no response. Not satisfied, he climbed into the loft, kicked at every bundle of hay, searched every nook. When he left, scattered hay almost covered the spare living space. Christmas wouldn't be happy, but he was still away hunting. Perhaps there'd be time to clean it up before he got back. Max would want that. *Verdammt, where are you this time, Max? I can't take anything else right now.*

A thorough search of the camp turned up nothing. Frank complained that this was the third time they'd had to search for Max since Valentine's. Someone needed to blister his hide. Several men agreed.

Across the yard, Erich spotted a man with broad shoulders and thinning hair a shade darker than Max's. His father, no doubt. Alf

stood on the cookhouse steps and gathered the men around. "We
struck out here, so we're expanding the search. Every Canadian
comes with us. We're going to search Horley."

"What about us?" Erich asked. Tension clenched his stomach.
He needed to do something.

"We don't need more people lost. You don't know the area, so
you'll stay put."

Sam cleared his throat and folded his massive arms. "I'm from
down Edmonton way, so I won't be a help. I could stay and find
you if Max shows up." Alf nodded his agreement.

The Germans sized Sam up. Several looked unhappy, like
youths who'd been told they had a babysitter. Erich swallowed,
recalling the press of that beefy arm against his throat. Lehrmann
said, "We can stay alone. Nowhere to go." A few others muttered
agreement.

Alf raised his hands for silence. "Sam isn't your guard. Get that
idea out of your heads. I'm trusting you all to stay and look after
things for as long as it takes. The women will be with Mrs. Schmidt,
so you have to cook and clean for yourselves."

In minutes, the Canadians were gone. With nothing else to do,
the Germans brought out the soccer ball.

Erich's team put him in goal, though he was so distracted
that he barely saw the ball coming. Moved too late to block it.
An opponent clapped him on the back and thanked him as his
own teammates swore. Nikel gave him a soft swat and told him to
pay attention. He tried but he kept wondering if those boys had
done something worse to Max. Burned him? Buried him alive?
Stop thinking!

The ball rebounded off him and crossed the goal line. Laughter
and swearing battered him in equal measures. Nikel pushed him
out of the goal mouth. "Go be useless somewhere else." This from

the man who was still limping. Erich stepped aside to let Nikel take over and retrieved his coat from beside the log turned goal post. It started to rain. The players inspected the sky, seemed to shrug as one, and resumed playing. Erich donned his coat, stuffed his hands in his pockets, and headed toward the cookhouse where Sam was smoking under the roof's overhang.

The overcast day turned shadows into lead and the cookhouse windows into sheets of silver. Anything or anyone could be hidden behind the glass. Erich veered toward the barn, wondering if he'd somehow missed Max's hiding spot. The soft snow took imprints of each step.

Some of the horses were in the pen behind the barn. Inside, the smell of musty hay filled Erich's senses. The dust tickled his nose. He called for Max, hoping against hope. A faint meow answered, but the barn cat stayed hidden. The silence reverberated, filled him with worry.

Erich leaned against the frame of the open door, anxiety building like a fire being stoked. Anxiety and frustration and a sense of helplessness. He was sick of feeling helpless. Lehrmann strolled across the yard toward him in a gait meant to look casual, but Erich could see the prisoner's tension in the squareness of his shoulders and his foreward-jutting chin.

That man's harassment was another thing he was sick of. Did he enjoy picking on someone so much younger? If not for the threat of Henry sending them back to Camp 133 if anything else happened, he'd gladly tell Lehrmann about Chuck. Erich frowned. No. He didn't want to be responsible for anyone's death, not even Chuck's. Which left him having to face Lehrmann. Erich eased into the open, unsure what was coming, knowing something was. Lehrmann stopped ten feet away. He spoke in German. "You're still looking for that foolish boy?" Erich didn't reply. Lehrmann spat. "I hope the *Dummkopf* dies in the wilderness. One less enemy."

He was baiting Erich, and though he tried to ignore it, he could feel his anger—a tide that had been rising for months. He forced himself to start walking away.

"You're a traitor," Lehrmann called after him. "You would join these enemies in a heartbeat. That girl only has to bat her eyelashes."

Cora again. Erich stopped, fists clenched. "She has never been friendly to me. Not once."

"Not for lack of you wishing. I've seen you imagining what it would be like to lift her skirts. We all think about that." Jaw clenched, Erich strove to remain calm, but Lehrmann kept talking, his oily voice worming its way into Erich's head. "Maybe we should bring her to our bunkhouse. Let her get to know us better. All of us. Not just you, though I'm sure you're eager to lose your virginity."

The thought was so vile, Gerhard might have said it. Lehrmann's face melted into his brother's and the need to strike back exploded. Lehrmann twisted away when Erich barreled into him, deflecting him toward the barn wall. He crashed into logs, rolled along them, pushed away. Erich stared at Lehrmann, his breath coming hard and fast. This is what Lehrmann had wanted, and he had given in. He shook his head, angry with Lehrmann, and with himself. Lehrmann stood in a ready stance, hands at his side, sneer on his face. The soccer players raced toward them, as if they sensed blood.

Erich wiped his aching nose, surprised it wasn't bleeding. "I'm sick of you and your threats. The Lanes have trusted us. Cora has only been polite, even though German bombs killed her relatives." His hands curled into fists. "For you to suggest—"

"See?" Lehrmann's sneer deepened. "Even now you are licking their boots." The other prisoners arrived to form a half circle around them. On the cookhouse steps, Sam stood, frown visible. Lehrmann raised his voice. "Those Canadians are filling your head with lies! They even claim Germany is losing."

Hostility rippled off Lehrmann. A flare gun went off in Erich's mind, giving light to stark truth. Lehrmann had once demanded, *Who is your master, Hofmeyer?* This was the moment he had to answer. Stand for the truth, or cower and let the lie continue. *For once I will not hide behind silence.* The only way he might beat Lehrmann was if the man was too angry to think. Erich straightened, spoke firmly. "The Canadians are right. We've lost. It's only fanatics like you who are too blind to see it."

A snarling Hubart lunged from the sidelines, but two men grabbed and held him. Lehrmann flushed. "You're a traitor to say that. And anyone who doesn't kill you for saying it is a traitor."

Erich had thrown the gauntlet. Now he had to persist. Fury overrode the fear that usually froze him. "*You're* the traitor, Lehrmann. And all the Nazis. You dragged us into a war no one wanted. A war that has destroyed our country."

"The Führer—"

"Lied to us." Erich spat on the ground. "Has lied to us from the start."

With a roar, Lehrmann attacked. For once, Erich was ready. Years of being the target—Gerhard's at home, Bechtel's in Camp 133, Lehrmann's here—fueled him. They exchanged a flurry of punches. Erich ducked under a swing, spun, and delivered a kidney punch. Lehrmann went down on one knee. From somewhere in the distance, Erich heard Sam yell at them to stop. In that split second of distraction, Lehrmann rose and swung, but his punches were losing power. Erich poured all the years of frustration, of not fighting back, into his attack. An uppercut to Lehrmann's jaw staggered him. Erich pressed. Lehrmann slipped. Erich kicked his thigh, sent him sprawling into slushy snow. Dove on top of him. Saw Gerhard below him. Pummeled his chest and head.

Finally hands dragged him off Lehrmann, who was dazed and bleeding. The men holding Erich patted him on the back. Erich was panting, knuckles bleeding, one cheek throbbing. He squeezed his eyes shut, opened them, blinked. What had happened? He squinted at Lehrmann, seeing only the beaten man. Not his brother. He flexed his aching fingers.

Rudolf patted his shoulder. "He had it coming."

Who did? Gerhard or Lehrmann? Both, maybe. He nodded, eyes on his bloody hands, blood spattered on the snow, blood on Lehrmann. So much blood. God, he wanted this war to be over.

Nikel had a hand on Sam's chest, and the hefty blacksmith seemed willing to be restrained by this small obstacle. He folded his massive arms. "John said this has been coming for a long time. Feel better?"

Erich shook his head to clear it. "I'll feel better when these two Nazis are sent back to the camp in Lethbridge."

A few men nodded. Sam spat into the snow. "Until Henry gets back I can only lock them in the bunkhouse." He indicated Lehrmann. "Doesn't look like he'll give you trouble any time soon."

Sam motioned for men to help Lehrmann, who groaned and turned his bruised face toward Erich. "This isn't over, Hofmeyer."

"Yes, it is. Even if they have to send me to that prison camp for anti-Nazis, I'm finished backing down from men like you." Like Gerhard. Erich scanned the prisoners, but other than a frothing Hubart, none looked interested in arguing. Nikel gave him a wink and organized the men to escort Lehrmann and Hubart to the bunkhouse.

As everyone left, Sam trailing behind like an overgrown sheep dog, Erich's remaining energy drained away. He sagged against the barn wall, glad for its solid strength. He touched his face, winced when his fingers reached his cheekbone. They came away red. He wiped them on his pants. His side and stomach were tender, though his coat had provided some protection.

Erich thought of Sam's words. *This has been coming for a long time.* Johann had been right to tell him that, but he'd had no idea how right. This had been coming for years, not months. Years of trying to keep his head down but still getting attacked, of trying to avoid his brother's taunts and cruelties, of shrinking under his father's derision, of cowering through Bechtel's beatings. A mix of emotions churned inside. A drop of satisfaction, or maybe relief, but mostly he felt empty. Shouldn't there be more of a sense of victory? More of something? There was no turning back. He could never return to Camp 133 now; his life would be worth less than a crumbled brick.

Beyond the barn's eves, drizzle ticked against the snow. All the men were out of sight, probably in the cookhouse. The soccer ball sat abandoned on their makeshift pitch. Would he ever play another game here? Ever eat another piece of Mrs. Lane's rhubard crisp?

A sound inside the barn made Erich turn his head. Again, a scraping, coming from the hayloft. *Max?* Erich hobbled through the barn and climbed the ladder with ribs complaining.

He stepped off the ladder to see Christmas brushing aside clumps of hay. He straightened and cocked his head. "You clobbered your own man."

Erich glanced at the small door for getting hay into the loft. It was cracked open. "He's a Nazi bully. He's needed that for a long time." He kicked aside a bundle of hay. "Sorry about the mess. I was looking for Max."

Erich needed to sit down before his knees gave way. He lurched over to the crate in Christmas's space and moved the unlit lantern to the floor. He winced as he pressed his ribs.

"Little Mouse?" Christmas crouched near his pack and rifle.

Erich nodded. "He's been missing since last night. All the Canadians except Sam have gone to the village to help search."

"Little Mouse isn't hiding. He's gone."

Erich straightened with a hiss. "You saw him? Where did he go?"

"He's gone into the bush."

46:

16 MARCH 1944,
LOGGING CAMP (8°C/46°F)

"The bush?" Erich repeated. "What does that mean, he's gone into the bush? Did you see him today?"

Christmas nodded. "Near his farm."

Frustration hit Erich like another punch to the jaw. "But *where*? He's missing. Tell me."

The boy gave Erich a narrow look.

"Please?"

Another nod. "I took a deer to be slaughtered by Max's father like Henry wanted. I got there late so left it hanging in the shed. Coming out, I saw Max leaving, so followed until he turned onto a trail. I stopped him. He said he was going to my trapping cabin."

"And you let him go?" Erich started to stand but sat back down with a wince.

"He said he needs to be alone. That I understand." He pointed. "I made him promise to wait for me on the trail by River of Ghosts, and I would walk with him. I came back to tell Henry I had left the deer and tell why I couldn't stay."

"Where is this cabin?"

"North of the Peace. The night you found him here he asked where the cabin is. He knows the way." His black brows dropped over his dark eyes. "But the Peace is restless this winter. Warm winds push the ice. Now, rain thins it. Not safe. So I told him wait."

"Where he's waiting, is it far?"

"Not far."

Erich touched his bruised cheek again. "We need to tell Henry and Max's father. They'll know where to look."

"Where are they?"

"The village maybe. Or searching neighboring farms. I don't know for sure."

"We can go to where Max waits, and you can talk to him. Like you did before. You are good with words."

"I can't just leave." And Sam wouldn't let him if he asked. So much could go wrong out there. For them and for Max. But Erich could almost hear his grandfather quoting a sampler that hung in his den. *Our doubts are traitors and make us lose the good we oft might win, by fearing to attempt.* Shakespeare and his grandfather were ganging up on him.

Christmas remained silent and watchful. Could Erich trust him? What choice did he have? Fear had crippled him all his life. Would he let it stop him again, after he had conquered it by fighting Lehrmann? Max needed him, needed them both if he was in trouble. To Erich, he'd become a little brother who needed protection. How could he deny Max the thing he had always wanted? He nodded to Christmas. "Okay."

Christmas picked up his gear and pointed Erich toward the ladder. On the main floor of the barn, Christmas grabbed two bridles. "Horses get us to the trail faster."

"Shouldn't we tell someone where we're going?" Not Sam. Nikel, maybe.

Christmas looked out a window. "Rain disappears tracks."

Erich sighed. "Horses then. We'll meet searchers along the way and can tell them what we know."

In the corral, horses bridled, Christmas motioned for Erich to mount. He had ridden, but never without a saddle. The other youth's steady gaze challenged him. Erich grabbed a handful of black mane, pressed his other hand on the horse's brown back, and jumped. He landed on his stomach, the bay's withers digging into his tender waist. He gritted his teeth, finished mounting. Pain folded him over the horse's neck.

Christmas leaped almost effortlessly onto the back of his sorrel and pointed at the corner of the corral closest to the road, to a gate Erich had never noticed. He opened and closed the gate without getting off his horse.

On the road, Christmas urged his horse into a trot. Erich did likewise, wincing at each jolt. They alternated between a few minutes trotting and a few walking. Wet-horse smell grew stronger. Erich pulled his toque from his pocket.

Trotting bareback was as uncomfortable as Erich had expected. His father had made him and Gerhard take riding lessons in an effort to fit in with the noblemen's children. It never made a difference; they were seen as pretenders. When the Nazis came to power they'd come to his parents' parties. He'd heard whispers that some noble families disliked the government, but they had made a show of loyalty, bowing to those in charge. Like he had, Erich realized. For years he'd been pretending a loyalty he'd never felt. After today, that was over.

Almost two miles later, as they were coming out of the hills and in sight of the first farm, they turned west onto a path Erich didn't see until they were on it. They entered a gully and followed an animal trail along its floor. It wended northwest then cut over a rise and into another valley. When they walked, the rock of the horse's gait was soothing.

They emerged from the valley and stopped. Erich figured they had come maybe six miles. "How far to this river?"

Christmas pointed north. "A day."

"What?" Erich swung his leg over the bay's neck. Landing on the ground sent a jolt through his midsection that caused him to hiss. "Where was Max supposed to wait for you?"

"Here." Concern wrinkled Christmas's brow.

Here was a meadow, maybe a field. Hills rose up behind them. The land sloped down to the north, a patchwork of stark white and mottled browns sprinkled with gray. The horizon was a blue-gray ribbon. There were no signs of human habitation.

Erich kicked at the snow. "He didn't wait? Does that mean he's headed to the big river, the Peace?"

"I think so." The frown deepened. "This is not good."

"We need to catch him. But how will we tell anyone where we've gone?" When no answer came, Erich tramped to a tree and broke off a slender branch. He drew an arrow in the snow, wrote "Max" by its stem. Erich's instinct was to turn back, find the searchers, let someone else shoulder this worry. But Max was out there, heading into the hinterland alone, and they were closer to him than anyone in the search party. Erich rubbed his bruised knuckles. "Where are his tracks?"

Christmas pointed to shallow depressions misshapen from rain.

Erich stared at him, then back at the shapes in the snow. How could he be sure? They could be anything. Erich pursed his lips. Alf and Henry had both remarked on Christmas's tracking abilities. All he could do was hope they were right. He rubbed his backside, damp from the wet horse. It would be sore soon. He hadn't ridden in years. At least his stomach felt marginally better, even if his cheek felt like a crowbar had whacked it.

They had left the barn around ninety minutes ago. Erich did some quick math. If it had taken Christmas the same time to get from here to the camp, then Max was three hours ahead. Maybe the horses had gained them some time, but they didn't walk much faster than a person. And a boy had boundless energy for running.

"We go." Christmas broke the silence.

Erich mounted. It wasn't as painful as last time.

Christmas reined his horse in beside Erich. "I see in your face you want to go back."

Erich shrugged. "But Max isn't back there, is he? I want more to help Max."

"Little Mouse is my friend too. We help him." Christmas started out.

Erich tried to not think about the trouble that awaited him when they returned to camp. He was AWOL—absent without leave. Being a prisoner, they might assume he'd escaped. Erich recalled that first talk with Henry when escape had come up. *You'd be running scared. All the men and boys, and half the women around here, are good shots with a rifle.* If they thought he'd escaped he might lose the chance to go to the anti-Nazi camp—he might get shipped back to a death sentence in Camp 133. Finding Max was the only thing that could win him some goodwill now. It wasn't just Max's life on the line here. He eyed the back of Christmas's head and hoped he was trustworthy. Max had always thought so.

An hour later Erich's stomach reminded him it was time for lunch. The flatter ground had allowed for some trotting so they had covered maybe four miles. They'd seen two different farmsteads, both over a mile out of their way.

They came to another small river valley and dipped into it. Another animal trail followed the frozen waterway. The horses kept to a fast walk on the level surface. When they reached a road, Erich turned the horse onto it and rode out of the valley to survey the land. There was a farm only a half-mile away, but no smoke rose from its chimney.

The enormity and possible uselessness of what they were doing sagged Erich's shoulders. They might not catch Max before dark—if they were even following his trail.

They continued along the stream's valley, which snaked mostly north. To pass the time, Erich told Christmas about the accidents at the camp and what he'd found out. He asked Christmas if he remembered the day he'd arrived in the camp.

"Did you see Chuck when you got there?"

Christmas, who had so far only listened to Erich's musings, tilted his head for a moment, then twisted on the horse's back and rested his hand on the red rump. "Yes. I walked with Jimmy and Miss Cora to the barn. Chuck came out of it. Didn't look at me... the way you don't look at me. He asked to take Miss Cora's horse."

Being compared to Chuck made Erich squirm. He pressed his lips together, knowing he couldn't defend himself. He *had* ignored Christmas, treated him almost like a servant. He searched Christmas's face, appalled to think that any Nazi teachings might have invaded his thinking, that he might have been treating Christmas as less than everyone else. This was the person who had found him in the forest and probably saved his life.

He cleared his throat. "What was Chuck wearing?" Jimmy had seen Chuck's coat hanging on the hook. If he'd really just grabbed someone else's to go to the bathroom, surely he would have gotten his own coat before he started his day.

Again Christmas gave the question a moment's thought. "Plaid coat. Not his brown one."

So Cora and Christmas had arrived right after Chuck hid the bolt cutters. Christmas faced forward again, done with talking. After awhile, he led them onto flatter land. Erich asked if they were still following Max's trail.

"He stayed in the valley. We cut across fields to catch him."

They came to a road, thundered down it for half a mile, then walked. Christmas got off and led his horse, so Erich did too. They passed a farm. Erich ran to the house, but returned when repeated pounding and calling determined no one was home. He had hoped to be able to tell someone what they were doing and where Max was headed.

The road dwindled to a trail. Mid-afternoon, riding again, they came to another valley. Erich reined in the bay beside the sorrel. "Is this the same river?"

Christmas nodded and led the way down the snowy slope. The rain had lessened to a mist, but a full day of damp had left Erich chilled and miserable. And hungry. In the valley, Christmas slid off his horse and examined the ground. He squatted, fingered a track. His eyes were black and unfathomable. "Little Mouse is still ahead." He squinted north as if he could see beyond the twists and turns, then pulled some strips of leather from a pouch at his waist. "Pemmican. Eat."

Erich sniffed it, tore a chunk off with his teeth and chewed. "What's in it?"

"Bear meat. Fat. Berries. Good."

Bear? Erich eyed it suspiciously, then took another nibble. "Not bad." He ripped off another chunk.

Christmas mounted his horse and kept going. The small river joined another in a slightly deeper valley. Erich asked, "Is this the Peace River?"

"Ksituan River. It joins Peace."

Ridges lined by trees bordered the valley. In places the banks had given way, exposing sand with tangles of roots shooting out from the sides like twiggy waterfalls. Other slopes were gentle sweeps of whiteness that might be grass in the summer. The snow was turning gray and blue as the sun sank below the horizon. Long shadows fell, shrouding the valley in gloom.

Christmas called a stop. "Rest. Moon will rise late. We will walk under it."

Erich eyed the sky. It had been cloudy all day. How could the moon give light? But he was too tired to argue. He eased to the ground. Christmas led him to a spruce tree leaning over the bank, and revealed a hollow below it where roots and grass held some soil in place, creating a roof for their shelter. Erich ducked to enter the cave-like space.

They had just settled when Christmas pointed. "Moose." The lanky animal crossed the valley, paused to look at the horses, then plowed through a deep snow bank with its long legs. Erich whispered, "Amazing. I'm sure I've seen one in the forest near the camp but always at a distance. It's so ugly, yet so graceful."

"Good eating," Christmas replied.

Erich laughed, which made the moose look back before it disappeared. His amusement died. He knew he was tired and needed to rest, but he couldn't shake the feeling that Max was gaining ground. Soon, he might be out of reach.

47:

16 MARCH 1944,
KSITUAN RIVER (3°C/37°F)

Max slipped. His knee jolted against the ice. He groaned and pushed to his feet. He'd been walking since before dawn and felt the ache of tiredness with every step.

Over and over through the day he had wondered if the note he'd left was going to work:

> *Dear Constable Mason,*
>   *I have left home. Please don't look for me. And please don't arrest my father because I tipped over the Anderson's outhouse. I was mad because the older boys are always mean to me. I know it was wrong, but you have to believe that my father would never think what I did was good and would punish me if I stayed. No matter what you think he really does like his new home, and he loves his farm, especially his pigs.*
>   *Sincerely,*
>   *Max Schmidt*
>   *PS: I hope Richard didn't get hurt.*

He had tucked the note into his math book. He should have left it on the table. They'd find it, wouldn't they? Maybe he should have left a second note, apologizing to his mother for taking a loaf of bread and jam. It was all he could easily find sneaking around the kitchen in the dark. His jar of water was almost empty. He pulled it from his school bag and took a sip, then screwed the lid on tight so it wouldn't leak.

He had his pocket knife (which he never took to school), his

KAREN BASS

father's filleting knife, his fishing pole, half a dozen hooks, some snare wire, and a rolled-up blanket. He wished he'd brought his comics, but they were too bulky.

He *had* brought his favorite *Superman*, though he wasn't sure he liked Superman as much any more. He used to believe the hero was real and was out there somewhere. He knew better now. Even if Superman was real, he was only worried about people in big cities like New York; he certainly didn't care about one boy in far off Alberta. He only worried about big bad guys. He expected you to take care of little bad guys yourself.

Except that hadn't worked out so well.

Max almost tripped again. He couldn't continue. He waded partway up the moonlit riverbank and found a spruce tree with hardly any snow under it. He crawled into the space under the branches and curled on his side with his bag as a pillow. Not long after, he woke. He was still tired, but walking was warmer than hunkering under spruce boughs.

When he rounded the next curve, he stopped and stared. A gray embankment towered above him and stretched to the east and west, like the biggest castle ever. He'd known that following the rivers north would lead him to the Peace. He'd been here with his father in the summer, but the river valley looked deeper and wider on a winter's night. Not as friendly.

He thought about Christmas's cabin. If he remembered right, he needed to follow the river west and north until he came to a big bend and a cluster of islands. A little lake lay northeast of the first big island, maybe a mile from the river, and on it stood a small trapper's cabin. His new home.

He felt bad about lying to Christmas. But he probably would have acted like an adult and tried to talk him into turning around. And there was no going back.

Below the wall of the north bank, the wide white surface of the frozen river beckoned. It would be so much easier walking in the open rather than in the shadows where snow was piled. Max marched onto the large river's ice.

48:

16 MARCH 1944,
KSITUAN RIVER (2°C/36°F)

Erich fell asleep curled against the earthen wall under the overhanging tree and didn't wake until Christmas tapped his foot. He felt heat before he opened his eyes to a small fire by their shelter. The flames licked a carcass on a crude spit. He didn't ask what it was. Christmas passed him a canteen.

After they had picked the carcass clean of its stringy meat, Christmas suggested they sleep for awhile. Erich scanned the darkness. "I guess Max will be hiding in a hole too. In this dark, we might miss something."

"You speak truth," Christmas said.

Erich inclined his head, then touched his bruised cheek. He poked the fire with a stick. The stirred sparks floated up on the fire's draft. Worry drifted through his thoughts like the embers, igniting images of things that could happen to Max.

Christmas said, "Henry will be angry at you for today when we return?"

Erich kept his attention on the fire. "Very angry."

"Police?"

"Maybe." Erich's frown deepened. They hadn't met anyone to send word to the searchers. Erich prayed Henry didn't believe he had escaped. Surely he'd realize Erich's concern had sent him after Max.

"Not good," Christmas said. "Police took my grandfather's brother away. He died in a cage. Cree need sky above, ground below. Not walls. Not fences."

"I understand completely," Erich whispered. It took him a long time to fall asleep.

Christmas woke Erich in the middle of the night. Most of the clouds had cleared. The half moon shone like theater lights turned low before a performance. Christmas pointed out the ring around the moon. "Snow comes."

They scrambled down the incline to the horses. Erich started to loop the reins over the bay's head. Christmas stopped him. "Horses need more rest. We walk."

"We can't leave Henry's horses in the middle of nowhere."

Christmas removed the bridle from his sorrel. "They'll go home with the sun."

Erich removed the bay's bridle. He didn't see the point of arguing. In this poor light, tracks would be impossible to see from atop a horse anyway.

Christmas took both bridles, and within a few steps had become a shadow in the night. Erich gave his horse a final pat and followed. The valley twisted serpentine. Sometimes he sensed slopes rising up on either side. They felt like guardians of a secret. He half expected a spirit to appear and curse them for entering a forbidden domain.

Their footsteps crackled. At least the moon gave them some light. "Why doesn't Henry have any electric torches? You would think he'd have at least one. We borrowed his horses. I would have gladly borrowed a torch."

"Torch?" Christmas slowed, allowing Erich to catch up. "What is that?"

"A handheld light that runs on batteries."

"Oh. Flashlight. Alf said all batteries go to the army." Christmas sped up again.

Having grown up in a city, Erich found the night too quiet, their footsteps too loud on snow that had melted and re-frozen. He didn't mind being out in the forest when he knew the landing and logging camp were close, but this felt too remote, like they were about to step off the edge of the earth.

The valley deepened, cut off more of the sky until it was only a ribbon above them. The moon cast weak, spotty light along the river's path.

"Can you still see Max's tracks?"

"No rain here. Tracks are clear."

To keep up, Erich marched as if on military patrol, counted steps that helped him stay moving. One hour passed. Two. Possibly more. Erich worried he would soon fall asleep walking, like some soldiers had on forced marches during his initial training. He must have been half-asleep. Christmas's arm across his chest jolted him back to awareness.

The sky was bigger again, much bigger, and steep hillsides seemed to soar upwards for a half-mile. The moonlight painted folds in the formidable walls, making them look striped black and gray, and giving the ridges high above an accordion look. The floor of the valley was vast and almost white under the moon. Behind, the smaller ravine they'd left was a slash of blackness.

"This is the Peace?" Erich asked.

"Yes," Christmas replied. "Here Ksituan joins its mother."

A whistle punctuated his amazement. "The river fills this whole valley? It must be bigger than the Rhine." What a huge and wild place he'd come to. And Max was in it somewhere, alone. "Did we miss where Max turned off for the night?"

"No. His tracks lead onto the ice."

"Didn't you say it was thin this winter?" Dread froze his insides as water seemed to gurgle underfoot.

Somewhere nearby a coyote yelped. Erich held his breath. That didn't quite sound like something wild. More like...

"Help!" came a faint cry. "Is someone there? Hello?"

"Max!" yelled Erich. "Where are you?"

"Help me! Help!" The voice was louder now, frantic. "The ice moved. I'm trapped."

49:

17 MARCH 1944,
ON THE PEACE RIVER (1°C/34°F)

Erich took in the expanse of white—that was all ice, ice that was moving, breaking up, opening to expose watery depths. He shuddered, remembering his own fall into flames and frigid sea. He wanted nothing more than to rant at Max for going onto the ice, but that would have been panic talking. He bit back the words. His fear would only make Max's worse.

They needed to...nothing came. Too tired. Too sore from the fight, the long ride, the middle-of-the-night walk with little rest. He didn't know what to do.

Christmas tugged his sleeve. "This way."

Relieved someone was taking charge, Erich followed. They went left along the edge of the broad Peace River, picked their way over ridges of ice and waded through snow drifts. Erich's gaze was repeatedly drawn up. There was no easy way back.

Max's voice became louder, his pleading more desperate. Erich finally spotted a mass on the ice between black gashes of open water. The two searchers stopped parallel with Max. His huddled silhouette was almost a soccer pitch away. Their silence, as they surveyed the situation in the steely moonlight, was deeper than the valley.

A crack split the stillness. Alarmed, Erich took a step back. Out on the ice, Max began screaming. Christmas said, "Max needs to get off the river."

Ice boomed again, setting Erich's heart jangling in its cage. "He's too scared to move." Max's cries scraped his nerves. High above, a coyote answered the cry with mournful yips. He yelled, "Max! It's Erich. Christmas and I are here." Quieter he asked, "What do we do?"

"We pray the river lets us get him."

"Get him," Erich repeated. "How?" Max called for their help, over and over.

Christmas commented, "Walking men fall through ice. We crawl."

Weight distribution, of course. "Right." They'd crawl. Under the ice waited water as cold as the Atlantic. Erich's breathing sped up. He inhaled deeply to push back the dread. "Max! Do you have anything we could grab? A walking stick?"

"You had your fishing pole," Christmas called.

Max's voice quavered, voice almost inaudible. "When the ice m-moved, my sack and rod f-fell in. I'm cold. There's water all around."

"We're crawling to you, Max. Stay calm." Erich hoped he could too.

He cursed the warm weather and his lack of gloves. On hands and knees, Erich tugged the sleeves of his coat down and walked on the heels of his hands. Christmas led. As they crept away from shore he became more aware of the water under them. The current brushed against the ice, whispered that it waited. Five minutes seemed to take an hour.

Christmas stopped. "Open water. Three feet."

Erich gritted his teeth, silently begged Christmas to keep moving. Water swished under their fragile floor.

After an endless moment, Christmas called, "The water narrows. Little Mouse, move west, away from Ksituan." Erich craned his neck. The moonlight showed Max on a vaguely oval slab of ice the length of a swimming pool. To the east, a triangle of open black water was dotted with islets of ice. To the west, one side of the oval looked like it was touching their larger section of ice.

"Toward the island?" Max asked.

"Yes."

Erich strained to see this island. Moonlight turned the white ice stark. The water looked like open wounds. "There's an island?"

"Not close," was the terse reply, barely heard over the water. So not a refuge. The three of them crawled west, keeping in a line, two on one side of the water, one on the other. Max wheezed with fear. Erich struggled to ignore the swishing murmuring below. Minutes later Christmas announced, "Here."

Erich looked around Christmas. Max's oval didn't quite touch their section. He swore under his breath. "There's still open water."

"Less than a foot. It get wider again."

Thirty centimeters, Erich thought. Under Christmas's direction, they sprawled on the ice, bellies pressed against the cold surface. Erich's feet pointed toward shore. He clasped Christmas's ankles to form a chain of two links.

"Little Mouse," Christmas called. "On your stomach, come to the water. Take my hands. Erich will pull us."

Erich tightened his grip, rasped a plea for safety. He rested his bruised cheek on the ice until the cold hurt more than soothed. Ahead, Max was gasping loudly.

Christmas jerked one foot. "I have his hands. Pull!"

Erich scraped across the ice toward shore, like a crab inching backward. *Drag Christmas's ankles, scuttle the body backward, don't think about the water. Drag, creep backward, don't think.* Sweat trickled along Erich's hairline, into his eyes. Salt water. He moaned. Hauled Christmas toward shore. Only a foot of water. His breathing grated. The need to be faster hammered in his ears.

"Almost," Christmas called. Drag, creep, drag. Erich's arms trembled. He wiggled backward some more.

A crack shattered the night; a splash followed. Max screamed that he was in the water. Christmas's ankles almost yanked out of

Erich's grip. More splashing. Frantic cries. Panic slammed into Erich as screams ricocheted in his mind. *I'm under the flames. Must get away.* They were burning. Screaming. Dying.

No! This wasn't the Atlantic. This was Max. In a river. Erich fought his frenzied thoughts. Pulled Christmas's legs. Squirmed toward shore. Pulled again.

Stay focused. Pull. Pull again. Christmas's feet yanked away. Erich reached out. "No!"

"We are out of the water," Christmas yelled.

On the ice. Erich panted. Christmas shook him, got him to hook his hand under Max's arm and drag him on hands and knees. The going was awkward, slow. Max was unresponsive, a dead weight. Halfway to shore, Christmas said, "Get up now."

Erich pushed himself to his knees, gasped for breath, then moved into a crouch. Stooped low, they dragged Max to the shore. When they were almost there, Christmas picked up Max, straightened, and staggered slightly under his weight, then hurried to solid ground. Erich stumbled after them, knees weak.

Behind them the ice crackled and groaned. Erich fell to his knees as Christmas released Max's limp body into his arms. "He's soaked," said Erich, conscious now of the shivers that wracked his own body. "So cold. We need a fire."

Christmas disappeared into a crease in the valley wall. Max shivered violently, teeth rattling. Erich searched the area in the dim light. He found a nook created by a fallen log and rocks, kicked away the snow, moved Max to the spot. He rubbed Max's arms and legs. His hands were chunks of ice. Erich tried but couldn't wake him up.

He heard Christmas and called out their position. A minute later, a fire was burning. They moved Max as close as they could.

Erich asked, "How did you start the fire so quickly? A Cree trick?"

Christmas held up a lighter. "White man trick."

Erich laughed, more from relief than anything. Christmas slipped into the night again and returned with an armload of spruce branches. They made a bed for Max. After three more trips, they had another bed and "covers" for each. They worked silently.

Christmas began to remove Max's clothes, so Erich helped. Staying busy kept worry at bay. They both removed their coats to drape under and over Max, then sandwiched him between the spruce boughs. Christmas spread the wet clothes on makeshift tripods to the right and left of the fire. Erich moved behind Max's legs and rubbed them. When Christmas added more wood to the fire, its radius of heat expanded. Erich stopped shivering.

"Do you think Max will be okay?"

"We will keep him warm and pray. We will take turns warming him from behind."

Erich stood. "I need the toilet."

When he returned from the trees, Christmas squatted by the fire, naked from the waist up, his shirt wadded into a pillow for Max. He motioned for Erich to join him. Erich crouched, took the offered canteen. The heat bathed away the chill of the night. His scarred shoulder ached. Christmas said, "You are brave."

Erich turned toward the oval face burnished copper by the firelight. "So are you."

Christmas offered his hand. "My name is Sîpîy Pimohtew."

The Cree words sounded strange to Erich. He took the hand. "It's good to know your name, See-pee-pimo..." His tongue tangled around the words.

He snorted. "Call me Christmas. I like this name. White man's Christmas is a time of happiness and gift-giving."

Erich smiled. "I don't deserve your friendship. I treated you badly."

"You did. But now we are friends. This is good."

"It is. I'm sorry I didn't realize you were my friend sooner, See-pimo—"

Christmas shook his head. "Learn it tomorrow. Now, sleep."

"Does your name mean something?"

"All names have meaning. What does Erich Hofmeyer mean?"

"Erich means 'kingly.' Hofmeyer means 'estate manager.' Ah, 'keeper of the village,' you could say." *Kingly.* That was almost funny. He'd always felt like a pauper in his family.

"A good name. Little Mouse is part of your village. You keep him safe."

Erich smiled. "What does your name mean?"

"In white man's words, I am 'River Walker.'"

"Also a good name. If you didn't know the way to the river and how to walk it, Max might not be alive."

They settled under their blankets of spruce boughs, scratchier than wool. Erich took the first shift warming Max's chilled body. His skin quivered, and hardly seemed touched by the fire's heat. *Keep fighting, Max.*

50:

17 MARCH 1944, BY THE PEACE RIVER (1°C/34°F)

Erich only dozed, startling awake every time the dream started, the same dream that had tormented him since his ship had sunk. Falling into oily flames and sinking under them into icy water. The hiss of damp wood burning made him shudder with unwanted memories. What time was it? He propped up on his elbow. Christmas added wood to a crackling blaze, nodded in their direction, and extended his hands to warm them. Max looked dusky in the early light. At least he wasn't alabaster anymore.

Christmas touched his own cheekbone and pointed at Erich. "You look like you lost a fight." He almost smiled, stood, and stretched. Still shirtless. *Amazing.*

Erich did smile, which made the bruise ache. "The other guy probably looks worse."

Christmas lifted one shoulder. He walked away from the fire.

A quiet voice came from near the ground. "It's all red and purple. How'd you get that?"

"Hello, Max. It's good to see you awake." He touched his bruise. "I had an argument."

"I thought you always kept your head down." Max's voice rasped.

"I guess you have to stand for something sometimes. How are you feeling?"

"I'm hot. Can we move away from the fire?"

Erich rested his cool palm on Max's forehead and heat soaked into it. "I think you have a fever. That's what comes of swimming in rivers in the winter."

Christmas returned with an armful of dead branches. He dropped them, took his shirt when Erich held it out. "We need to get Max to a doctor."

"Dunvegan is closest without climbing out of the valley. They have horses to get him to the white doctor in Spirit River."

"Let's go." They got into their coats and helped Max dress. Erich hauled him to his feet, supported him with an arm around his waist. Max hung onto Erich's neck and Erich gripped his wrist.

Christmas put out the fire. He gathered his belongings, his rifle, the bridles, and walked toward the river.

"Will we have to go on the ice?" Max's voice quivered.

He looked relieved when Erich replied, "Beside it."

Their pace was set by Max's labored steps.

Behind the ridges above, the morning sun threw long shadows. The light didn't reach the river. It was cool in the valley, but walking kept Erich warm. Outside. Inside, a chill of worry frosted everything. He studied the depth of the valley, its breadth, the white and brown heights, shadowed with blue. The place felt as stately as any castle. Immense and timeless.

They neared the smaller valley of the Ksituan River that had been their path yesterday. Christmas's arm shot up as he pointed to an eagle soaring on morning breezes to the east. They stopped to watch. Erich felt Max sagging, and with a grunt he swept him up, struggling for a few steps, then found his balance. Any bigger and he wouldn't be able to carry the boy.

They had just reached the mouth of the Ksituan when a voice boomed out of the smaller river's valley. "You can't escape, Erich Hofmeyer. Release your hostage and give up."

A bullhorn. Police. Erich held Max tighter as the voice repeated its demand. The words echoed, rang in his ears after they faded.

They thought he was trying to escape, that he was using Max as a hostage. His stomach threatened to twist inside out. He half turned and met Christmas's gaze. This wasn't how it was supposed to go. They were supposed to walk out as heroes, the people who had saved Max. How could he have been so stupid? He was the enemy here. He should never have forgotten that.

Christmas faced him. "What will you do?"

He shook his head, not knowing. Finally, a thought came. "You should leave. I don't want you blamed for any of this. When they see me carrying Max they'll see they are wrong."

"Will they?" Christmas didn't sound convinced.

Erich ignored that. "Before you go, I want to say your name right."

After six tries, he got it: *See-pee-Pim-oh-tay-oh.*

Christmas said, "Walk carefully, my friend."

Erich inhaled the crisp air and walked into the mouth of the Ksituan River, past someone crouched by a tree with a bullhorn. In his arms, Max had fallen asleep, or passed out. He turned a bend on the smaller river's icy path. About twenty men were arrayed across the river and partway up its banks. He hesitated, then approached the middle of the line, where Henry stood by a policeman. Max's weight pulled at his arms and strained his neck.

"My boy!" a voice to the left called out. Then, "What have you done?"

Erich stepped around a lump of ice. A blast echoed the instant after a bolt of agony slammed into him. As his body crashed backward, he saw blue sky and the eagle flying away.

51:

17 MARCH 1944, BY THE PEACE RIVER (1°C/34°F)

Hitting the ground jarred Max awake. His body sprawled uncomfortably across something warm and limp. He groaned, half rolled, and tried to push himself up. He glimpsed Erich's pale face, flopped back onto Erich's stomach.

His head spun as he tried again to sit. This time he saw blood. On Erich. On the snow. "No," he whispered. Horror tingled over his body.

A policeman knelt beside him. Constable Mason. Max cringed away but the constable held his shoulders steady. "The boy seems fine. Looks feverish."

"*Gott sei Dank. Gott sei Dank.*" Max's father hauled him away from Erich's body and folded him into a bear hug.

"Wait," Max said. "Is Erich okay? He saved me. Him and Christmas."

The policeman didn't touch Erich, just looked at him, then asked, "Who shot the prisoner?"

Was Erich alive? Dead? Why didn't he check?

"I did." Chuck stepped forward and handed his rifle to the officer with a sneer.

Max tried to lunge toward him, but his father held him back, turned him away. He saw Christmas striding toward them from the open mouth of the river, bridles swinging and rifle propped on his shoulder. Several rifles turned toward him, but Henry waved them down.

Christmas stepped to within a foot of Erich's body and crouched, frown in place. He looked up. "Chuck shot Erich because Erich knows he caused the sloop accident."

Chuck's sneer sharpened. "What would you know about it, Chief?"

"Erich told me all he knows as we traveled."

"We're supposed to believe a German prisoner and an Indian?"

"They're my friends!" Max tried again to escape his father's embrace. "They're telling the truth!"

Christmas pointed. "I saw Chuck that morning, in a plaid jacket. He came out of the barn where Erich found the hidden bolt cutters."

"Lies," Chuck said.

"Truth," Christmas replied. "Miss Cora was there. She saw too."

Henry scowled. "She's a witness?" Everyone turned toward Chuck in his brown coat. Henry said, "You never wear red plaid, Chuck. Why that day?"

Christmas stood. "All hunters know to use disguise. If anyone saw him they would think it was another lumberjack."

Why were they all ignoring Erich? Was he dead? Max's knees buckled as dizziness whirled the valley into a blur of white and brown and red plaid. His father held him up.

"Interfering, troublemaking—" Chuck spun away. "I'm not listening to this shit."

He started to leave. At a signal from Henry, two men stopped him. One was Frank, who looked daggers at Chuck as he clutched his arm.

Max said, "Christmas is telling the truth."

Henry replied, "Yes, I believe he is."

Chuck roared a crazed mix of rage and grief. "Let go, Frank. You're my partner."

"Not in this," Frank said. "I was afraid you were causing those accidents, Chuck. I've got no use for those Jerries, but that don't make it okay to attack them. Like Henry said at that dance, if we treat them like they treated our families, we're no better."

Chuck's face contorted into ugliness. "They killed my sister's boys. She has nothing. They deserve to be hung. Every one! Dammit, Henry, they've got *your* boy. You should want to be rid of them, but you protect them. It's not right!"

Frank gave his boss a sad look. "Henry, I should've told you what happened the day John Nikel got hurt. Chuck wandered off at lunch and never came back until we were in camp. I heard shouting, but didn't go help. Didn't want to see proof Chuck had done something."

Chuck turned the air blue with swearing. Max's strength gave way. His father eased him to the ground beside Erich and the patch of red snow.

"Don't leave, Erich," Max whispered. "You stood up for me. Rescued me. Pulled me out of the water." Death waited under the ice. No one seemed to care that Erich was falling through the ice.

Christmas squatted beside him. "The doctor has a blanket for you, Little Mouse. Let him care for you, then he can care for our friend."

"Will you stay with him?"

"If they let me."

52:

18 MARCH 1944,
SPIRIT RIVER (3°C/37°F)

Everything was white. Was this heaven? Erich squinted. Would heaven have a water stain on its ceiling? He tried to turn his head but quickly abandonded the effort. Every flinch hurt like the blow of a sledgehammer. Definitely not heaven. He explored his surroundings as much as possible with his gaze. White ceiling. White walls. White window frame. White sky. White curtain between him and footsteps.

A woman in white swept through an opening in the curtain. "Good, you're awake," she said. "Look at those blue eyes! Girls must swoon." She took his wrist, tapped a finger as she counted his pulse, then returned his hand to his side. "Do you remember what happened?"

Erich raised his right hand to his chest. The movement made him quiver in pain. He inhaled noisily.

"Be still. I expect you have a headache from cracking your head on the ice. You were shot above your right lung. You lost some blood so you'll be weak. There was some bone damage, but you're lucky. A few inches down or to your left and you probably wouldn't be with us."

Erich remembered avoiding a lump of ice. Stepping left. If he hadn't done that, the bullet would have hit him dead center. Dead. He focused on breathing slowly. The bullet might have missed his lung, but it still hurt to breathe.

"I'm to tell you there's a policeman outside your door, so escape isn't possible." The nurse snorted in an unladylike way. "As if you could even get up."

Erich felt iron encircling his ankle. He was chained to the bed, though he guessed the nurse was talking about his injury. He offered a weak smile. She smiled back. "They said you speak English. I see you understand." She patted his hand. "I'll tell the doctor his patient is awake. A few people are waiting to hear that news."

The doctor's visit drained the last of Erich's puddle of strength. He felt himself drifting. Heard Max's voice in the hall. When he next woke, the window pane was black. The curtain was open, allowing light from the hallway to fall across his bed. Electric light. He stared at the one bulb he could see and dreamed of warm showers.

He was cool. Almost cold. Except for his arm. That, for some reason, was warm. He raised his head carefully. Max had a hand curled around his forearm. He was asleep in a chair, slumped forward so the bed was his pillow.

He lay back and tried to ease his arm from the grip. Max sprang up. "Are you okay, Erich? Please be okay. I've been really worried." He drew a long breath. "I thought you had died."

Erich's voice came out croaky. "I wondered that myself for a few moments."

Max eyed him warily, then tested a smile. "You don't tell funny jokes."

"I guess I don't." Erich exhaled carefully.

Max's eyes flicked back and forth. "Stay awake," he whispered. "I'll be right back."

Voices tiptoed into the room. Erich's headache had receded to a dull throb, but he didn't want to risk turning his head, so stayed facing the window. Christmas appeared in that scruffy worn-out coat he always wore, not quite smiling, but looking pleased.

"Little Mouse promised to get me if you woke." He spoke softly.

Max added, "We had to sneak by the nurse. She wouldn't let Christmas come in."

"What about the policeman outside my door?"

Max blinked. "Was there a policeman? He's not there now. Are you under arrest?"

Erich didn't mention the manacle heavy on his ankle. "I don't know. I did leave camp without permission." He changed the subject. "Who shot me?"

Max briefly told him the story. "Constable Mason wasn't going to believe Christmas, but I said he was telling the truth. When the doctor was bandaging you, Christmas told about your fight with Lerhmann. He saw it from the hayloft. And I told about the time at the dance when you said you hoped the Allies would win. Henry wasn't surprised that's how you feel. Constable Mason made him tell us what he meant." Max furrowed his brows so he looked like a comic version of an angry adult. "Why didn't you tell me your grandfather is English?"

Erich worked his jaw, but that pumped his headache up a notch. "Liking people because of their bloodlines is what Nazis do." He exhaled slowly and turned to Christmas. "It's what I started to do with you, Christmas. I was wrong. I'm glad we got the chance to become friends." He offered his hand. Christmas gripped it. Erich gave a pained smile. "Grandfather taught me to value freedom and to see all that was wrong and dark in Nazi teachings. I often wished I'd delayed my return to Cologne the summer of 1939. Then I might have gotten to stay with my grandparents during the war."

"Where do they live?" Max asked.

"Stratford-upon-Avon."

"Where's that?"

"In England, in the town where Shakespeare was born. I saw a lot of his plays in the summers I stayed there." His voice creaked as he spoke. He licked his lips.

Max reached for the glass of water on the table beside the bed and helped him take a sip.

Christmas cleared his throat. "We should let you sleep."

"I feel like I've slept the day away."

"You did," Max replied. "Henry said something about you having a second concussion in under two months, but the doctor thinks you're out of danger and that sleeping will help you heal. He had to operate to take out slivers of bone." Max said that with awe, as if it was something wonderful.

Erich's grimace deepened. Thinking of it made his shoulder ache.

"I wanted to watch," Max added, "but the doctor said that I was too sick. I've seen lots and lots of blood, especially when Father butchers a pig."

His casual attitude told Erich he didn't know how serious the gunshot wound had been.

"This winter," Max continued, "I spilled a whole pail of it on me. I was in so much trouble. And that stuff is really sticky." He twisted his face into a look of disgust.

Christmas smiled. Then laughed, as clear and crisp as the coldest winter's day. Erich joined in, then groaned because of how much it hurt.

Henry's voice made them all start. "What are you, the Three Muskateers? I can't even keep you apart when two of you are sick. The nurse woke me because she heard voices." Erich turned his head so he could see everyone.

"I'm not sick anymore," Max replied. "The doctor is letting my parents take me home tomorrow."

"Good for you, son. Don't you think you should let Erich sleep so he can get better too?"

Max's mouth opened and closed. He looked sheepish. "I just wanted to say hi when he woke up. He did help save me."

"Yes, he did. But he got into trouble doing it. You know that, right? You need to stop running away, Max. Look what happened this time."

Max lowered his head and kicked at the bedpost. Erich winced. Christmas moved Max back a step, and he realized what he'd done. "Sorry, Erich. And I'll try, Henry, but it's really hard to be somewhere awful, somewhere you don't want to be."

Henry crossed his arms. "What's so bad about Horley?"

Max bit his lip, so Erich replied. "Boys at school are brutal to him, Henry. He's tried to deal with it himself, but nothing helps."

"Tipping over an outhouse in the middle of the night and breaking a boy's wrist isn't how to deal with anything."

Max looked alarmed. "Richard broke his wrist?"

"Max tipped over an outhouse?" Erich couldn't keep the amusement out of his voice. He saw Christmas start to smile too.

"That isn't funny, son." Henry's tone was chilly.

"No it isn't," Erich replied. "I think you should call the police."

"The Andersons already have."

"Good. And I'll be a witness to the cruel way that boy treated Max." Erich held Henry's gaze without blinking.

"No!" Max blurted. "Erich, you promised."

"Promised what?" Henry said.

Terror blanketed Max's face. Christmas squeezed his shoulder. "I saw your injuries that night in the hay loft, Max. Erich is right."

"Injuries?" Henry's voice was tight.

"I'm sorry, Max," Erich said, "but if this boy's parents are sending the police after you over this outhouse tipping, then the police should know how that boy and his friends almost hanged you." He kept his attention on Henry, whose face turned stony.

Silence thudded into the room. Henry looked at each of them in turn, but lingered on Max the longest. He addressed Erich. "Was that after the dance where you got attacked?"

Erich managed a small nod. "That must have given them the idea. I saw the rope burn."

"So did I," Christmas said. "He tried to hide it but his collar moved as we talked."

Henry exhaled slowly. "We'll work this out, Max, but you'll have to tell us everything. And by us, I mean your parents, Constable Mason, and me. I'll stay with you and make sure they listen to whatever you have to say. This has to be cleared up. Understood?"

Head still down, Max nodded. With slumped shoulders he headed out the door. Henry stopped him by gripping his arm. "Don't blame Erich for telling me this, son. It takes a real friend to help get a hard truth into the open."

Max returned to Erich's bedside and extended his hand. "Are we friends?"

"Of course we are," he said, shaking Max's hand. Pain throbbed in his shoulder. "Come see me tomorrow before you leave."

When Max left the room, Erich said, "Thank you for not letting me bleed to death out there, Henry."

The man's brow's furrowed. "Don't think it wasn't tempting." Christmas snorted and Henry swatted the sound away. "You're a trouble magnet, Hofmeyer. Do you have any idea how long I've spent on the police telephone here in Spirit River, talking to the prison-camp warden in Lethbridge? He was pleased you helped rescue Max, even if you did make us all think you'd run off. I didn't want to believe it, but the evidence sure pointed to it. Didn't help that someone saw you from a distance on one of my horses."

"Where was that?"

"West of Spirit River. They said you came out of the river valley, saw their house and wheeled back into that valley before they could let you know they were there."

Erich remembered the road they'd crossed. The farm they'd seen. There'd been no sign of people around, no smoke in the chimney. Obviously someone had been there.

Henry said, "I told that warden what Christmas told me, that he couldn't have pulled Max from the river alone and would have likely been pulled into it by him. Your strength saved both of them, Christmas insisted."

"His name is Sîpîy Pimohtew."

Henry glanced at Christmas. "I can't spit out those Cree words. Wish I could." Christmas gave a small shrug. Henry said, "The warden was satisfied with the outcome, except for that hole in your chest. He ordered you to heal up. I had to talk fast to stop him from sending some Veterans Guards to watch over you."

Dread shivered through his bones. Erich opened his mouth, but nothing came out. He tried again, forcing out the question in a hoarse voice. "Are you sending me back?"

"Gonna have to send all the prisoners back soon. Season's pretty much done, especially with all this danged warm weather." The light from the hall created a halo around the bald top of his head. "Lehrmann and Hubart are already gone, in handcuffs. The warden was upset that two Nazis had snuck onto the work detail."

Erich sighed. "Lehrmann is the fanatic. Hubart is mostly a follower." He recalled his grandfather's opinion. There were too many Hubarts in Germany right now. And too many people, like his father, who followed because it benefited them. "How long... before I have to go?" The thought of returning made the pain in his chest blossom. His breathing rasped.

"Got to heal first." Henry tapped his thigh. "You'd go to a different camp, one in Ontario for POWs who don't like the Nazis. The prison warden figures your life isn't worth a plugged nickel in Lethbridge."

Erich guessed that a plugged nickel had no value. "I was at that point when they sent me here. Please tell me when, Henry. I'd like to know how long I have to...enjoy some freedom." He shifted his chained foot. At least he wasn't surrounded by barbed wire.

"That's up to you. I've asked the warden if I could keep two workers. Alf has a farm in the valley where he keeps the horses in summers and grows feed for the winters. He's clearing more land and needs help to harvest bigger crops. Danged hard work. Long days. And believe me, you haven't seen a long summer day until you've lived in the Peace Country. Sun doesn't hardly go down until eleven o'clock."

"What are you saying?"

"Don't turn stupid on me now, son. I know you're young, but you're a good worker. I need men I can trust, who will work unsupervised and won't give Alf trouble." His hand skimmed over his bald pate. "That trouble thing almost counts you out, but Nikel assures me he can keep you in line, especially with Chuck gone to Grande Prairie to face a judge."

Erich felt his energy leaking away. He closed his eyes. "You know I want to stay, Henry."

"Maybe so, but that warden insisted I hear it from you directly. These work assignments are voluntary." He cleared his throat. "I'm going to thank that nurse for letting us visit at such an ungodly hour. We should go, Christmas." He started to turn, then looked back. "Almost forgot. Cora hopes you get better soon."

"*Cora?*"

"Maybe you getting shot has softened her up a bit." Henry winked and paced into the hallway. His footsteps faded away.

Christmas paused by the foot of his bed. "Miss Cora is nice. Get shot again and maybe she will give you a kiss."

Erich choked on laughter that racked his chest with pain. He rested one hand on his ribs. "Thanks for pushing me to go after Max with you. I'm not usually a brave person."

Christmas gripped the metal rail and leaned forward. "You are when it matters. I saw you stand up to an enemy. It's easier to stand up for a friend."

"Sometimes the problem is figuring out which is which."

"And now do you know?" He gave a questioning smile.

Erich closed his eyes and released a slow breath. For someone who was supposedly smart, he sure could be a slow learner. "It took awhile, but yes," he said, smiling at his friend. "Now I'm certain."

AUTHOR'S NOTE

During the course of World War II, the Canadian government housed 38,000 German prisoners of war. The two biggest camps were in Alberta. Over the years I had heard a few anecdotal comments about German POWs in northern Alberta (in one case, the person claimed they'd been only seventy-five kilometers from where I grew up), but it wasn't until I visited the archives in Lethbridge that I discovered proof in the form of a newspaper article. That was enough to jumpstart what became Erich's story.

The inspiration for Max's story was far more personal. Shortly after my first novel, *Run Like Jäger*, came out, a long-time friend of my deceased father called to tell me he had read the book. During our conversation, he began telling me about his own childhood during WWII, as the son of German immigrants. So I owe my heartfelt thanks to Hartmann Nagel for sharing his memories that first time, and in subsequent interviews. Many, but not all, of Max's difficulties, came out of those talks.

The character of Christmas also rose from my childhood. I named him after an older Cree man my grandfather introduced to me. All I know is that, years before, he had worked for Grandpa on his farm from time to time, and that he was a shy man with a kind smile. My character is a tribute to both him and my grandfather.

Hartmann also helped me get the details right for the logging camp without electricity. He caught some mistakes in an early draft and suggested details I'd missed. And he regaled me with fascinating stories from logging camps in the 1950s and '60s. I learned a bit about my father along the way. And I gained a friend.

While he helped me on the research end of things, the fantastic team at Pajama Press assisted on the production end. I can't thank Gail Winskill enough for seeing the potential in *Uncertain Soldier*, and her team for helping me work toward achieving it.

A special thanks goes to my amazing editor, Linda Pruessen, who guided me through several rounds of major revisions, transforming the story in so many ways. She was a hard taskmaster, but as always her vision helped clarify my thoughts and my prose.

I might write the words, but creating a book is a group effort—of that I am certain.